ABOUT THE AUTHOR

daughter of a bookseller, Ewa Dodd has been writing he was young – starting small with short self-illustrated for children. More recently, she has delved into novel g, and is particularly interested in literature based in .d, where she is originally from. *The Walls Came Down* is rst novel, for which she was shortlisted for the Virginia for Fiction. She is also a graduate of the Creative Writing ramme at City University.

wa lives in Highbury, north London with her husband.

First published in the UK in 2018 by Aurora Metro Books
67 Grove Avenue, Twickenham, TW1 4HX
www.aurorametro.com info@aurorametro.com

Editor: Cheryl Robson
Production: Simon Smith
Aurora Metro Books would like to thank Marina Tuffier, Anthony Crick, Peter Fullagar and Ivett Saliba.

We are grateful to ea Change Group www.eacg.co.uk for sponsorship of The Virginia Prize for Fiction.

Printed by 4edge Limited.

ISBNs:
978-1-911501-15-2 (print)
978-1-911501-16-9 (ebook)

THE WALLS CAME DOWN

Acknowledgements:

There are many people who contributed to bringing this book to life.

Firstly a big thank you to my mum whose experiences as a twenty-something year-old living in Warsaw formed the basis of the 1980s backdrop of this book. Her upbringing was so different to my own and I've always found it interesting.

Thank you to the team at Aurora Metro – Cheryl, Simon, Andrew, Ellen and Mary, who worked with me through multiple edits to make the story as good as it could be and to help the characters come to life.

Thank you to my first readers, Poppy, Agata, Sally, Nina and Beth, and to everyone who encouraged me to persevere with finishing it, including Suzie, Sophie, Rosie and Deeps (who along with Poppy gave some great cover ideas). It's been a long but exciting journey.

I am also very grateful for the resources from ITAKA, Poland's central search and support organisation for missing people, and from the European Solidarity Centre in Gdańsk. Both helped to add credibility to the events surrounding Adam's disappearance.

And most of all, thank you to Giles, for everything.

THE WALLS CAME DOWN

EWA DODD

AURORA METRO BOOKS

1988

Chapter 1 – The Beginning
Warsaw

The crowd slowly swelled out of the building, breaking up into angry fragments and then coming back together, rippling down the road in an undulating sea of red and white banners.

The young men in front of her were screaming something incomprehensible. Some of them were jumping on one another's shoulders, slapping each other's backs as if to offer encouragement. To the left of her, in the shadows of a greying block of flats, a teenage boy was urinating freely, his flag still hanging out of his pocket.

Monika wasn't sure why she'd come out into the streets that day. She must have been sucked in by the excitement of her neighbours, by her sister's shouts about this day being 'history in the making.' The Communist government would be put in its place and finally everything would change. There would be no more pitiful wages, no more working one third of a job (just so they could say that everybody was employed), no more waiting for hours in a queue for meat, only to be turned away at the last moment because it had run out and all that was left were onions.

She wasn't sure whether she shared the swarm's belief that the Solidarity party had it in them to make the change happen, but even a glimmer of hope was good enough for her.

Monika rushed out of work early, after Mr. Rakowski had told everyone that the factory would be shutting at midday to prepare for the strikes. She gave up waiting for a bus and ran the three kilometres to the twins' playgroup to collect them, flustered, just as the doors of the building were shutting. She felt the uncomfortable perspiration beneath the armpits of her tight linen jacket.

She was planning to take the children home – to give them their lunch and then leave them with their aunt – and only then to go out in the streets herself to find out exactly what was what. But they were so excited to be part of the crowd that they wouldn't allow her to leave without them.

"I want to see the flags," Adam had insisted, pulling down on her arm, and she gave in, of course she gave in. She couldn't say no to him after everything that had happened.

They didn't have Solidarity flags, so they had to settle for the large rectangular national flag which Monika had sewn herself when she was sixteen. She rushed upstairs to get it as the children waited outside the block. She noticed that it had a large wine stain on its lower left hand side. Never mind – it would have to do.

"Mama, look!" Joanna yelled. She was pointing to a group of teenage girls, rolling out of the local school in their navy pinafores. They all had armbands on – red smudges against the white sleeves of their shirts. "Mama, can we have one?"

"No Joanna darling, look you have the flag. I brought it for you." But before she could place it in her daughter's outstretched arm, her son snatched it from her and began to run down the street making car noises. One of the girls must have noticed that Joanna was about to burst into tears, as she came over with a big smile, pulled her armband off and gave it to her.

"Thank you," said Monika gratefully.

They were now in the middle of Grójecka Street making their way slowly towards the centre of the city. She had to keep calling Adam back as he disappeared amongst the throng of people emerging from the side streets. Finally, tired out from the excitement of the day, he came back and she wound her fingers around his thumb, as this was the way that he always wanted to hold hands.

"Mrs. Malicka!"

She turned around to see Mrs. Barska, one of her neighbours, calling her over from the other side of the street.

"I can't believe they managed to organise this! Do you know; I heard that there are similar strikes going on in Gdańsk, Dąbrowa Górnicza and Bielsko-Biała…" She reeled off the cities on her fingers, "Thousands of people involved."

"Really?" asked Monika, "Do you think that it will actually lead to anything this time?"

"Definitely! Mark my words. This is the beginning of the end; they're all saying it."

Beside her, a tall bearded man with a large camera was conducting an interview with a particularly incensed youth, who seemed to be shouting revolutionary phrases into the microphone.

"What sort of message do you think the strike is sending out to the government?"

"That the workers have spoken! That we won't stand for this anymore! There is no dignity left when prices continue to rise and wages fall!"

"But there have been years of this. Years of economic hardship. Years of broken promises. Why do you think that the change will happen now?"

"It's got to breaking point. It's too much. We've realised that this is not a country that we want our children to live in if these things continue and so we have mobilised ourselves…"

"You look well," said Mrs. Barska, momentarily drawing Monika away from the ranting. "You've caught the sun and you have some colour in your face. It's so good to see. And that suit is a great cut."

Monika gazed into the woman's face searching for a hint of mockery, because surely, nobody could think that she looked anything but tired, worn out and ragged. She knew full well that she was too thin and lately she didn't even bother with doing her make-up in the mornings, because what was the point really? There was nobody who she wanted to impress.

But Mrs. Barska gazed at her with a calm and genuine simplicity which made her realise that the compliment was sincere and well-meant.

"Thank you," she muttered awkwardly.

"I'm so bloody glad that this has happened. It should have happened years ago, you know. Then things could have been different for me and you. As it is, we need to make sure that it's better for the young ones," she said, seriously, "Now my son is a hooligan, but you have two great specimens of the next generation to fight for. Fight for them Monika – fight for them to live in a democracy, to have proper jobs with proper pay!"

She yearned to be truly infected with the revolutionary passion, but the fire inside her refused to spark up. It was as if her kindling was just a tiny bit too damp, the lighter fluid not quite strong enough. And no matter how hard she tried, she couldn't shift the leaden weight that pressed down on her mind with such force that it sometimes took her breath away. It was heavy and dark, like a tank, leaving nothing but a dull emptiness in its wake. But the very least that she could do was to keep up appearances, to show the world that she was coping – no, not coping, but participating.

"Yes, I will. I am determined to…" She suddenly trailed off as she realised that her right hand was now hanging loose by her side.

On her left, Joanna was sucking her thumb, half nestling her cheek into her mother's skirt. Monika felt herself suddenly go cold.

"Where's your brother?" she asked frantically. "Adam! Adam!" she yelled into the street. Her voice was caught on the wind, drowned out by the excited screams of the throng.

***

Monika sat in the dark. Her body felt frozen despite the warm afternoon. There was a low rhythmic hum around her, a swoosh of movement. The shrieking sting of panic had left her body. The aftershocks were still pulsing in her temples, but they were weaker now. When she looked down into her lap, she noted with some surprise that her hands were still. She had imagined she would see them moving, dancing to the tiny tremors of her heart.

Somebody was speaking to her, but the voice came through a blurred haze, as if they were underwater. She didn't make an effort to hear them. Whatever they had to say was not important.

And then her right arm moved, her fingers circling the air, as if seeking out her son's thumb.

"Have you eaten anything?" her sister repeated. The threads of words eventually wove themselves together into some form of coherent whole.

"Yeah; I had something earlier…"

"It's almost seven in the morning. You should try and get some sleep. He *will* be found you know…"

"How can you be sure?" she asked. She stared at Irena's face – the blue eyes, just marginally too big for the face, were red-rimmed and swampy.

"Because the ground can't have swallowed him up..." her sister began, and slapped her hand over her mouth.

"What I mean is that they'll definitely find him," she recovered, "The police are doing a thorough search. He's probably just hiding somewhere, thinking that this is all a great game. Maybe he followed a group of protestors to another part of the city and he couldn't make his way back. But he knows his address, so he'll be able to tell whoever finds him."

"Maybe he's gone to Mysłowice?" Monika mumbled into her lap.

"What? How would he get there? He doesn't even know how to get to the train station. Monika, he's barely four years old."

Monika's shoulders began to heave, but no tears came out. And then it returned – the rhythmic, unhealthy speeding thump of her heart against her rib cage, the clouding of vision. The walls were closing in on her and she needed to run – more than anything she needed to run, but she couldn't... she wouldn't be able to escape before the complete darkness descended and then it would be too late. She would be left an empty core, a fish left out on deck losing its battle against the elements.

Something warm and feathery nestled into the nook of her elbow. She looked down to see the crown of a small blond head.

"Has Adam come back yet?" the sleepy voice asked.

2010

Chapter 2 – Matty
London

Matty looked out at the grey haze of rain pounding down on the heads of commuters as they spilled out hurriedly from the brightly lit mouth of City Thameslink Station. Fools. They weren't privy to his secret of travelling into work an hour early. That way you avoided the worst of the awful, clammy crowds. Either that or they weren't mad enough to get up at 4.45am every morning.

But being an insomniac, 4.45am and 6.45am made no difference to Matty – it was the silver lining to a sleep free existence. And now he sat in the corner of the Chipston Capital Funds office, with full view of the open plan trading floor that was still quiet but would, at any moment, begin filling up with the swarm of worker bees.

Matty treasured this time. He used it to check the news while sipping on his triple shot espresso. Sometimes, he halfheartedly tried to get ahead on some work – currently he was in the process of getting a volatility analysis finished for Jason Lyons, his boss' boss. He had recently mastered the art of 'managing your manager' and now told Jason exactly what he was going to send him and when, *just* before his emails pinged in, signalling his own planned work deadlines.

But today was one of those days when Matty's mind particularly wandered, perhaps because it was the first full week back after the Easter bank holiday weekend and he realised that he had at least forty-five hours to put in before Saturday. He minimised the window with the report on his PC, in favour of the BBC News site. He scanned the headlines. *More footballers tell of sexual abuse – 96 dead in Smolensk air disaster – Security tightened at Hatton Garden – Substance abuse blamed for prison 'rage' – Reaction: Everton 1 – Man Utd 2.*

The mention of Hatton Garden put Matty in a bad mood. Because Hatton Garden meant jewellery, and jewellery meant rings, specifically engagement and wedding rings. It was something that he just didn't have the brain space for right now. He'd suspected for a while that Ellie was expecting a proposal any day. They had recently both turned twenty-six and the last summer had brought with it the first flurry of weddings and the relentless queries of *When you gonna pop the question, mate?*

The truth was that the thought of marriage filled him with a cold, wet dread. It wasn't anything to do with Ellie – it was just the whole finality of it, the sense that he would have to root himself down. And that was something that Matty hated more than anything. He lived for the thought that he could take flight whenever he wanted, and go wherever he wanted.

Today, gazing out of the window at the drab greyness that filled the world outside Chipston Capital, he visualised himself on a beach in Italy, preferably somewhere in the south. It would already be warm at this time of year. He would lie down and soak up the sun, his cold beer half buried in the sand.

But quite honestly he wouldn't mind being anywhere rather than here. He could settle for Helsinki or Prague. He would lounge around, eating dumplings with Ellie and making love until mid-afternoon.

"Morning."

He forced his attention back to the present as Arun carefully folded his gangly frame into the chair next to him. For such a tall man, he moved with an admirable degree of grace.

"You heard about the crash?"

"Hmm?"

"Can't figure out if there'll be any impact on us."

"Nah, stuff like that doesn't have an effect," said Matty knowingly.

"Well, not usually, but this plane had half the Polish government on board."

How had he missed that? He always prided himself on being first when it came to significant news stories.

"Terrorist attack?" he asked weakly.

"Don't know. They haven't said. But the President was on there with his wife, the leader of the National Army, the Head of the National Bank, 18 members of Parliament – you name it, they were there. I *doubt* that it was an accident."

Matty brought up the page on his computer. The BBC had already got hold of many of the headshots of the victims, and a wall of solemn black and white photography filled his screen.

"Who *does that*? What sort of a country puts all of their most important people on one plane? It's almost as if they're playing into the hands of the terrorists."

He shook his head and then a soft prickling sensation developed in his gut as he noticed Jason making his way towards them at speed. At an animal level, Matty was intimidated by Jason – he admired his stockiness and his ability to simply, yet forcefully, make his views known. Matty yearned for those qualities, which he was painfully lacking. He couldn't even blame his build – it was something deeper than that, a charisma, a presence.

"What's our Sterling-Złoty exposure? We don't want to get caught with our pants down again," Jason told him, perching casually on the edge of the empty desk behind him. There was no 'Good morning.' Jason didn't need to greet anyone.

"Don't you want the emerging vols piece first?" he asked weakly. He knew that this deadline wasn't until tomorrow, because he had set it himself.

"I need both today," Jason said simply. "By midday latest." And then he sauntered off, just like that, his heavy frame swaying between the rows of desks where his worker bees were already on the phones, already in full swing, eager to bring him home the honey.

Matty lay his palms flat on the desk to steady himself. The unfairness boiled within him and, as was usual in situations in which life wasn't working out quite how he wanted it to (and which happened increasingly often), he took a walk. It was only a break away from what he was currently doing that could clear the redness which flooded his mind.

He paced up and down the corridor, his fingers drumming against the side of a newly painted radiator, and his mind took off. He was lucky of course. Matty was among a minority of his friends who had managed to get work despite the crippling recession that had started almost two years before. Most of them, despite their university degrees, were still doing admin work or lowly paid 'internships', and that was if they'd been fortunate enough to fight off the throng of competitors to get there. He felt guilty about how comparatively easy it had been to get his position at Chipston Capital and how quickly he'd managed to clamber up the first few steps of the ladder to success. He knew that by joining the firm, he'd become one of the hated crowd of fat cats who of course were to blame for the country's economy falling to pieces. He knew that while they congratulated him, his friends were visualising him digging a knife into their backs.

But what else was he to do? He turned up every day in his pressed shirt and his suit from Gieves & Hawkes which, even though it had been four years, still made him feel as if he were poorly acting a part in a production in which he'd been blatantly miscast. And the bottom line was that he wasn't getting anywhere and, more importantly perhaps, that he hated it all.

He would have to escape, if only for a short time. He would plan it tonight. He took three deep breaths, as instructed once by his childhood GP, and braced himself to walk back in.

But that night, he didn't get home until a quarter to ten. He'd somehow managed to reassure Jason that their Sterling-Złoty positions weren't substantial, and then spent four and a half solid hours catching up on other work he'd side-lined.

He collapsed on the sofa next to Ellie, who sat cross-legged beneath a thick wool blanket, a pile of exercise books on her lap. She was in her pyjamas, her face washed and her hair dishevelled, but even in this state Matty was always amazed at how beautiful she was.

He lay down with his head on her lap, knocking the books into disarray.

"Let's get away somewhere," he muttered, yawning.

She ruffled his hair.

"You know we can't afford it."

It was true. They'd spent a lot on a trip to New York at Christmas, and Ellie wasn't earning a lot as a teacher.

"We can," he insisted. "Come on."

"Well…" she said slowly, "I suppose we could do a long weekend. But I'm still really worried about it being too expensive."

"It won't be if we avoid the tourist hotspots. We could go to a random European city?"

"Which one?"

The news flickered on the TV in front of them and he caught a glimpse of the carcass of a plane, lying on its side in the dense fog, surrounded by forest. It sparked a sudden idea in his head.

"Warsaw?" It was the last place people would be flying to following an air disaster, and there were bound to be knock-down rates.

He picked up Ellie's battered laptop and brought up a flight comparison website. He wasn't wrong. There were several flights leaving around half term time which were less than fifty quid per person. It was a no brainer.

"I suppose," Ellie shrugged, "I don't mind where we go." Her cheeks were flushed and a tiny smile began spreading across her full lips.

The panic rose in Matty's stomach. She thought it was an engagement holiday. He momentarily considered calling off the idea altogether, but the urge to get away was stronger than the awkwardness of Ellie's hopeless anticipation. Yes, he would get the leave signed off tomorrow and they'd be off.

Half an hour later they were lying in bed, his cheek nuzzled against the warm space just behind her ear, his hand on the crevice of her hip bone. He fell into the novelty of a wonderful, undisturbed sleep, happy in the knowledge that something was about to happen, a break in the monotony, a chance to escape.

Chapter 3 – Tom
Chicago

Tom's appointment coincided with a snow flurry in Chicago, which had arrived unseasonably late, as it was already the start of spring. He'd woken up to a whirlwind of white outside his window, and in those first few moments of wakefulness he wondered whether he was still dreaming. But what was a dream and what was reality had lately become a puzzle to him. His mind had begun to produce strange images – blurred memories appeared before him in the middle of the day, when he was resting with a book, or watching a baseball game on TV, as if they were really happening, right there in his living room.

He blamed it on exhaustion at first, and the difficult readjustment from what had been an incredibly busy working life, to one which had recently become the exact opposite of that.

"It's what retirement does to you," Mitch had told him, only half-joking. "You stop doing useful things and your brain turns to mush. You become bone idle, and then that bone idleness tires you out, and you become a shadow of what you used to be."

So maybe at first, the tiredness was exactly that. But since his sixtieth birthday at the end of January, it had become progressively worse. Sometimes Tom was so tired, that he couldn't bend his arms to lift himself out of bed in the morning. And he wasn't hungry. Often he would accidentally miss breakfast and lunch, surviving until five in the afternoon on nothing more than a mug of black coffee.

By late March the vomiting had started. He'd suspected food poisoning – it was quite possible that the chicken he'd cooked for dinner that day had a tinge of pink inside. But then it happened again two days later and again at the end of the week. When he felt a dull ache in his stomach, he begrudgingly rang his doctor – a young, eager trainee, who referred him straight to the hospital.

So Tom forced himself into his stiff corduroy winter trousers noting with some anxiety the gap between the waistband and the cold, pale skin of his abdomen. He put on a thick cotton vest under his shirt, doubled up his socks, and emerged into the falling snow.

The unexpected snow had slowed the city. His bus crawled at a snail's pace through the western suburbs, the driver apologising over the intercom about 'delays due to poor visibility'. Tom, as always, had left himself plenty of time to get to his destination so he wasn't worried. He gazed stoically out of the window at the blizzard, enjoying the ethereal feeling that it created, until it suddenly, unexpectedly, brought with it the hot sting of nostalgia. Snow always reminded Tom of his youth and now, in a moment of remembrance so strong he could almost have been there, he saw his younger self as he hurled his body onto the white ground, spreading his arms wide and waving them up and down, to create the imprint of an angel. He had long forgotten what it had felt like to be so spontaneous, so carefree.

The vision was still in his mind when he finally emerged in front of the grey monolith of the University of Chicago Medical Centre. The snow had since turned to an unpleasant sleet, which raged across the square, swirling among the chaos of ambulances and taxis. He breathed in deeply, bracing himself for a morning of unpleasant waiting.

The foyer was filled with people and wheelchairs, all moving in different directions. He took his place in the queue that had formed in front of the reception desk, and was directed to the seventh floor, where, after a few wrong turns, he eventually managed to find the right department.

He was asked to sit on a grey plastic chair in a waiting room filled with an assortment of people of all ages and backgrounds. He surveyed them for signs of illness, but to his disappointment, there was nothing obvious. No hacking coughs, nobody clutching their stomach, nobody even looking particularly pale.

The chair that he was sitting on had a hard and uncomfortable backrest, and a slippery seat, so he was constantly having to reposition himself. Fifty minutes later, his surname was finally called and he went in to see the consultant.

The door was opened by another absurdly young man. Tom almost laughed aloud, because, with his white coat and the stethoscope casually swung around his neck, he looked like a caricature of a doctor. He smiled broadly and motioned for him to come into a brightly lit, white room in which there was nothing but two hardback chairs and a desk. Behind this desk, a woman with a high forehead and a pair of round, old-fashioned glasses on her nose was typing. She reminded Tom of a cartoon owl. The young doctor indicated one of the chairs and said, "She'll be with you in a minute."

Eventually, The Owl stopped typing and raised her eyes – looking straight at Tom, but with a blank expression, as if he were quite invisible and the seat before her was in fact filled with nothing but air.

"Hello Mr. Mason," she said slowly. So she could see him after all.

"How are you feeling?"

He was stunned by the question.

"Very bad actually," he said without hesitation, "That is why I'm here."

"Yes of course. But I meant, how are you feeling in relation to your visit to the doctor a couple of weeks ago?" She consulted the notes. "How are the symptoms?"

He took time describing his symptoms. He knew that she could see the notes about the weight-loss and the vomiting – that hadn't changed, so he didn't mention it. Instead he brought up the itchy skin and exhaustion, and he noted that she raised her eyebrows. He groaned internally. He shouldn't have said it. Who complains about itchy skin? She will have already written him off as a time-waster and a hypochondriac, and those were two things which Tom Mason prided himself on not being.

"And you have a history of alcoholism. Is that correct?"

He liked that she didn't beat about the bush. Others had called it 'a slight problem with his drinking', 'an overindulgence.'

"Yes, I did," he admitted, "I did for many years. But I have been sober since 2001."

"Right."

"And your appetite hasn't improved."

"No. I wouldn't say so. No."

Tom wondered why she wasn't typing. Surely, she should be frantically hitting the keys in response to what he was saying? He'd assumed that like many in the medical profession, she was constantly in a hurry, ready to get through her quota of patients for the day with as much speed as possible. He had seen constant news reports on how over-worked doctors were.

But The Owl put her hands flat on the table (he noted the bitten down fingernails) and looked at him long and hard, with a sad seriousness. There was something in her facial expression that made the beetle crawl of anxiety start up in his stomach.

It was at that moment that he considered the real possibility that he could be truly, seriously ill. Until now, he was treating the whole thing as a mere collection of annoying symptoms that he needed to get rid of, so that he could get on with what he was supposed to be doing, which was enjoying himself. Wasn't that what retirement was? A chance to relive your youth with all the knowledge and the money that forty years of hard work brings with it? And he had a more than decent amount of money stashed away in the bank, and nobody to spend it on but himself. He'd planned to start painting. It was a desire that he still had after so many years. He'd even gone to a store on North Lincoln Avenue back in December to buy an easel, some canvases and oil paint. But then his health troubles set in and he'd never actually gotten round to picking up a paintbrush.

He considered for the first time what it might be like to die. Who was it who said that we all essentially died alone? Tom had never understood what this meant. He supposed that the speaker was referring to the fact that no matter how many people you had around you, the physical act of dying was happening to nobody but you. It was a horrible, intimate event in which by all intents and purposes you were alone. Family and friends could only make the run-up to it more bearable, and he wouldn't even have them, well apart from perhaps Mitch and Sally.

"So, what happens now?" he asked weakly.

"Right, well – we need to do a few tests to enable me to eliminate a few things."

"You think I have cancer," he blurted out.

The Owl seemed annoyed at this outburst. He wasn't playing along with the conversation that she had planned for him – she presumably had the same dialogue prepared for all of her patients.

"No. That's not what I said, is it?" she asked in a tired voice. "We need to rule out some possibilities so that we can then move onto diagnosing you properly. That's how medicine works."

Tom wasn't at all sure whether that was how medicine worked, but he thought it better not to say anything.

An overwhelming sense of fear had gripped him with such force that he felt suffocated by it. He had the ludicrous thought that if he were going to die, he would prefer to go right now, before he found out any bad news.

"Are you OK?" asked the young doctor, who had been hovering at the other end of the desk. "Can I get you a glass of water?"

Tom ignored him.

"Do you think it's *likely* that I have cancer?" he said, not looking at either of them.

There was a momentary silence before The Owl spoke.

"It's possible. I wouldn't say that it's probable, but it's certainly possible. It's not right for me to give you any percentage of likelihood at this stage. We're going to do a scan of your abdomen and we'll go from there." She gave him a date for the scan, which was on Thursday of the same week, three days away. Weren't there usually weeks and weeks of waiting for these appointments?

"So soon?" he asked weakly.

"Yes, we had a cancellation. And it's better to get these things done as quickly as possible," she said.

When Tom left the hospital, the ethereal snow had disappeared for good, and the rain pounded down from a blanket of thick, dark grey cloud. It was time to get back home before he got drenched, but he was too tired to run to the bus stop. He was too tired to do anything anymore.

Chapter 4 – Joanna
Warsaw

As predicted, Marek barely looked up from his desk as she entered.

"Ah, Joanna. Thanks for coming." He pointed at his phone half-apologetically and motioned for her to wait.

She hovered before his desk, unsure of whether or not she should take a seat in the chair opposite him. He had summoned her into his office and she waited to find out whether she was going to be made redundant. She hadn't been given any proper work in weeks, so it was most certainly on the cards. If she was lucky, she might receive a decent pay off.

"Yes," she heard him repeat to whoever was on the phone. "We'll run the conspiracy angle. I don't care if you don't believe it. The readers want to know all the possibilities. The Russians sent the plane. That's a fact. Some say it's a convenient way to get rid of our entire government in one fell swoop. What? Yeah, obviously include the weather conditions and poor visibility. We need a summary of all the theories…"

Joanna waited. It had been almost a week, and the office was still buzzing with the Smolensk Air disaster. The whole thing filled her with a sick feeling – not a personal guilt, but a guilt on behalf of her entire profession. Marek had dubbed the incident as the 'best piece of news that he'd come across in his career.' There were 96 people dead, and all he could think about was media angles.

He finally turned towards her. Joanna noticed that he'd put the phone down on whoever he'd been speaking to without saying goodbye.

"Sorry about that. Now, I called you in here because I want you to write our next feature."

"What?" She'd been waiting to be given a major feature project ever since she'd started at the company almost a year ago. "Are you serious? Have you already settled on the subject?" she asked, still not quite daring to believe what she'd just been given.

"Yeah, finally." He motioned with his hand that she should sit down. "Look, we need something different to all this disaster coverage. People will soon get sick of it. I was gunning for coverage of our biggest football achievements of the last hundred years, you know, ahead of the Euro? But Krystian says it's bullshit. He thinks every other media outlet from tabloid to broadsheet will be running that kind of thing and that our readership won't be interested. What do you reckon?"

Was he genuinely asking for her opinion or just testing her to see whether she would agree with him? Krystian was the non-executive director of the company, who was always sticking his nose into editorial issues that weren't really his concern. He was small, snarly and mean-spirited, and Joanna hated him.

But on this occasion, she was forced to agree with his opinion. She was bored by everything that she'd seen so far to do with the Euro. The adverts with their three-dimensional eye-popping footballs seemed to scream out at her every time she turned on the TV, waited at a bus-stop or searched for something online. And she failed to believe that this was the sporting event that would 'put Poland back on the map – make it great again.' It was just another money spinner, which would have them paying back for the stadium building through taxes for the next three decades.

And that was when it happened. People say that emotions are on a higher level, beyond the body. But Joanna experienced every intense emotion as a deep, physical sensation. At that moment she could clearly feel a dull tickle at the base of her stomach that developed into a deep itch of frustration. The months of being ignored and overlooked when it came to proper news and feature stories, being treated constantly like the office intern, having to brush away the chauvinism and the patronising comments, seemed to come to a head and blend together into an unexpected rage.

She wouldn't be grateful, oh no. She had deserved this months ago. And she would say exactly what she thought.

"I think we can give them something different," she managed, in what she thought was a neutral tone, "I think they'll have loads on the Euro everywhere else."

To her great surprise, Marek conceded quickly. It was as if he didn't have time to get into any further debate about it.

"Fine, fine. Maybe we'll run something smaller on it. So in that case your other option is 'Missing People'."

"What?"

The blood rushed to her cheeks.

"I think it could work very well for us," he continued. "To be honest, I don't know why we didn't come up with it before. Do you know that over 15,000 people are reported missing in this country every year? Many of them are found within 24 hours of course. But there are always those who are never found," he announced dramatically.

"I want to report on a mix of the highest profile cases over the past few decades. Some of them have been closed for a few years, but you need to scout out how much information the police will give you. I want you to start working on it as soon as you can. I'll send you all the info that we've found so far. I don't think you need me to tell you that if you get this right, it will be amazing for your career."

Her body had gone rigid. She wanted to lift herself off the chair, to move out of the stifling heat of the room, but an invisible force weighed down on her. The momentary elation that she'd experienced in voicing her true thoughts to Marek had vanished instantly. It was replaced with a sense of intense fear.

"Are you alright?" he asked, arranging the pages scattered across his desk.

"Yes, of course. I… I'll get on it straight away."

"Fantastic. It'll go out in the second issue of June, so I want to see the first draft by 10th June at the latest. I've given you a bit more time than usual as this is your first one. Well done. Have a great weekend. Take some time to think about how you want to structure the piece."

With that, he shut his laptop and began to put on his coat – a sign that the conversation had ended. Joanna wasn't sure how it had happened, but she eventually managed to get herself out of the building onto the cold, dingy street. She realised with shock that she hadn't even thanked Marek for the opportunity.

She wandered into the empty parking lot still dazed from the conversation, and struggled to locate her car. She eventually identified it by its broken, off centre bumper and climbed into the driver's seat.

She turned her key in the ignition, but then hesitated and laid her head on the steering wheel. She suddenly couldn't face the simple task of driving home to her empty flat.

The image of the first Christmas without her brother came flooding back to her. It was always there, as if imprinted on the insides of her eyelids, but it was at particular moments that it returned with a painful sharpness.

She saw the smiling faces of her young cousins around her aunt's dining table; the Christmas tree with its folded top which didn't quite fit in the hallway, and the swirling silver candlesticks, which her grandmother feared would set fire to the tablecloth. Apparently they had already done so once when Joanna was just a baby.

She remembered her grandfather's prayer before they sat down to dinner. Being the patriarch of the family, he took it upon himself to read from the Bible about Mary and Joseph's journey to Nazareth. Then he calmly wished health and hope to everyone, "even those who could not be with us today." It was upon these words that Joanna's mother had uttered the most piercing wail that her daughter had ever heard. She remembered covering her ears and throwing herself under the table to escape the sound.

Her aunt had stepped in at just the right moment.

"Monika. Shhh… Come with me. You need to get some rest." She led Joanna's mother through to one of the bedrooms and the Christmas dinner proceeded as if nothing had happened. It was somehow wordlessly decided by the family that it would be better this way.

Joanna was seated next to her grandfather who fed her tiny morsels of fish and smiled at her sadly. Her mother didn't return to the table that evening. She also wasn't there for the midnight church service or for the festive breakfast the following day. In fact, she didn't get out of bed until the snows had melted and it was almost half way through March.

Four-year old Joanna couldn't rid herself of the gnawing feeling of aloneness and spent much time wondering about why she was the only one amongst her friends who seemed to be losing family members at a very rapid rate – first her father, then her brother, and now her mother was near enough gone. She remembered that she'd spent the winter of 1988 wondering when she herself would begin to fade away. Surely it was only natural that she disappeared too? Maybe then she would be reunited with the others?

The oddest thing was that she'd almost come to terms with her father's disappearance. She could remember very little about him by that stage, other than his musty smell and the prickly texture of his beard when she had run her fingers over it. But her feelings about her brother were very different. Joanna could sense that he was alive, she was certain of it. Whenever one of the multitude of tactless kids in her class asked her about his whereabouts, she would say confidently: "He got lost and he's just trying to make his way back."

She never accepted that Adam had disappeared for good. As a teenager, she had fought with her mother to keep his case open, but after 20 years with nothing but a few false leads, the police had decided that they had reached the end of their search.

What was worse was that since getting out of bed in the spring of 1989, Joanna's mother had decided that the only way that she could carry on living was by pretending that Adam had never existed. She went as far as selling all of his clothes, giving his bed away to the neighbours and cutting up pictures of her children when they were little, leaving only the parts that featured her daughter. The problem was that Joanna and Adam had done everything together and the pictures ended up looking very peculiar, with a disembodied hand holding Joanna's as she walked, or a tiny slither of a shoulder leaning on hers.

No, she wouldn't put herself through it again. All her reserves of endurance and hope had finally left her. She'd ring Marek later that night and tell him that she couldn't do it. Even if it meant working on minor film reviews for the rest of her career.

Chapter 5 – Matty
Warsaw

"I feel sad for the young women, you know?" said the taxi driver.

"Sorry?"

"The stewardesses who died in the crash. They were twenty-four, twenty-seven years old. Nobody write about them in newspaper. Everybody forget. President funeral more important. But I think about the parents of the stewardesses."

"Sure. It must be devastating," Matty agreed, "They were so young." Then, at a loss for what else to say on the subject, he pointed out of the window.

"What's that building?"

The taxi driver glanced to the left and rolled his eyes in the rear-view mirror.

"Shopping centre of course. They are everywhere – French, English, American. My daughter go away to Australia in 2005. She come back last year and she cannot recognise Warsaw, you know? Was all grey blocks before. Now – foreign investment, you understand?" He rubbed his fingers together – the international sign for money being made.

"Everybody say that life is better now," he continued, "but I think… is too much, you know? You want to see real Poland?

You go to countryside. Honest people there. Here is just money, money…"

Matty noticed that despite his complaints, the driver gladly accepted a hefty tip, grinning to himself as he deposited their luggage outside the Lennard Hotel, a comical multi-coloured building jutting out from the end of a long terrace.

"You need to go anywhere, you call me. I give you best rate." He beamed at them and offered up a meaty hand.

The hotel was much more elegant than Matty had expected. A plush red carpet led from the swivel glass front doors to the reception desk. Their room was on the ninth floor with an impressive view over the city. At the forefront he recognised the palace of Science and Culture which looked like a rocket ready for take-off.

Ellie had chosen the hotel, primarily because it had a special sale on. It was reopening after a long period of renovation and they were clearly eager to reel the tourists back in. It was luxury really for the price they were paying, so he couldn't complain. But he'd wished they'd chosen a bed and breakfast, or even a youth hostel – something with a bit more character.

He sat down on the bed facing the large floor to ceiling window. Pop music whined in the hallway just at the threshold of his hearing and he suddenly felt so tired that he could curl up on the bed and fall asleep. Outside the window, a delivery boy pushed a cart laden with cakes. Gloomily, he watched a gaggle of office workers spilling out from the tram and dispersing in all directions. Of all the places to come on holiday, why had he chosen here?

"I'm ravenous," Ellie declared, "Let's go and find a good place to eat."

He got up wordlessly and began to unpack the contents of his suitcase into the sliding wardrobe. Within minutes they were going back down to reception in the glass-fronted elevator and Ellie made a beeline for the concierge.

His eyes flitted across the arrangements of the decorations in reception – paintings of figures in traditional dress, a statue of a white eagle wearing a crown, and an arrangement of red and white flags. And for the second time since his arrival in the city, a shadowy memory appeared. It took the form of a dusty flag, billowing against the wind. Was it a real memory, a dream or some indecipherable combination of both?

He stepped out into the street behind Ellie who was staring at a folded map, her nose wrinkled, her long hair piled haphazardly on top of her head.

"She's told me of a couple of good places to eat just down here," she announced, stabbing the paper, "We want to go in the direction of 'Centrum'. We'll reach a roundabout and that big palace will be on our left."

As they walked down the street, Matty got a full sense of what the taxi driver had meant. He was struck by the oddness of the architecture. The greying blocks of flats that they were passing looked like they hadn't been touched for fifty years. Cream bits of paint were flaking off the front doors and graffiti slogans obscured the blue plaques with the building numbers.

A huge moving billboard on the side of one of these buildings advertised a mobile phone company in garish pinks and purples.

Then, like a mirage in the desert, they were greeted with a glistening sheet of curving glass emerging in waves from behind the concrete block labelled 'Central Station'.

"What is that?"

Ellie scrutinised the map in his hand, "Another shopping centre. This one's called 'Golden Terraces.' It's the most bizarre mix that I've ever seen," she muttered, "You have old and you have new," she said spreading her hands, "but there's nothing in between. Why don't they spend some money renovating the old blocks of flats instead of pumping it into state of the art shopping centres? I mean people actually live in those places."

Matty copied the taxi driver's hand movement. Money. Money was the reason why anything ever happened.

Ellie's face dropped and her eager happiness seemed to evaporate in the face of such obvious materialism.

He kissed her gently and pulled her close and they walked off into a side street behind the main station, having passed the famous Palace of Science and Culture.

"It says here that it was given to Poland by the Russians in the year 1955. It used to be named after Stalin," said Ellie.

"Stalin's Palace?" He couldn't help laughing when he saw that even this relic of communism had been redeveloped to accommodate the commercial world. On one of its sides was a bright yellow and orange sign saying 'Kinoteka'. "It's a cinema. Ridiculous."

They walked further up the main side street and saw a church. A big dark plaque outside it was balanced on top of what looked like an artist's easel. Upon closer inspection he realised that it was there to commemorate those who had died in the air disaster. In the centre were two larger photographs of the president and his wife, and around them the smaller headshots of the other victims.

"I bet they're holding memorial masses for them all over Poland," said Ellie sadly.

As they walked on, the dark roads gave way to smaller dimly lit alleyways and Matty felt suddenly uncomfortable. There was an unfamiliar buzzing in his ears and in the pale grey haze of the early evening a desperate anxiety took hold of him. The dirty concrete around them brought on a sense of claustrophobia and he experienced a strange suffocating sensation, a tightness in his chest. He stopped walking, leaning his hand on a cold wall, densely covered in graffiti. *Death to the police. Down with Polonia FC.*

The wall belonged to another long stretch of flats in particularly bad shape. Fragments of the outer plaster had fallen off exposing the raw metal framework beneath. Were there still people living there?

There was a strange odour about the place, the earthy smell of concrete mixed with a sharp, acrid smell of urine and it tugged on something within his mind, attempting to free it from the dense scramble of his memory. And then a small and hazy cloud emerged, a half-formed thought. He was young, very young and running with somebody – another girl or boy, he wasn't sure… They were racing across a courtyard, racing each other and laughing. He was laughing so hard that he failed to look beneath his feet and all of a sudden he was flying through the air – with nothing to stop his fall except the palms of his hands, which were skidding on the rough concrete with an unbearable stinging pain, and coming to rest in front of a bin store, the blood mixing with the silt-like dirt that puffed up into plumes.

"Are you OK?"

Ellie's voice pulled him out of the memory. He shook himself free.

"Fine." But he wasn't. It was then that he realised for the first time that he was far from fine. The trouble was that he couldn't articulate what was wrong.

Ellie tucked her arm under his and they walked to the nearest restaurant. It served hearty Polish cuisine – pork chops in bread crumbs, dumplings, roast duck in apple sauce.

He helped himself to the jug of hot chicken soup in the centre of the table ignoring the internal turmoil that refused to lessen.

"Shall we go to the old town? Apparently it's really nice; they play jazz in the evenings and there are all sorts of little bars around."

But he could barely register the words that were coming out of her mouth.

"Yeah…"

"And then tomorrow maybe we can go to the Army museum? Or there's another new museum about the Warsaw Uprising. It's supposed to be really interactive."

"Sure, let's go." The restaurant was stifling. He felt a light trickle of sweat moving down the back of his collar.

"What are you thinking about?"

"Oh, nothing." A dull pain was eking its way slowly into his temples from the top of his spine. A wet fear swept through him, and then he sensed the awful feeling of his chest constricting.

"So what do you want to do tonight?"

"Erm… I don't mind. You choose."

A young waitress with heavy cat-like eye make-up came to take their order.

"Dziekuje," Matty muttered.

"Prosze," said the waiter.

Ellie stared at him. "What does that mean?"

"Hmm?"

"What you just said? You just said 'Jen…' something."

"Did I? Oh, dzienkuje. It means thank you. I read it in a guidebook or something."

Air. He needed air. He felt as though he was breathing through a straw and his heart was pounding in his chest as if at any moment it would let rip and free itself from his insides.

Close your eyes and count. You're not dying. You're not dying…

But his brain and heart wouldn't listen. They had freed themselves of his control.

"There's a gig on tonight at this place near the Old Town called Asphix… Sixties music – rock, Motown. It's happy hour all night apparently. What d'you reckon? I think…"

But he was already standing up. He automatically threw her his wallet and walked out quickly into the darkening night. The sky was the colour of pale charcoal and a few street lamps were already lit. In the half-shadows everything took on an unreal hue. Even the graffiti, so garish in the daylight, now looked as though it was part of a theatrical set.

He walked, as if driven by a magnetic force, back towards the wall by which he'd stood just half an hour before. It took him some time to locate it, but it was no less imposing in the dark. He leaned on it, his hands on his knees, breathing hard. Time passed. Above him, the half-moon disappeared, concealed by a smattering of clouds, and for a few moments he could only hear the heavy hammering in his own chest, which gradually slowed, until it was normal, or somewhere close to normal. Around him, the city was filled with that same distinct yet indiscernible smell, as if the very air here was thicker, more significant.

In answer to his previous question about whether the building beside him was inhabited, an old woman in a floral apron emerged onto one of the balconies to hang out her washing.

He caught her gaze and had a strange desire to call out to her, but he had no sense of what he wanted to say. She shuddered in the coolness of the night and retreated into the flat, frightened.

And then again, the flicker of a vision. Him as a young boy sitting on a balcony, his legs dangling through the railings, observing the passers-by. Another child's hand pouring a collection of petals into his open palm and him taking them, delighted, and emptying them out over the moving heads in the street below.

Frustratingly, no matter how hard he focused, he could conjure up neither the building he was in nor the face of the other child, and both of these facts seemed important. They seemed vitally important.

Matty stared back down at the pavement. The tessellating pattern of rectangular paving slabs stretched out down the road, left-right-left-right. He would have to go back and find Ellie. She had the map. He would struggle to locate the hotel on his own in the dark. Had he taken his phone? He patted his pockets. He must have left it at the restaurant. Which direction had they come from? He couldn't be sure.

He chose at random and turned abruptly to his left, colliding with a tall, bald-headed man in a hoodie.

The guy leered at him and shouted 'Spadaj!' The word produced an unpleasant echo in the empty neighbourhood and prompted Matty to run. He bolted down the street, his blood pumping. The man would catch up with him at any second. He could hear his pounding feet, but his chest wouldn't allow him to run any faster. He waited to feel the rough tug of a hand on his shoulder, but there was nothing.

"Matty? Is it you? God. What's happened?"

She was standing in the middle of the road, her dark hair illuminated by the light from a nearby lamppost.

"Oh God Ellie, the guy." He stopped right in front of her and rapidly turned around. There was nobody there.

"What's going on?" Her fear gave way to anger.

"I just… I thought somebody was chasing me."

"Why did you just bolt out of the restaurant like that?"

"I…" He searched his brain hopelessly for an explanation. "I felt sick. I needed some air." It wasn't really a lie, but he knew that it also wasn't the whole truth.

Chapter 6 – Tom
Chicago

Spring was in full swing. Tom could sense it in the air when he opened the windows and he could finally switch off the central heating which had worsened the itch on his skin.

Lately, even small tasks seemed impossible, so he pretty much spent his entire time in front of the TV. That was where he first learnt of the Polish plane crash. The beautiful young woman on the news relayed the details calmly and he took them on board with a stoic detachment. It's as if his tired brain couldn't process the enormity of what he had just heard. It was only later, when he was lying in bed, convincing himself that the news story had been real and not a figment of his exhausted mind, that he experienced the catastrophe on a personal level. Almost 200 people dead, and most of them younger than him. So many important figures, so many political leaders, economists, thinkers… so much unfinished business, so many unspoken conversations with family members, so many unresolved arguments. These were things that he was all too painfully aware of and they unexpectedly brought with them a raw guilt that he thought he had buried too deeply for excavation.

Tom avoided watching TV after that and chose to sit outdoors instead. He'd been meaning to sort out the garden for so long that Sally finally felt sorry for him and had offered to 'help out'. The crocuses that she'd planted a few months earlier had already come and gone.

"They're to celebrate ten years of our friendship," she'd announced.

He couldn't believe that a decade had passed since he'd moved into Cardinal Drive, right next door to Mitch and Sally, a kind, vibrant couple whom he now considered to be his best friends. Sally was a dab hand when it came to gardening and he was already looking forward to the summer plants that she had in store for him – the damask rose, the hosta and the lavender, which did well in Chicago's changeable climate.

By mid-June the amaryllis would be out, the carnations would be beginning, and the irises would be in full bloom. He liked to sit in his chair in the living room window and visualise it all – but he couldn't rid himself of the fear that he might not see it because he was dying. There was a chance that he could be gone by the peak of summer.

He had liver cancer. The Owl had told him so two weeks ago now, a deep and genuine sadness in her green eyes. He accepted the news calmly. If he were being honest with himself, he had subconsciously known it for a while.

"There are many things that we can do, of course," she said hurriedly. "We can start you on a course of chemotherapy right away."

Many years ago, after watching his colleague Fi go through chemotherapy for an aggressive form of breast cancer, suffer and then slowly, slowly and painfully die, Tom had resolved that he would never put himself through it.

"No," he said, "No thanks. Not for me."

"Well, it's your decision of course and you don't have to make it right away. I know that it's a shocking piece of news and there is a lot to consider."

But The Owl was wrong. The news wasn't shocking. It just filled Tom with a dull, aching sorrow. He told Mitch and Sally about it the very same day with as much calmness as he could muster.

"I'm going to need help," he admitted. It's what he'd been told by the nurses, after he'd categorically rejected the chemotherapy. "Maybe not straight away, but soon." He was already having trouble making his own food, because his hands shook, and the other day he'd sat down on the stairs and couldn't get up again for a full fifteen minutes.

"We'll *obviously* help in any way that we can. You don't have to ask," said Sally. "You shouldn't be worrying about dinner. Let me at least do that. I always cook for myself and Mitch anyway, so one extra portion would honestly make no difference to me. In fact, it would be a pleasure."

"That's really kind of you. It is," he said, looking into her wrinkled, anxious face. "But we both know that it's going to be a lot more than just the food. The nurses say that they're going to need to send a carer. Because one day soon I won't even be able to get myself to the bloody loo."

They were sitting at opposite ends of his big, oak dining room table as he said this. It was the only piece of furniture in the entire house that he took pride in. The thick, knotted and unvarnished wood reminded him of childhood. He'd seen it in a junk shop window only a couple of weeks after moving into the neighbourhood and even though it was huge and bulky, and didn't in the slightest match his other furniture, he knew that he would have to get it. He couldn't bear the idea of an absolute stranger making food on it, having discussions across it, cleaning it.

"Well, we'll make sure we find you a good one," Mitch told him, "and a good *looking* one, eh? A proper young babe?"

He winked encouragingly, but Tom ignored him. He felt too tired to even hold up his head, so he placed it in his hands and continued to speak to them whilst staring down at a rough, brown mug stain.

"I don't want anyone else in this house. I can't bear spending my last days one on one with somebody who's being paid to look after me and who most probably doesn't want to be there!"

He was shouting now, the last few words spat out furiously into the middle of the circular stain. This isn't how it was supposed to be. It couldn't be… surely it couldn't be his recompense for four decades of work? He'd hardly ever taken holidays, often worked much later than his designated hours, gone into the dealership on Saturdays, even when he had the flu. And now he was finally supposed to be paid back for all of those missed weekends, the toil, the hardship…

"You know it's not your only option."

He forced himself to look up at her. Despite being a full two years younger, Sally exuded a motherliness which had made Tom warm to her immediately all those years ago.

"What do you mean?" he asked carefully.

The silence swelled between them. Sally opened and closed her mouth a couple of times as if fearful of the effect of her words.

"I don't want you to take this the wrong way," she said eventually, "but there is a very good nursing home that I know of. My niece used to work there before she moved to New York. I honestly wouldn't recommend it if I didn't believe that it was good. They treat people well and the staff are truly special."

"You mean *Sunshine*? Hell, I remember it," said Mitch suddenly, grateful for something helpful to say. "I swear to you, I said to Sal when we went to visit that I wouldn't mind staying there myself. Didn't I say that?"

"You did, you did."

Tom stared at them both. He was about to object, but strangely, when he thought about it, he wasn't as repulsed by the idea as he first thought.

"What's it like?" he asked hesitantly.

"Well… it's bright, it's huge – it's got these acres of gardens. And the patients… the people in there do stuff together. They play cards, and eat together, and talk all the time. It was completely the opposite of what we'd expected. Anyway, why don't we go so you can see for yourself? You don't need to make a decision either way. You could just get a feel of the place?"

Tom could see that she was rambling now, desperate to make sure that she hadn't upset him.

"OK," he said resignedly. What else could he do?

***

They drove to *Sunshine* that weekend in Mitch's car. His grandchildren had recently been to visit, so Tom had to squeeze himself uncomfortably into a back seat that already housed two child seats. He was shocked to see that he had lost so much weight that he could fit in quite comfortably in between them.

His mood had been dark from the moment of waking and he was beginning to regret his decision. The leaden weight of inevitability pressed down on him so hard that he could barely focus on what he was doing. He sat in the back of the car not speaking, and focusing on nothing else but the rhythmic rise and fall of his chest. He wasn't gone. Not yet.

And then they pulled up into what he could only describe as a white manor house. The building had checked royal blue curtains billowing in the breeze, and pots filled with blood red pelargoniums outside the windows. When he managed to pull himself out of the car, he noticed that the 'manor' was perched atop a hill, and the beautiful view of the green valley spread out below it, giving way to a thin yellow sliver of beach, and finally the endless crashing sea. He'd always loved the sea. He was drawn to it like a fisherman or a ship's captain. There was something calming about its vastness and depth, which made him feel so small in comparison.

Sally took him by the elbow and nudged him gently in the direction of the porch. Mitch led the way, his bulky torso swaying gently from side to side as he ascended the stairs. At the top, he turned and waited for them to catch up. Flanked by the elaborate columns of the entrance way, Tom thought that he looked like a British lord from the Victorian times, surveying his land.

But before he could press the doorbell, a woman emerged to greet them. She was short and energetic, with dark, coffee-coloured skin and a shock of curls.

"Hello. Mr. and Mrs. Jefferson?"

"That's us."

"It's lovely to meet you. Welcome to *Sunshine*. And this is?"

"This is Tom."

"Hi Tom. I'm Clara. I'm one of the senior nurses here. Today, I'm just here to give you a little tour if that sounds OK?"

"Yes."

And that was all. No pity, no questions about his condition, no fake smiles or other nonsense. Clara merely motioned for the three of them to follow her, and led them straight into a spacious room with clusters of tables and soft, antique-looking leather sofas. There was music emanating from a corner, and Tom identified a David Bowie track.

He was shocked to see that there were people of all ages filling the room. Many were old, or 'older' (as he considered himself), but there were some who were middle-aged, and others still who were really quite young. To the left of him, a girl with a bald head, who looked no older than twenty-five sat laughing at a black and white film being projected onto a screen above the fireplace.

Just behind her, three men sat at a card table mock-arguing about who'd won the last round of the game. Two of them were focussed on counting the cards on the table, but the third – a small man with receding ginger hair and an eager expression looked up and grinned at him.

"Are you a potential newbie?" he asked. "I'm Dustin. I'll save you a seat," he motioned, pointing to the empty space to his right.

And that was when he knew. He hadn't even seen the rooms, met the other nurses, or discussed any payment details, when he begrudgingly admitted that he would make *Sunshine* his home.

Chapter 7 – Joanna
Warsaw

Joanna stared at the blinking cursor on the screen and willed her brain into focus. She scrolled through the pages of text that she'd amassed so far. Paragraphs of tiny letters in different fonts, which she'd meticulously pasted from a range of different sources, stared back at her. There was so much to get through, and so little time in which to get a structure together, select her case studies, conduct any interviews if necessary… But she was ready. She's been prepared for this moment for months, training herself up for the starter's pistol. She was desperate for the piece to be a success, and she realised that the only way to guarantee this was by making herself entirely detached from the subject matter, a casual observer. And it would all have been fine, if not for her treacherous memory which kept pulling her back from the present, demanding attention, today of all days.

It was her birthday. She usually hated working on special occasions, but today she felt grateful for having an excuse not to go out. She shut the laptop and lay her head in her hands, allowing herself just the briefest of pauses from the endless reading. Somewhere from the murky depths of her tired mind, a small hand emerged, its helpless fingers gripping the empty air. She reached out, her adult arm extended, so freakishly large in comparison. She could grasp hold of it in time, if only she could stretch out enough – but the sudden piercing sound of her house phone ringing brought her back to consciousness and sent her fevered mind racing. For a fleeting second the usual mad thought struck her that it could be her brother.

The fantasy of him ringing on this birthday played itself out in her head every year. She waved it away physically, with a flick of the hand, and ran into the kitchen to pick up the receiver.

"Joanna?" asked a man's voice.

"Hello. Who is this?"

"It's Marek. You're not picking up your mobile," her boss said accusingly.

"Oh sorry. Maybe it's out of battery. I've just been working on the piece you see…"

"Ah, that's great to hear. I knew I could rely on you to get started straight away. How's the research going?"

"Yes, very well. I've got access to the national newspaper archives online. I also have the name of the person to get in touch with at the local police department and at DELTA," Joanna answered truthfully, "I've developed a sort of… relationship with them."

"DELTA?"

"The foundation that supports the families of missing people."

"Oh, right. Well it seems that you've done quite a lot," said Marek impressed, "So where are you going to start?"

"Well…" she said weakly, "I suppose I'll go and visit them and go through the cases on their files – obviously the ones that are open to the public – and then work from there?"

"Sounds good. Tell them it'll be good publicity for the families of the victims too."

"Of course," she said, not quite registering what she meant.

"You know, we can feature the photos of all the cases you select. We get good readership figures. Those families will be craving coverage, particularly if their case was closed years before. Loads of them would have been battling to keep their story in the press."

"Yes… I'm sure they will ," Joanna mumbled, a wet feeling of nausea forming out of nowhere at the back of her throat.

"OK, well I'll leave you to it," he said happily, and hung up the phone without saying goodbye.

Joanna picked up her laptop from amongst the stacks of paper and dirty crockery on her desk and pulled it into bed with her. She knew it was hopeless, but her fingers automatically typed 'Adam Malicki' into the search engine. She eyeballed the results on the first three pages, but she could tell that there was nothing new, no antidote to the hopeless anticipation that maybe, just maybe something might appear.

There was no sense of order to dealing with a missing family member. No manual that would help you through, guide you along your painful way. In hindsight, she realised, it was not too dissimilar to grief, which even years later continues to churn up memories that you thought were long buried.

And sometimes the rage would descend on her unannounced. She would overhear conversations between the girls at work and the fury would build and build in her until she wanted to collapse with the bursting enormity of it – they spoke of failing an interview or having a row with their boyfriend or a two-day power cut in their flat, and she wanted to scream at them – 'You don't know what pain feels like! You don't know what it's like waking up every morning and sometimes not knowing who you are, because all of the people who were closest to you – who had made you who you were – are essentially gone.'

She should have rang Marek days ago to tell him that she wouldn't do the feature. Surely if she'd explained why, he would have understood and given her another chance on a piece with a different topic – anything – she could even cover that sports piece that they were planning further down the line. She yearned to be objective, to distance herself from the subject matter, but every time she tried, the memories came back stronger. But today's phone conversation with Marek had cemented her certainty that she would do it.

It would mean going back to see Stefan at the police station. She had spent so many hours with him that they were on first name terms. He was always painfully polite, but he was probably sick of the sight of her, of the manic persistence of her search.

It would be decent to email him, she thought, to at least warn him that she would be coming. He'd looked so annoyed when she waltzed through the door last time, unannounced, demanding to look at her brother's files for the umpteenth time.

"You're not going to find anything new in there," he'd warned her, but she'd insisted. She'd felt she might have a brainwave if she looked again at the facts from that awful day – that worst day at the end of the miserable eighties. Of course, she'd left with nothing but a feeling of dry hopelessness.

Hi Stefan,

Hope you've had a great Easter break. I wondered if I could come and see you tomorrow? Don't worry; I'm not going to root around in Adam's stuff again. I'm writing a feature piece for the magazine on missing people. Not my idea – the editor's.

Let me know when works for you,

Joanna Malicka

She put the laptop on the floor and curled up again into a foetal position. Maybe she'd been too brusque in her email. Her impulsive nature often led her into trouble.

Had she always been like this? She tried to remember her behaviour as a child. She had been shy, mostly. She would never have run off into the crowds without her mum. Why had Adam run away? She waved the question away. It wasn't the right one. *Did* Adam run away? Her theory was that the answer was 'no'. He may have been different from her, more spirited, but he wouldn't have just left without reason. Joanna didn't believe her mother's theory that he'd gone to search for their dad. Adam would have understood that he'd died, surely? They'd had a memorial service for him, for God's sake.

If therefore, he didn't run away, he must have been snatched, and the strike had been a perfect opportunity for that. But why would someone want to snatch a little boy? And how would they have managed to keep him hidden for so many years? Here is where Joanna's theory stopped without any further progress.

"You have to let go," her Aunt Irena had said that very Christmas, "If you don't let go you'll end up like your mother."

She would give up, but for those moments of peaceful certainty that Adam was there. No matter how far apart they were, no matter how much they were split by time and place, there would always be that thin invisible thread binding them together, which could stretch into infinity. And every now and then, she could feel that reassuring, imperceptible tug at her brother's end.

'One final chance', she said aloud. True to her nature, she made the decision instantaneously and she would stick with it. If she was going to write this piece, she would feature Adam's case in it. No, she wouldn't just feature it. It would be the leading case – so leading, that Marek couldn't edit it out.

Chapter 8 – Matty
London

She was already in there, her pale, freckled hand clasping the neck of the wine glass. When he was small he loved looking at her hands, so pale that they were almost translucent, the purple latticework of veins just visible through the papery skin. She would gently hold him with these hands when he had nightmares and wasn't able to speak. That was in the days when she still insisted on being called 'Mother'.

She was sitting at her usual table, stoic and composed, rifling through a glossy brochure filled with photos of new builds, period homes, sixties 'classics', mock-Tudor mansions split into flats and any other type of property that most young couples in London would dream of owning, but in reality could never hope to afford.

She was wearing a tight, elegant and well-cut dress, one of many in her wardrobe which, in her own words 'instantly took a decade off her' and gave an air of nonchalant confidence which was very necessary in her line of work. And when it came to peddling property in what was, quite frankly, the hardest market in at least twenty years, Celia was the don.

The trick, as she'd divulged to Matty and Ellie, was not caring. You went in, showed your clients around, carelessly highlighted some of the key features of the home, which they would be stupid to miss out on, and then swiftly took them back towards the door, creating the impression that whether they were interested or not was really neither here nor there, because there were simply plenty of others lining up to nab it.

Celia always chuckled happily about another unsuspecting prospective buyer that she'd managed to snare into her net. "And, he ended up paying at least thirty grand more than he had to," she divulged, winking at them and raising a toast to her own success.

Then there was talk of all of the red carpet premieres that she'd been to lately. One of her friends from drama school – for Celia, in her youth, had been intending to be an actress – had achieved great things in Hollywood, and she'd miraculously remained friends with Celia through it all, inviting her to many of her award ceremonies in London and other celebrity events. She was notoriously brushing shoulders with somebody famous.

"So I met Kimmy last night. She's a new and up and coming director – she's got a son your age. I was telling her all about you actually…"

Matty inwardly rolled his eyes. Celia was known for always embarrassing him. When he was at school she would brag to everyone about his latest exam results, when he'd gone to uni, she would slip in 'Cambridge' at every opportunity, and now it was 'My son the financier,' a description that he despised.

He had studied maths for the worst reason, it appeared. It wasn't because he yearned for wealth or success, or due to a sense of entitlement, but simply because he loved numbers and he was good with them. Some people were good at writing, or painting, or engineering – and his huge, and luckily quite respectable passion, was numbers. As a child, Celia indulged him in this hunger and did everything to fuel it. She allowed him to take control of the food shopping budget, and, aged six, challenged him in the supermarket to work out in his head, as they walked around the isles, the running total cost of the items they put in their trolley. She bought him the latest mathematical puzzle computer games, and once even enrolled him in an international maths challenge when she realised the stuff that he was learning at school just wasn't stretching him.

The trouble was that he couldn't concentrate enough to revise for the paper, as his mind was too busy to ever focus on one thing for two long. Maths was something that he had stuck with the longest, and now finance had followed. But he was increasingly feeling that he was reaching the end of his tether with finance too. He knew better than to tell his mother that.

Celia poured out her previously ordered expensive bottle of red wine into their glasses, without asking whether they wanted it.

"So what have you been doing with yourselves recently?" she asked breezily, now that she'd had enough time to give a thorough report on her life.

"Well, my class is doing alright. We had a school inspection the other week, but I think it all went alright. We won't get the results for another couple of weeks, but the head teacher seems positive," said Ellie with forced happiness.

"That's good." That was it. There were no other questions, and not even a flicker of interest from Celia. Matty was angry with her for caring so little, and he wondered at his mother's behaviour. Ellie was so kind, so inoffensive. Surely it couldn't be anything to do with her? Would his mother have acted the same towards any other girlfriend that he'd introduced to her? He never had, so he didn't know. He was increasingly suspicious that it could be jealousy that was driving the coldness. Ellie's main fault in Celia's eyes was probably that she was taking all of her son's time.

"And how is everything at Chipston Capital?" she asked, turning swiftly to him.

"Oh, it's fine, you know. The same," he lied.

"You look tired." She gently stroked the back of his hand. "You should take a break. You work too long."

"I'm fine. I'm getting enough sleep," he said, pre-empting her question. "We've even had a small holiday recently."

"Oh?"

"Yes, just a long weekend. We went on a city break."

"I wasn't aware," said Celia drily. She took a heavy gulp of wine, "Where was it? Paris? You two are so romantic."

"No actually. We thought we'd do something a bit different. We went to Warsaw."

"Warsaw? Why Warsaw?" Her left hand turned her ring round and round the finger on her right at an increasing pace and she swept a sheet of blond hair onto her back.

"Oh you know, we didn't want to do any of the typical touristy places." he said quickly, "And we found out that flights to Poland were cheap and that there were quite a few places to see."

"Interesting choice," she said, casting them a strange look, "Is there anything exciting to see there these days? I remember thinking that it was all rather boring."

"You were there?" asked Matty, "When? Did we go there when I was little?" Perhaps that was the explanation, the reason why he'd felt the way that he did… The relief swept over him in waves. He should have known that there would be a reason.

But she was quick to refute it. "No, don't be silly. I went there before you were around, with one of my old boyfriends."

In the dim candlelight her face had gone a strange colour – a sallow, larval white.

"Oh right. And what made you decide to go there?" Ellie asked her politely.

She hesitated before answering and there was again that strange, almost melancholy gaze as she looked over at Matty.

"We were travelling around Eastern Europe. He was interested in all of those Soviet Bloc States," she said eventually, "I can't think why…"

"Celia…" He had been preparing himself to ask her the question for weeks now. It wasn't the right time really. But then, when had it ever been the right time? She'd always been honest about his adoption. She'd told him from the moment that he was old enough to understand that she hadn't given birth to him, but it didn't mean that she wasn't his mother, or that she loved him any less or any differently from those mothers who had given birth to their children. But there seemed to be an unspoken rule that he should never ask any more about the adoption.

He'd tried once, aged eight or nine, out of pure curiosity about his own background. At school, they'd been learning about different jobs and speaking about what their parents did, and Matty was keen to find out where his birth parents had worked. Had they been good at maths like he was? And if they were, what did that maths lead them to do? It was a valid question, when Celia clearly had such different skills from him – her power after all lay in words, and their manipulation.

It had been a brilliant Sunday in late summer and they had spent the day baking, and then eating their home-made cupcakes with strawberries and thick, clotted cream that oozed through the gaps between his milk teeth. And even as he asked the question, Matty experienced an impending sadness at the prospect of potentially ruining such a perfect moment, one in which everything – the taste of the soft buttered sponge between his lips, his mother's laughter and the parachute balls of dandelion heads dancing in the breeze – had combined so beautifully together, only to have him upset it. And he did upset it, or rather he upset Celia, who answered his innocent question brusquely and swiftly returned indoors explaining that she had work to do.

And now, twenty years later, Matty experienced the same sense of desperate trepidation. Perhaps he should have called her 'Mother' to soften what he was about to say.

"Yes?" she asked, her usually flat forehead creased with concern.

"You know my adoption papers… can I see them?"

Her fork juddered in her hand, but she recovered quickly, her voice solid and silky smooth. He noticed that it had gone up an octave – it was the tone that she usually used when delivering a sales pitch.

"Of course, I'll have to dig them out. I'm not sure where they are. But why?"

"I just wanted to see if I could find out something, you know… about my heritage."

"You won't," she said calmly, putting a forkful of salad in her mouth, "Your birth parents wanted to remain anonymous. I've told you this many times. So you won't be able to find out anything about them. I'm sorry Matty. I can't stop you looking, but I just think it's a waste of your time."

And that was it.

As they walked back through the darkening streets of Soho, still heavy with the pedestrian traffic of drunk office workers, he wondered whether he should have asked the question at all. It was evident that she wouldn't follow up on his request anyway and he would only have to remind her.

But he felt that he had to ask. A memory had been unlocked within his mind – the hazy, blurred image of something which he knew was so vital. The carefree lightness of a few weeks ago had evaporated and left nothing but an icy sense of foreboding.

"It must be painful for her," said Ellie, linking her arm with his, "She's the one who brought you up and she's scared of being displaced. I think she already feels threatened enough by me, because I'm with you all the time."

"It's life though, isn't it? Most people's kids move out eventually and get girlfriends or boyfriends. Plus she's got Kimmy and the celeb gang. They should keep her busy."

He stopped and looked at her directly. The setting sun blinded him, causing pale blue dancing dots to appear between them. In this light she looked beautiful, even more so than usual, her dark hair framing her elfin face. In moments like this, he was struck by how lucky he was to be with her. Out of so many men walking the streets of London, so many better looking, more successful, funnier men, she had chosen him. But she didn't understand him fully. She couldn't.

"I want to know about myself, Ellie. You don't know what it's like – not knowing. There must be something. Even if there's no record of their names, there must be something."

"You could contact the adoption agency?"

"Celia says it no longer exists. It's closed down."

She shrugged her shoulders. "Surely there are organisations that can help with this sort of thing?"

"Maybe. But in order to search properly, I need to have the documents in front of me."

"She said that she'll give them to you. Give her a chance."

"Fine." He would. He decided then that he would press her for them for as long as it took.

Chapter 9 – Tom
Chicago

Something strange had happened to Tom since his arrival at *Sunshine*. Six weeks had passed in a blur of document signing, removal vans and adjustments to his new life. He could barely believe that it was already May. He had fully expected his symptoms to get worse, but strangely, if anything, he felt that he had more energy now than before his diagnosis.

"It's what the place does to you," Dustin said on the first day that he moved in when Tom admitted he wasn't feeling all that bad. "It stalls you a bit. It's as if your body knows that you're now in safe hands and you don't have to worry. Don't get me wrong. It's not like you're cured or anything. But maybe for a little while, you're a bit better than you were. Enjoy it. What are you in for?"

"What?"

Dustin laughed – a deep belly laugh – and slapped him on the back.

"I mean, what do you have? What's wrong with you?"

"Oh. Liver cancer."

"Nice. Got the crustacean myself, but of the lung variety. Seems like we both overindulged, eh?"

"How long have you been here?" Tom asked. He had the impression that people never stayed long in God's waiting room.

"Ten months and five days so far," Dustin announced proudly, "I'm hoping that I might make it to a year."

He was shocked at this news and a little amazed. He wanted desperately to ask whether Dustin's symptoms had worsened, whether he was feeling much sicker now than when he started, what the doctor's prognosis was for him. But it was too early, far too early for details like that.

"It's not usual, you know."

"What isn't?"

"The amount of time that I've stayed here. Most people are six monthers at most," he said sadly. "I've already said goodbye to two of my poker opponents. It doesn't make it easy, I can tell you that."

"No; I'm sure it doesn't."

"But I have a feeling about you."

"Yeah?"

"I have a feeling that you might be a hanger on, just like me."

"Oh, I don't think so."

Lately, he'd been thinking how lucky he'd been to get this far at all. With the constant wars and disasters on the news, he'd wondered how it was possible that all those thousands of people were dying and not him. There had been the Polish plane crash, and the Baja earthquake in California, and countless other tragedies, and that was just in the past few months. Both incidents of course were freak accidents, but he couldn't help but feel paranoid. His mother's words came back to him: 'We live in times in which you can trust nobody but yourself.' It was an exaggeration of course, but it was a true reflection of the times in which he'd grown up.

Now, of course, things were different. The awful news stories had been followed by Obama speaking about the efforts to support those affected by the tragedies. He was a good man, the current president. For the first time in years, Tom felt that there was some sort of stability in the political system that he found himself in. But he was filled with a sad certainty that it wouldn't last.

"Well, let's have a bet, shall we?" Dustin asked him now. "I bet you that you'll still be here come Christmas. How about that? It's a good bet to enter into for you, because if you're not here then you don't have to pay me back," he said, slapping Tom on the knee, and laughing.

The deal was so ridiculous and the laughter so infectious that Tom couldn't help but join in.

By the end of the second week, he'd managed to settle into a form of routine. In the mornings, his breakfast would be brought to him by the lovely, curly-haired nurse who had shown him round. He was glad that out of all of the nursing staff she'd been assigned to him. It wasn't because she was kind, or efficient in her work, although she was both of those things and they were qualities which Tom greatly admired. It was because there was something about her that was captivating, something interesting that lay there simmering below the surface. He longed to find out more about her.

After breakfast, every other day, the doctor would come and check in on him. He was still quite young, but prematurely balding. Unlike The Owl, he was friendly and open, and didn't wear the doctor's usual attire of a white coat, all of which meant that his visits were far less daunting than they otherwise could have been. He measured Tom's blood pressure, checked his skin and eyes and prescribed painkillers that made life on the whole quite bearable.

Early afternoons were Tom's favourite. He spent them in the living room with Dustin and the others and every day was different. Usually it would involve watching an old classic film, playing poker or checkers, or listening to the young girl, Susie, whom he'd seen on the day that he was shown round, play guitar. He had to admit she was very talented.

But today, Dustin was feeling particularly talkative, and Kyle and Andy, the two men who used to accompany them at cards were engrossed in 'It's a Wonderful Life.' They were both decent men. Kyle, a large, red-faced fifty-year old with a fast-acting brain tumour; Andy still in his late thirties, a leukaemia sufferer.

"You got a wife?"

"No…" said Tom. He didn't want to go into it. Not now. But Dustin was insistent.

"No, as in not now? Or no as in not ever?"

"Not now. I did in the past."

"How many?"

"Two."

He wolf-whistled. "Two eh? What happened to them? Did they pass on?"

Tom hated it when people said 'pass on'. Where had the saying come from? It stupidly reminded him of the phrase used to describe somebody deciding not to eat a particular dish or take part in a game. No thanks, *I'll pass on that.* Except in this case 'that' was 'life' and there was no choice involved.

"No, they haven't. Not as far as I know, anyway. They left me."

It wasn't strictly true. Well, in one case it was. In the other, it was quite a different scenario. But Tom didn't want to explain this.

"I'm sorry," said Dustin.

"It was years ago. How about you?"

"Dead. She was the love of my life. The most beautiful woman that I ever laid eyes on."

Tom groaned internally.

"Clichés, I know. I could probably express it better, more originally. But it's true and it's the plainest way of putting it."

"Do you have a photo?"

Dustin was pleasantly surprised by his sudden interest.

"Of course. I have some in my room, but look – I can show you on here." He pointed to the row of desktop computers lining the wall at the far end of the room. Only one of them was occupied by a large Asian lady who seemed to be carefully typing out an extremely long email using just two fingers.

"You store your photos on there?" Tom asked, with shock. He had a fundamental distrust of computers. In his experience, they were unreliable electric boxes which were forever shrinking in size and ironically causing people to lose contact with one another. He'd successfully managed to avoid them during the many years that he worked for *South Shore Autos*. Until the mid-nineties, they had got by very well without them, and by then he was the boss – so all of the computer admin could be outsourced to his more junior staff. In terms of his personal life, he hadn't needed to go near them. He had nobody to email whom he couldn't write a letter to, and he was luckily still able to do all of his banking in person.

"No, no. I don't have them saved on there. They're just on the internet – on social media."

And before he could protest any further, Dustin patted the seat next to him in front of the computer screen, and there was no way out.

Tom watched as he logged into his profile. He knew that it was Dustin's profile from the large photo that filled the left-hand side of the screen. His colleagues at work had once shown him their own profiles with a similar set-up. From the photo, a noticeably fatter Dustin, in a velvet suit and a glitzy bow tie grinned at him.

"It was taken at my daughter's wedding last year. She's the one with photos of Mandy."

"Right."

Dustin moved the mouse and clicked on something on his screen which caused another profile to pop up, this time featuring a blond girl with a shock of curly hair.

He clicked on the picture and a small white arrow appeared on the screen to the left of it. This apparently enabled him to view a whole album of other photos.

"This is her, look – this is Mandy on the left with our two daughters. That was just before the last stroke. We went on a road trip round Scandinavia. It was before Hayley graduated from uni."

He could see that Dustin's boasting hadn't been misplaced. The woman in the photo really was stunning – a striking olive-skinned lady with a broad smile and large green eyes. He'd clearly done very well for himself.

"She's beautiful," he told him, to his great pleasure.

Dustin continued to flick through to see if there were any others.

"How do you do that? How can you see all of those?" Tom asked, despite himself.

"What d'you mean?"

"Are there endless pictures? Do people all over the world just put up reams and reams of photos for everyone to view?"

Dustin stopped and looked at him.

"You've never been on social media?"

He shook his head.

"You've never had the temptation to catch up with people, to share memories? Even to spy on people that you used to know and then lost touch with?"

"Yes, but there's no guarantee that the people you want to connect with are on there," he said dismissively.

"No, you're right," Dustin admitted, "But I read in the paper that there are around 360 million people on here at the moment, so the odds are in your favour. You want me to help you set up a profile?"

The question caused the familiar beetle crawl to develop in the pit of Tom's stomach. He was gripped by a rare anxiety coupled with another very peculiar emotion, which he hadn't felt in years. He mumbled something non-committal to Dustin and said that he would get back to him. It was only when he returned to his room later that afternoon that he realised that the emotion wasn't worry, it was a flutter of something like hope.

Chapter 10 – Joanna
Warsaw

"I haven't seen you in a while," said Stefan. Joanna wondered whether he was being sarcastic, but he appeared to have a genuine smile on his face. He looked much older than the last time that she'd seen him. The webs of wrinkles around his eyes had deepened and his features seemed somehow looser. She watched as his stubby fingers tapped out an impatient rhythm on the desk.

"I know. I tried to 'relax' about it, as you asked me, but Adam never seems to leave me alone," she admitted, sitting down in the chair opposite and looking Stefan straight in the eye.

"So your editor actually asked you to write a piece on him? It's a bit insensitive, isn't it?" There was outrage in his voice, but he was looking at her with that peculiar expression – a mixture of gentleness, and acute interest in what she had to say. Not even Irena paid her this much attention. The last time that she was here, Joanna had left with the intense feeling that he had been on the verge of asking her out to dinner, but in the end he hadn't said anything and she was grateful for it.

"No, the piece is generally about missing people," she explained. "He doesn't know about Adam. You might find it strange to hear this, but only my closest friends know about my brother. I just don't think it's important to... I just don't think I have to..."

"Don't worry, I understand," Stefan cut her off, "But how did you want me to help you?"

"Well... I wanted to collect a variety of case notes belonging to different people. Those who went missing when they were very young, like Adam, and those who disappeared at an older age. I want to cover different parts of the country and include cases with varying degrees of evidence, where you're authorised to give it to me of course. It would be good to have a mixture of cases – some resolved and others closed without a resolution."

"You do realise this is information which I can't release to you under the Data Protection Act?"

"I'm not looking for *sensitive* information, only things that are available in the public domain. Newspaper clippings, reports given to journalists – that sort of thing. It would save me hours of trawling through the media archives."

Stefan looked at her and seemed to consider something. She noticed his right eyelid twitching – a trapped nerve? There was something endearing about it, this symptom of tiredness, of overwork. How old was he? Probably late thirties, she guessed, although his hair was turning grey at a rapid pace. She wondered how many years he'd been here, sitting at his desk, puzzling over the reams of notes, incomplete evidence, false statements. Did the rare success of capturing a known offender make up for all the times in which Stefan must have felt inadequate and hopeless?

"How many do you need?" he asked eventually.

"I think about twenty. That would be enough for me to select some interesting content from."

"Right, well… I obviously won't be able to get them to you straight away, but I can have something for you by the end of the week. Are you… are you going to feature Adam?"

"Yes; I want to. And don't look at me like that, I've got nothing to lose by doing it and I don't believe that it will uncover anything new. It would just… well, it would feel wrong to write about this and not feature him. It would be as if I was denying that it ever happened."

"What about your mother? Doesn't she read *Prawda*?

He gave her a sad smile and she suddenly remembered the first time that she'd met him. She was seventeen at the time. It was a time in which her mother still managed to hold it together, at least in public. She had come to the police station in her wool skirt and jacket, holding her black umbrella with the duck head handle. She had made a few polite enquiries and seemed to accept everything that Stefan told her, whilst Joanna fumed. In public, her mother maintained an impeccable demeanour at all times and spoke of Adam's case as if it were a sad story that had happened to a close friend.

She wondered what Adam would have thought if he saw Monika now, sitting in her nursing home staring quietly into the middle distance, occasionally rocking backwards and forwards to a mournful tune that only she could hear. She was barely 57, but she already looked like somebody who was twenty years older.

"Depression" was the simple diagnosis, but it was evident to Joanna that it was more than that. It almost seemed as if she was an Alzheimer's sufferer, so powerful was her detachment from everything and everyone around her.

"No; I'm afraid she doesn't," Joanna answered simply. It wasn't a lie. She hated lying.

"Fine," Stefan sighed, "I promise I'll prioritise it all for you. I know that you probably have urgent deadlines.

She sensed that he wouldn't do it for anyone else.

"Thanks; I appreciate it."

The air outside the station was cold and crisp. It pierced her cheeks with a metallic sharpness, making her pull her scarf tightly around her lower face. She was grateful to Marek for allowing her to work from home until the first draft had to be submitted in three weeks' time – there was no way that she could get her thoughts together in the office.

She walked back home dreading what she was about to do. The small suitcase at the bottom of her wardrobe hadn't been opened for almost three years and Joanna couldn't remember when she'd last read through the yellowed, musty newspaper cuttings and the rolled up sheets of notes, meticulously typewritten.

She decided to take up the task as soon as she got home, knowing that she would never get started if she began stalling. A haze of dust emerged as she pulled it out from its tight, safe storage, and carefully began lifting out the contents.

She had only managed to salvage four photographs, which wasn't much to show for a life, particularly of somebody with whom you'd spent nine months in such immediate proximity. The first was a family portrait, which she'd always studied with a sense of detached disbelief. She and Adam must have been around three years old when it was taken. She was sitting next to him on a sofa, and although it wasn't obvious from the picture itself, she was somehow certain that this was part of an arranged photoshoot. There had been cushions placed on either side of them so that they would stay put, but Adam's expression belied the fact that he was desperate to wriggle away. Joanna looked much more stoic and composed in her pinafore and frilled socks.

The two pictures that followed were portrait shots of Adam, in the same style as the previous shoot – they had presumably been taken by the same photographer. And behind these was the picture that Joanna wouldn't let her mother cut up – one of her and Adam in puffa coats playing in the snow in the square outside their block of flats. Her four-year old equivalent was laughing and wriggling as her brother pushed a snowball down her collar.

A few years ago, in December, she'd had the mad idea to recreate the experience. She took her then boyfriend with her to the exact same spot and told him to throw snow down her back. She'd hoped that it would jog her memory, enable her to remember something, anything about her brother. She didn't realise quite how hard she was praying for this to happen until she lay on the white ground minutes later, sobbing uncontrollably. Her stupid, useless memory refused to co-operate and left a wet trail of misery in its absence.

Joanna unrolled the case notes and lay them down flat on her desk. She used a coaster and a tube of hand cream to hold down the rolled edges, and began re-reading the familiar words.

Name: Adam Malicki.
Aged: 4.
Missing since: 1st May 1988.
Place last seen: Warsaw, area near Central Station.
Height: 97cm
Description: Short, straight brown hair, mole on right cheek.
Last seen wearing: White short sleeved shirt, blue dungarees, brown lace-up boots.

The next ten or so pages were covered in scribbled notes of where the police had searched in the immediate days following 'the boy's' disappearance. At the end of each of their entries was the dreaded phrase written in bold capital letters, 'NO RESULT, NO FURTHER LEADS'.

In the third week of May, a team had been sent to Mysłowice on her mother's instruction to comb through the area surrounding the mine where her father used to work. The notes documented the cruel glimmer of hope when a local child, a girl of about ten, claimed to have seen a boy of Adam's description sitting on the corner of one of the local streets. It had turned out to be Marcin, a six-year-old who had recently moved to the area with his parents.

The search continued in Warsaw well into August and then September. There were minutes of recorded interviews with Adam's friends from nursery and a detailed transcript of an interview with Joanna herself. It was always strange to re-read her own words from twenty years ago.

Did you see where your brother went on the day of the protest?
– No. I only saw that he'd gone when mummy realised.
And do you remember where you were standing?
– Next to mummy and Mrs. Barska and her friend with the big zoomer.
Can you be any more specific?
[Shrugs] – No.
Where do you think he could have gone?
[Shrugs] – Maybe to grandma's?
Anywhere else?
– I don't know.
What did… what does Adam like doing? Do you play together?
– Yes, sometimes we play tractors.
Tractors?
– Yes, like on grandma's farm. Adam always drives.

The interview went on in this vein without any helpful clues. She could almost read the frustration in the voice of the policeman. She doubted whether children ever provided useful leads in investigations.

She left the scattered papers and went into the kitchen. She switched the kettle on and leant against the fridge, cooling her forehead on its white exterior. She was surprised to find that she was suddenly angry at her four-year-old self for not watching her brother, for not seeing where he'd run off to, for not capturing any useful information. She was the person who was supposed to be closest to him, to think like him, to have an inseparable bond.

She always tried hard to hold Adam in her mind as she was falling asleep, so that maybe she'd dream of him. She never did. Or rather she dreamed of him constantly, only not as a presence but as a painful absence: a warm breeze blowing through her flat, the hand of a small boy turning and waving through a dirty window, a small scuffed pair of boy's shoes still hidden in the depths of her cupboard.

Often she felt that she could see his dark little head amongst the crowds shopping in the city – to her he was always a boy, stuck in his eternal four-year-old body. There were times when she would push through the irritated shoppers to catch up with this vision of him, but he always ultimately escaped her.

In the cruellest of her recent nightmares, she heard Marek's voice on the phone laughing at her, saying that Adam had been living in the apartment next to hers all his life and was now a successful businessman employed in one of Krystian's other businesses.

Joanna had always believed that she would know when her brother had died, but today, for the first time, she wasn't so sure.

Chapter 11 – Matty
London

The sunlight made its way through the thin membrane of his eyelids and no matter how hard he tried to capture it, sleep eluded him again.

How long had it been? Three weeks since he'd slept properly – three weeks since they'd arrived back from Warsaw. He lay there, the same uncomfortable feeling gnawing at his stomach. He shifted and twisted, deliberately turning away from Ellie, ensuring that their bodies weren't touching. He wished that he had a separate duvet, so that he could cocoon himself within it and properly begin work on deciphering his half-formed memories. He was certain that if he were to somehow achieve the perfect conditions, a harmonious equilibrium in which all other thoughts were dispelled from his brain, he could delve into the real crux of the matter which lay there, hidden among the debris. But somehow he wasn't able to bring about the atmosphere needed for self-discovery.

Instead, another painful epiphany consumed him. Over the past few weeks he'd realised with some shock that the overwhelming emotion that he felt towards Ellie was anger. It was an unfair kind of anger. After all, it hadn't been her intent to shift the ground beneath his feet, to deliberately heave doubt into his mind.

'Doubt' was a good description – nothing concrete, just an unnerving feeling of impending doom. If somebody asked him, he wouldn't even be able to say what he was doubtful about. All he knew was that there was a painful imbalance within him. But was it new or had it been there all along? Had he ever felt happily moored?

Recently in these sleepless morning hours he experienced the absence in his life of something vital. There was a loneliness inside him, which his connection, his *relationship* with Ellie failed to fill.

He felt a sudden sharp kick at the base of his spine and turned around to see her stretching.

"Morning," she whispered, grasping his hand under the duvet. Her eyes were still half-closed with sleep. They were the feature that first drew him to her – so large, unusual, and such a deep blue.

"Do you want to go to the market today?" she asked him, "I've finished all my marking. We can mooch around the galleries, maybe grab some lunch at that new pie place?"

It was Saturday. He had forgotten. He hadn't expected Saturday so quickly. The thought of spending a whole day alone with Ellie pretending everything was fine filled him with trepidation. And if she asked him what was wrong again, he felt that he might implode.

"I erm… I said that I would meet Dan for the football. I forgot that you said you would be free today." It was only a half-truth, an incomplete deception. Her face rearranged itself into a look of disappointment.

"Can't you cancel? You see him all the time."

"I don't…" he began, but she cut in.

"Never mind. I'll ring and see whether I can meet Meredith."

"Sure, sure. Sorry."

Until recently, Saturday mornings had been his favourite time of the week. He and Ellie would roll into the kitchen at around 11am, free from any nagging alarm clock. Then he'd go to the café down the road and pick up some chocolate croissants, and they would eat them with coffee while reading the paper and lolling around in front of breakfast TV. But without her raising any objection, the precious routine had now been ignored for three weekends. Ellie hadn't said anything – she was too kind for that – but he still roused himself out of bed with a sting, before she could lean in for a hug. He quickly pulled on his clothes and was out the door in minutes.

As he walked down the few roads that separated their home from the old, terraced house in which his oldest and best friend Dan lived with his mum, the honking noise of vuvuzelas accompanied him through the open windows. It was the World Cup fan's instrument of choice. He'd never heard of it before this summer.

He unlatched the gate and swung it open, savouring the familiar creak. He felt calmer already. He'd always loved this crumbling red tile path, the messy front lawn with its circles of yellow grass where Nadia, Dan's mum, had accidentally left an upturned washing basket or plant pot. It had always felt more like home to him than the spacious, tastefully decorated yet strangely soulless house in which he'd grown up.

He strolled straight through the peeling front door without knocking. It was always open, and somehow the Gilberts had never been burgled. The luck of the naïve?

"Get a bloody move on!" Nadia was pounding up the stairs carrying handful of scrunched up plastic bags, "Hi Matty," she called over her shoulder, "sorry I'm just trying to get that idiot to pass me down some boxes."

He laughed. He'd always loved the way that the two of them spoke to each other. There was no sense of rigid politeness, no 'would you mind awfully' or 'thank you darling'.

"What are you doing?"

"Oh I'm trying to get rid of some junk from the attic. I've decided to get a conversion done. Then we can get a lodger in for some extra money as this no good friend of yours doesn't look like he's going to move out anytime soon."

Dan's pink flushed face appeared at the top of the ladder.

"There's so much crap up here, I don't even know where to begin!"

"Just pass down the boxes and we'll sort through it downstairs!"

"I'll go and help him," Matty volunteered and pulled himself up the ladder in two swift moves.

"Thanks. I appreciate that. I'll make you some food," Nadia said, and vanished into the kitchen before Dan could protest.

He hadn't been exaggerating. The place was heaving with dusty cardboard boxes, disintegrating bin liners filled with old clothes and discarded furniture. A lurid yellow cradle occupied one corner of the room.

"My bloody old bed," said Dan, following his gaze and laughing.

"We won't get half of this done before the game."

"I know. I know. We'll just take some stuff down so that she gets off my arse. Grab those off the top first."

Matty lifted the first box. It held a pile of small red booklets with Dan's name and different years scribbled in felt tip pen.

"School reports. I had a look through some of them earlier. We had a proper laugh. Top of the class and all, wasn't I? Clever little git."

"Course you were. Shame it didn't last."

"Watch it!" He aimed a playful punch at Matty's left shoulder, causing him to fall into a mound of ancient-looking bed linen.

"With you it was a different story, wasn't it? Took you a while to master your speech."

"How do you mean?" asked Matty distractedly.

"Well let's just say that you weren't the brightest crayon."

Matty threw a bin bag at him in protest. Dan was known for his colourisation of the truth, and his exaggeration which sometimes bordered on outright lies. He loved playing up to his audience, even if his audience was just Matty.

"Outrageous. I beat you in every test," he retorted.

"Yeah, later you did. But not to begin with. You had a proper funny way of speaking too."

"Huh?"

"Doesn't matter. Look just take those two. I'll go down the ladder and you pass them to me."

They worked methodically and soon half of the second floor corridor was filled with piles of boxes. Dan insisted that they'd done enough and could now go and watch the game. But Matty's enthusiasm had gone. He suddenly felt deflated.

"Come on, we should be able to beat the Yanks! They can't play 'soccer'!"

A sweet tangy smell emanated from the kitchen. Nadia came out with a plate of steaming jerk chicken wings. Matty often wondered how Dan managed to remain so skinny with the amount of delicacies that she sent his way.

"Hey, what did you mean earlier about me speaking funny?"

"Oh, get over it. I just meant you talked a bit weirdly when you first joined school. You sort of stressed the wrong words… Bloody hell!" he shouted, pummelling his fist in the direction of the TV. "How could he have missed that one? How bloody embarrassing!"

"Don't listen to him," said Nadia, ruffling his hair, "You just had an accent that's all. Nothing funny about it."

A chill spread through his insides.

"What sort of accent? But I'd always lived in London."

"I'm not sure that you did, Matty. Your mother said that you'd moved from the north. I can't remember where exactly. I personally always thought that you didn't sound as if you were northern, but accents are weird things aren't they? Kids loose them so quickly when they're in a new environment. With adults it's harder of course. Ian Nelson down the road has been living here for more than fifty years and he still has the thickest American drawl you can imagine and…"

But he was no longer listening. The cold that had nestled itself in the pit of his stomach began to slowly expand, seeping its way through his body, rising up in waves of nausea. He'd lost his appetite entirely and a lump of hot, undigested chicken lodged itself painfully at the top of his throat.

"What else did she say?"

"Who?"

"Celia."

"Oh nothing, Matty. You know that she's never been a fan of mine, so I wouldn't have been a person for her to open up to. I mean, surely you could just ask her if you were interested?"

But he couldn't, of course. He couldn't ask Celia. Even talking about the past unlinked to his adoption was difficult. She would wave it away with her hand, as if it was irrelevant. "You don't think about the past," she'd told him once, "There's nothing you can change in it. It's all about the here and now, and the future. Those are the things that you can do something about." But Matty suspected that the real reason she refused to speak to him about it was that it pained her.

He'd overheard her on several occasions in the kitchen talking to one or other of her glamorous friends, her words thick with wine. She would tell them of her ex-partner Cal, a no-use alcoholic who bankrupted her, forced her to move home and struggle through life as a single mother. It was only through sheer determination and her love of property that she'd managed to get to where she was today.

For years, Matty had remembered nothing about his adoptive father, not even a fragment.. But recently, he'd had the niggling echo of a voice somewhere at the edge of his memory. It was a deep male voice, a kind voice, which he couldn't quite match up with the awful description that Celia had given him. And with the impatient look that she gave him, he'd been sorry for ever asking about his father at all.

"I'll try," he told Nadia, but he realised how unconvincing he sounded.

"You coped very well, Matty. And you turned out OK," she said ruffling his hair, "You really did. I mean, Cambridge… Not many people can say they went to Cambridge. You're really quite something, eh?"

"Debatable," Dan muttered, grinning.

Nadia continued to smile at him, piling chicken wings onto her plate at an impressive speed, but there was something about her tone that was unsettling.

He was about to ask her what she meant by 'coped well' but she was now fully engrossed in the match.

As he forced himself to focus on the twenty-two men running around on Dan's widescreen TV, an idea took root in his confused mind. He would do some investigation without telling Celia. It was safer that way. But where to begin? His thoughts fluttered back to Dan's school reports. He went upstairs to use the bathroom at half time and picked up the one lying on top of the pile. It was from Year 2 and contained a solid description of Dan written by the teacher next to his grades, which were mediocre at best.

Surely his own might provide some clues? They had to exist somewhere. Knowing Celia, she would have stored them neatly and carefully in a perfectly colour-coordinated box in her wardrobe. He just needed to find it.

Chapter 12 – Tom
Chicago

It was a boiling hot morning, the day that Mildred went missing. Tom had woken up naturally, which was strange in itself. Usually, he would be roused by the sound of Clara entering the room and pulling apart his curtains. He checked the clock on the bedside table. It was already gone 8am. Something wasn't right.

And sure enough, Clara burst into the room ten or so minutes later, when he had already sat up and begun to dress himself. Not only was she late, but her usually perfect curls were dishevelled, and she looked as if she'd been crying.

She composed herself as she neared the bed, swallowed hard and smiled at him.

"I'm so sorry Mr. Mason. Your breakfast."

"Thank you. Is everything… are you OK?"

"Yes, of course," she said, busying herself with tucking in a bit of his bed sheet that had come loose.

"It doesn't look like you are," he said boldly, surprising even himself. Lately, he found that he no longer cared what people thought of him. At some stage in the past few weeks he'd resolved unwittingly to live freely, by his own rules, not worrying about anyone's reactions.

She sat down on the edge of the bed and looked straight at him. There was something painful in her eyes which he'd never noticed before – a mixture of resignation and fear.

"What's happened?"

"Nothing, I…"

"But something has," he said quietly and watched as her shoulders began to gently shake.

"It's just Mrs. Patterson…"

"Mildred? What about her?"

"Well… I shouldn't be telling you this, as a patient. But well, she's gone missing. I was the last one to see her last night and I think I might have forgotten to lock her door. I've been a bit distracted, but that's obviously no excuse."

"Have you searched all of the grounds?"

Mildred was an elderly woman in her early eighties who was suffering from an advanced form of dementia. She lived in a different part of the building to Tom, on the other side of the large living room, but Tom saw her at dinner time and during the early afternoon. She was sweet-natured, but her behaviour was erratic and it was clear that she flitted between different levels of consciousness. On a good day, you might even have a relatively normal conversation with her, but on a bad one, her ramblings were pure nonsense and she seemed entirely unaware of who she was speaking to.

"They did one sweep and found nothing. They're doing a second one now, going beyond the gardens."

"Can I help?" Tom asked, pushing away the breakfast tray. He suddenly felt a renewed energy within him and he yearned to do something useful.

"I don't think it's a good idea. You should be resting up until eleven…"

"It won't hurt me to do something active a few hours earlier. It's not like I'm preparing myself to do physical exercise in the afternoon."

And before Clara could say anything more, he was already on his feet, wrapping the chord of his dressing gown around his waist.

"Can I see her room?" he asked Clara, who was hurrying after him.

"You should get back to bed…" she told him helplessly, but her resolve was weakening.

He turned back to her.

"Room 19," she said weakly. "The door is open. I'm going to check if Marie's found her. She's been searching the gardens."

Mildred's room was almost identical to his own. It had the same dark green curtains in the windows, a large bed with a thick mattress, and a slightly battered oak wardrobe and chest of drawers. The major difference was that the room was filled with photos – they rested, in their higgledy-piggledy colourful frames on every available flat surface.

Tom couldn't help but stop and look. A younger Mildred was visible on a few of them, her arms around a couple of toddlers, presumably her grandchildren. In the spaces where there were no photos, greeting cards were arranged in neat rows. Tom peered briefly inside and found that they all contained different handwriting. It wasn't just one person who was writing to old Mildred – she had many people who cared about her. They cared about her so much in fact, that they continued to write to her, despite knowing that she most likely wouldn't be able to respond. In comparison to this display of love, Tom's own bedroom resembled a showroom. He could move out of it tomorrow with one bag and nobody would know that he had ever been there. This realisation filled him with a cold hollowness.

He sat down on the edge of Mildred's bed to gather his thoughts. If he were her, where would he want to go? Presumably to visit one of these loved ones. But where do they live? It was highly unlikely to be within walking distance, which meant that the journey would at the very least involve a bus or a taxi ride. Both of those involved the use of money to pay the fare, which Mildred wouldn't have. This meant that if she had gone outside, she wouldn't have gotten far.

He remembered Mildred during Film Evening a few nights ago. She had been coaxed into coming along by one of the other nurses, but she began to whimper as soon as the lights were turned off. She was scared of the dark. That meant that if she had left the building, she wouldn't have done it in the middle of the night.

The more Tom thought about it, the more he became certain that Mildred was actually still in the building.

It was then that he spotted the sticky stain on the duvet to his left. A faint sickly sweet smell emanated from it. Cough mixture. The offending brown glass bottle stood on the bedside table.

Even in her confused state, Mildred hated mess. On his second day at *Sunshine*, he remembered seeing her in the living room carefully sweeping crumbs off the table with a small wooden brush. He'd mistakenly thought at the time that she was a member of the cleaning staff.

The obsession became even more evident when Mildred was in the midst of a conversation or activity and would suddenly catch sight of a fleck of dirt on somebody's clothes, or a small cloud of dust by one of the skirting boards. She would immediately drop whatever she was doing and run to get rid of it.

If Tom were a betting man, he would bet that Mildred had woken up with a cough, tried to administer her own medicine, and caused a spillage, which would have bothered her greatly. So where would she have gone to clean it up?

Tom got up and began to slowly walk in the direction of the cleaning cupboard which was at the end of the long kitchen.

He was so certain that he was on the right track, that he was dumb-founded when he found the cupboard locked. He put his ear to the door just in case. There was a small possibility that Mildred could have locked herself in, although if she had, she would have no doubt caused an almighty racket. But there was no sound coming from inside.

So if not the cleaning cupboard then where? Of course. He had been stupid. The cleaning cupboard was filled with mops and hoovers. They wouldn't have helped Mildred. She would have simply wanted to change the sheets. So where was the laundry done? And where were the new sheets kept?

The kitchen and living room area was quiet. Patients hadn't yet emerged from their rooms after breakfast, and the heat was already stifling. He didn't dare to imagine what the place would be like when it was filled with bodies. Yesterday, the oppressive clamminess was so unbearable that he called Sally to ask whether she and Mitch would take him for a walk by the river, where there was always a cool breeze coming off the water. It had been a pleasant day, but he was shocked to find that he could barely manage five minutes of walking before having to sit down to take a rest. They had been patient with him, walking as slowly as he did, pretending that it was a perfectly respectable pace at which to move. He knew that the heat and the anti-nausea drugs were partly to blame for his tiredness, but it was more than that of course.

Now, he emerged through the large patio doors at the back of the room into the gardens, the sun mercilessly beating down on his head. A faint sound of shouting reached his ears and he looked down the slope of the hill to see three figures, dispersed evenly across the grounds, conducting a thorough search of the region. He sighed. He would have to wait until they came back. As much as he wanted to go down there, he knew that his legs would not be able to carry him. Increasingly, he'd begun to develop a fear of falling over in public.

"Mr. Mason?"

He spun around. She was sitting under the shade of an umbrella by one of the outdoor tables, cradling a cordless phone.

He walked over and took a seat opposite her.

"What are you doing?" he asked.

"I'm getting ready to call one of Mildred's children," she said quietly, suddenly forgetting the formal address that she used for most of her patients. "And then we're going to have to call the police. There's no other choice. I'm beginning to think she might have been missing since last night. Only God knows where she might have wandered off to by now…"

Her shoulders were slumped in resignation and something else – shame perhaps at not having prevented this incident from happening.

"Don't do it yet. Don't call them. Tell me first where you do all of the laundry."

"Sorry?"

"It's important. Please tell me where you do all your laundry."

"The laundrette is in the lodge," she said, pointing to the small house, separated from the main building by just the garden path. "But I don't see how?" She was angry now, and her voice had a frantic edge to it.

"Can I go in there?"

She looked at him with impatience.

"Why?"

"I just have a hunch that she could be in there."

"Fine, yes – if you want. But there won't be any staff in there. They don't start until 2pm."

"It doesn't matter," said Tom. In fact, the news made him even more certain that Mildred was in there. "Come with me?"

She lifted herself up from the seat hesitantly, but he took her hand and they walked together in the direction of the small, squat building, covered in dense ivy.

The door was open. A fresh aroma of lavender filled the hallway, and to Tom's disappointment, there was no noise.

"Where is the fresh linen kept?"

"It's that last door on the left."

He walked over boldly and opened it… It gave way with a small push.

He hadn't been wrong. There, spread on the pile of chemically ironed bedsheets was Mildred, fast asleep on her side and snoring gently, oblivious to the mad search parties which were currently shouting her name outdoors.

"No! Oh my God!" Clara's eyes filled with tears of relief. "How did you know?"

"A tiny bit of detective work," he said with satisfaction. "She had a medicine spillage in her room and she's always so… keen on cleanliness, so I thought…"

"Of course. It hadn't even occurred to me. Thank you so much. You don't realise what a problem we would have had. You quite genuinely saved…"

"It's nothing, honestly. Do you want me to help you move her?"

"She should be fine to get up. We'll just wake her." And Clara, still visibly dizzy with happiness proceeded to gently pat Mildred's face. Sure enough, the old woman woke up within moments and they managed to lead her, with no further problems, back to her room.

***

That evening, Clara spent longer in Tom's room than she normally would. After administering his pills and giving him his hot lemon water, she sat down in the wicker chair in his room and looked at him. He felt as if she was noticing him properly for the very first time.

And then suddenly, out of nowhere, she started laughing, a deep chuckle that came from deep inside her. Her thin body shook with merriment and her eyes began to stream.

"Sorry, sorry Mr. Mason. It's just that in hindsight it was so funny seeing her there like that, and with everyone stressing outside. She reminds me of my granddaughter, you know. Who was it who said that we come full circle? That as old people, we revert back to childhood? Anyway, my Lucy always hides and we find her somewhere random. She once even curled up in the fireplace and covered herself with the grate."

He didn't even notice when he'd started laughing too. It was impossible not to join in.

"How old is your granddaughter?" he asked.

"She's still small. She just turned five."

"I love small children," he admitted. "They're so unpredictable, and that's what makes them so fascinating."

"Well… my daughter is always asking if I can look after her. So perhaps I will bring her in one day?"

"That would be really nice. I'd love to meet her."

When Clara left that night, he felt happier than he'd done in years.

It was only when he shut his eyes and found himself in that dazed realm of near-sleep that the nightmare returned, quite unannounced. It hadn't plagued him for months but it now returned with full force. He saw the small, podgy hands reaching out for him. He was so close that he could breathe in the soft, talcum powder smell, but yet the hands eluded him. They were just out of reach. And when he tried to grasp hold of one of them, his fingers met with nothing but thin air.

Chapter 13 – Joanna
Warsaw

She lay on the sofa in her small living room relishing the thought that she could stay in tonight. She'd made no arrangements with anyone and the long blissful hours stretched out in front of her. There were no bigger decisions to be made than which takeaway to order or which favourite from her black and white film collection to re-watch.

Not so long ago, there had been Friday nights when Joanna's phone would ring incessantly with friends wanting to see her. They would demand that she met them in town to go to a gig, or to a bar, or if it was warm, just to wander up and down the bank of the Vistula searching for a good spot to have a few drinks. And she enjoyed these nights out. She would wake up on a Saturday at midday, like many people in their mid-twenties, hung over, slightly regretful, but generally content.

And then, slowly and quite unnoticeably over the past few months, she had begun to ignore her friends' calls and to pretend that she wasn't home. To begin with, she experienced flickers of paranoid guilt when she did this, as if the callers could somehow see into her house and witness her so obviously rejecting them. But slowly, she grew to believe that she had the right to solitude, and she didn't have to explain herself for wanting time alone.

"How are you ever going to meet anyone if you don't leave the house?" her aunt had asked over dinner a few weeks ago.

"I do leave the house," Joanna would say, irritated, "I've come here, haven't I? I go to work every day. And what do you mean by *someone*?"

"You know what I mean. Someone to fall in love with," said Irena boldly. "By the sounds of it, there are no likely candidates in the office, so you may have to leave the house for other destinations. This man, or woman (Irena was unexpectedly open-minded about this) is not going to find you at home."

"What if I told you I was fine on my own?"

"I wouldn't believe you."

"Well, we'll just have to disagree on that. The next thing you'll tell me is that most people are married with children at my age." It wasn't strictly true, but Joanna liked to say it for effect.

"I wasn't going to. I was just taking a stand against you being alone… and lonely."

The conversation went on in this vein and made Joanna increasingly defiant. She wasn't single through lack of offers. She'd had brief relationships at uni, and then a few short-term flings. There were men who had eyed her up in bars, asked for her number, even left their own, scrawled hastily on a cocktail napkin.

And it wasn't that they were awful – in fact, there was one whom she had liked rather a lot. But she feared that they would stand in the way of her obsession, for even she recognised that it had developed into more than just a hope, or even a habit, and they would surely want to stop her, to heal her, which was something that she just wasn't ready for.

So she would stay single for now, and if she was lonely, it was a loneliness that was barely noticeable because her mind was so preoccupied with the search that really there was no time to think about herself.

But today, she looked again at the phone, confused. A small part of her wanted to escape Adam. To go out, to lead her life, to laugh and get blind drunk. But as always, she would stay at home working. She would often imagine where he was and what he was doing. The only difference was that now she would also read through the documents of several other missing children and adults. It made her feel strangely at ease with her own plight, thinking that there were thousands of other families out there likely going through the exact same series of emotions.

A few years ago, when she'd visited his office several times in one month, Stefan had suggested that she join an organisation for the families of missing people. She'd laughed in his face.

"What, is it like an alcoholics' meeting?" she'd asked, "My name is Joanna, and I have a missing brother?"

Now she thought that maybe it would have been a good idea to speak to someone who was going through the same thing. Who knows? Maybe it might have even saved her mother's mind.

She picked up a file from the kitchen table and poured herself a cup of coffee. *Roman Gierski* read the front of the document. Stefan had left a sticky note for her on the front that said 'Found after nine years'.

Joanna fixated on the word 'nine'. Admittedly, it wasn't quite as long as twenty-two, but it was a significant number. Had his family given up hope? Or did they continue to search until he was found? It was this vital information which she most needed and more often than not, it was unavailable in the carefully printed documents.

She opened the file and looked at the sepia portrait shot of a boy with dark curly hair and a serious expression. The front page of his case notes told her that he was originally from Wesola, just outside Warsaw. He had gone missing on 5th March 1993 and had been found on 3rd January 2002.

He had allegedly disappeared following a football match at the Legia stadium in Warsaw, which he had attended with his father and brother. There had been only one sighting of him walking off with an elderly man, but the witness was unable to provide an accurate description of the suspect and, according to the notes, became increasingly nervous upon continued questioning. The police team had scoured the stadium and surrounding areas, and had even done an extensive search of the nearby stretch of the Vistula river.

It was five years later that the match footage was reviewed for a sporting documentary – one of the cameras, used only to document action near the home goal, happened to hover for some time over the cheering crowds, the young Roman amongst them. It captured the boy walking to the exit of one of the stands holding the hand of an elderly looking man wearing thick, dark glasses. The still produced from the camera footage was blurry, but it was widely publicised in the media and on posters around Warsaw under the capitalised order 'CALL US IF YOU HAVE SEEN THIS MAN'

After a week of the photo being made public, the police had received fifty-seven calls from across the country from people who were all 'certain' that they had seen him. Through a process of elimination, which took well over a year, they finally ascertained that the person in question was Jacek Nosak, who had by then moved away from his home in Warsaw and was nowhere to be found.

It was only following his death four years later, that he was recognised as the man from the police search, and Roman was returned to his family. He had allegedly been living a peaceful life with Nosak's family in the south of Poland and nobody ever seemed to get to the bottom of what prompted the man to abduct the small boy in the first place. Loneliness? Mental illness? Simple opportunity?

Joanna felt a mounting feeling of anger in her stomach when she finished reading the newspaper clippings. How had it not occurred to the police to look at the footage from the game earlier? Everyone knows that there are cameras at football matches. Granted, in the mid-nineties they may not have had security cameras like they do now, but the TV footage was surely worth a careful look?

She sighed heavily. It wasn't the first time that she was frustrated about the police overlooking obvious pieces of hard evidence. She remembered watching a recent crime documentary in which a husband had been accused of plotting the murder of his wife by contacting a hit man. The police seemed to interview everyone – the husband's family, the wife's family, the couples' friends, the man apparently hired to do the killing, even random 'potential witnesses' who lived in the area in which it had allegedly happened.

"Why don't they just listen to the calls made on his mobile to the hit man?" Joanna had asked Irena.

"Maybe he destroyed the phone?"

"Well, I'm sure the network provider keeps a record. If they really wanted to, they could do it. They're either covering something up, or they're incompetent or lazy…"

"Or it makes for good TV?" Irena dared to suggest.

It occurred to Joanna that part of the problem in Adam's case was that there was no technology which could provide clues to his disappearance. There had been little official footage of the Warsaw strike of 1988 and that which was available was from a different part of the city, where the local Solidarity leaders had assembled. From everything that she had managed to glean over the years, it was obvious that the strike that they were taking part in was nothing compared to the size of the other strikes happening across the country at the same time.

But then, out of nowhere, a niggling thought wormed its way into her head. 'Zoomer'.

She flicked back to the interview with her four-year old self.

And do you remember where you were standing?

"Next to mummy and Mrs. Barska and her friend with the big zoomer."

Could it be that the 'zoomer' was a camera? Is that what she would have called it?

Why didn't the policeman ask her what she meant? She re-read the interview again, although she knew it off by heart. There was no further mention of the word. She frantically forced her mind to remember a man or a woman with a camera. It was useless. She didn't even remember Mrs. Barska, let alone her friend. She knew that her 'memory' of the day that Adam went missing was entirely fictional, created from the scraps of recollections belonging to her mother and her aunt, and the police documents that currently lay in front of her.

Nevertheless, this 'zoomer' could hold the vital information. She rifled through the pages of notes to find the names of the witnesses. There she was.

Anna Barska
Age: 36
Occupation: Shop assistant
Marital Status: Married

The address was that of a street in the Ochota district, near to where Joanna, Adam and Monika had lived when they first arrived in Warsaw. There was no phone number.

Would she still live there? Unlikely. But it was it was a scrap of something that she could hold onto, a tiny ribbon of possibility that needed to be unravelled.

Chapter 14 – Matty
London

Matty felt the dull anxious nausea mounting in his stomach. It caused him to triple check every room to ensure that Celia wasn't home. He'd deliberately chosen Monday morning, knowing that she always had her sales meeting at 9.30am. She wouldn't have missed that even if she was half-dead from flu – it was her only opportunity to show off how many deals she had clinched and how many contracts she'd signed in comparison to her incompetent colleagues. So Monday morning for Matty was a safe bet. It had been easy enough to call his boss and say that he needed the morning off for an emergency dentist appointment.

It was stifling, this feeling of breaking into your own house. He wondered if Celia remembered that he still had a key. If she did, she presumably thought that he would never come here in her absence. Every time he came back, and this admittedly had been rarer and rarer in recent years, he was struck by the fact that nothing had changed in his absence. Even now, when he walked into his old room, he found it exactly as he had left it before he went off to university. The *Lord of the Rings* posters were beginning to peel off the cupboard doors, but his old books were all neatly arranged, not a speck of dust in sight, and the room was permeated with the usual scent of Celia's expensive detergent.

'Where would she keep them?' he muttered to himself. His immediate thought was her main wardrobe in the spare room (which was really a dressing room), but he soon realised what a ridiculous thought that had been. He opened it, half expecting a Narnia-like door to emerge before him, but there were only tailored suits, silk dresses still in their dry-cleaning bags, and racks upon racks of shoes.

He tried the kitchen drawers, then the cabinet in the living room. He felt that he was spending ages on his search, as he had to be meticulous in replacing everything in exactly the same place in which he'd found it.

The cupboard under the stairs held nothing but old mops, brushes and other cleaning equipment. He ran upstairs, checking his watch with annoyance.

A sudden scuttling sound caught him in his tracks. His stomach lurched, as a furry figure emerged from the shadows of the second floor. Otty. He'd almost forgotten about her existence.

He ran his hand across the cat's back, feeling the raised beads of her spine and the sharply angled shoulder blades. He couldn't help but be taken aback by how frail her bones felt beneath the tortoiseshell fur. She had seemed such a solid creature when he first brought her back from the cattery. How old had he been? Twelve? Thirteen at most.

But now when he picked her up, she felt bird-like, insubstantial, barely there at all. She was purring, rubbing her face into his fingers in the same way that she had always done and she looked up at him with a reassured, trusting expression. It was then that he'd realised how much he'd missed her. When he was at secondary school, Celia would often return hours after him, and Matty hated the emptiness of the house when he walked in. But then Otty would meow and dance round his legs in figures of eight, and he couldn't help but laugh.

For a moment, Matty considered the possibility of taking the cat home with him, but the thought was ridiculous. To begin with, it meant that Celia would know about his secret visit.

As he entered her bedroom, he was aware of the floorboards rippling and undulating beneath his shoes and he hesitated, wary of moving anything in his mother's sacred chamber. It was likely that her skittish mind would notice even the slightest shift in the position of objects, but it was a risk that he would have to take. He would deal with the consequences later.

He decided to go through the drawers of the dressing table and he came across all manner of brushes, bottles and make-up products. The third one down was obviously the medicine drawer, full to the brim with tablets of all colours and shapes. He picked up a few and recognised several varieties of sleeping pills.

He continued searching in his old bedroom, the loft, and even the bathroom cabinets, but he came up with nothing. Had Celia locked all of their documents elsewhere? Perhaps in a safe or a storage unit, to ensure that he never came across them? But it seemed unlikely that even she would go to those measures.

He went back into her bedroom to assess whether he'd missed anywhere obvious. Under the bed? He lowered himself to look beneath it, but he soon remembered that the bed was solid. He lifted the edges of the duvet and saw that there were large drawers on either side, presumably for storing bed linen. He yanked open the one on the right hand side, but it wouldn't open. He then walked round and tried the one on the left. This one slid open easily, displaying its contents of floral duvet covers and pillow cases.

Matty tried the first drawer once again, checking that it wasn't just stuck. He slid his toes under the bed to get a better hold and pulled. There was no give at all. He peered at the drawer more closely and noticed a tiny, barely noticeable sliver of something orange emerging from beneath the surface. He ran his finger across it – super glue.

Maybe the door was just broken and Celia had glued it down so it wouldn't keep falling off? Matty sat down, looking at it puzzled. She couldn't store anything in there, because she wouldn't be able to get to it herself without smashing the bed frame. Unless of course you could access the space from another angle… perhaps from above?

He slowly began to shift the mattress off the bed, trying his best not to change the arrangement of the pillows. It slid along much more easily than he'd expected. Dust clouds emerged from beneath and hit the back of his throat, causing him to double up coughing.

Through the slats on the left hand side of the bed, he could see the outline of two cardboard boxes and he carefully eased the panes of wood apart so that he could lift them out. The layer of dust on the lids was proof that Celia hadn't opened them in a long time. This meant that if he was careful in putting the bed back exactly how he'd found them, she would also likely not realise that they were missing.

He slowly took the lid off the larger box and peered inside. He lifted out an envelope labelled *Matthew – November 1986.* Bingo. Inside he found several photographs of a young looking Celia with curled blond hair, holding his smaller self. Beneath it was a small stack of documents, including his searched-for school reports. And below it, half hidden between two folders, the blurred headshot of a man with a black moustache and beard, and thick framed glasses. His father? His heart quickened as he stared into the man's eyes. But there was nothing about him that he recognised. No glimmer of recognition, no shadowy memory.

He eagerly opened the larger box and began to look through its contents, unsure of what he was hoping to find. To his disappointment, this appeared to hold Celia's own documents – her university certificates, a bound copy of her dissertation on Stanislavski's method acting, and an old address book.

Otty nestled into the space vacated by the boxes, sniffing at its unfamiliarity, brushing her fur against the dusty interior. She gave Matty a satisfied look, as if commending him for the discovery of this secret place.

He sat back down on the bed peering more closely at the photo of the moustachioed man. He carefully studied the contours of his face, wanting desperately to learn something more from them.

It was only when the antique clock from downstairs began to strike that he realised with a start that it was almost eleven. He made the panicked decision to take only the smaller box with him. He dropped the other one back through the bed frame, put the slats back in place and arranged the mattress on top, carefully tucking in the duvet covers on either side. He opened the window slightly to allow the dust to escape. Then he checked the other rooms to ensure that nothing looked out of place, and put the box in the boot of his car. He ran upstairs to shut the window; double locked the front door, and started the engine.

Chapter 15 – Tom
Chicago

"Can you search for anyone on there?" asked Tom fearfully.

"Yes of course. You just enter the name in this box, look. And you type it in."

They were back in Dustin's favourite position in front of the computer.

"Say you wanted to search for your family members, you would put your surname in here," he demonstrated putting 'Mason' into the box.

"It won't work for me," said Tom honestly.

"What? Why?"

"Because I changed my name when I moved to America."

Dustin's eyebrows disappeared under his fringe, but he pretended that he wasn't surprised in the slightest.

"Right… What was it before?"

"Malicki."

"How do you spell that?"

Shall we do it another day?" asked Tom desperately. He wasn't ready. The crawl of panic was beginning in his stomach and he saw his hands beginning to shake in his lap. "Why don't we look at some of your… some of your people?"

To his great relief, Dustin was all too happy to oblige.

"The thing that is best about all this social media malarkey is that you can see how people have changed over the years," he said, grinning and winking at Tom. "I like to have a little look every now and then. It's shocking when you see the difference between those who have really looked after themselves and those who have completely let themselves go. Look at this. Would you believe that these two women are almost exactly the same age?"

He brought up two photographs on the screen – one of a svelte blonde in a tight fitting red dress and a face of heavy make-up (Tom was certain that she'd had some surgical help to enable her to look the way she did) and the other a grey haired, dowdy looking woman with laughter lines around the eyes, and a genuine smile. He knew who he would rather spend an evening with.

"I had a thing with Nancy," he said, pointing to the blond and smiling slyly. "It was many years ago of course, and just before the wedding.

"Before whose wedding? Yours or hers?"

"Mine of course. A last jaunt before I settled down to a lifetime of monogamy. Oh come on, don't look at me like that. Are you telling me that you never had an affair?"

Tom coughed. The familiar anxious beetle crawl was spreading through his insides. He was free to confess. It would make no difference now, and the words were there on the end of his tongue, at the edge of his mouth, ready to spill out. But they wouldn't.

Dustin threw him an odd look and then turned around to examine further photos of Nancy at various stages of her recent life. Tom observed that she seemed to wear nothing but short, clingy dresses in which she pouted seductively, always deeply aware of the camera. He hated photos like that – posed, ridiculous. When he'd collected enough money to buy his first camera – a bulky, heavy thing with a huge lens and an impossibly difficult film mechanism – he liked nothing more than to take photos of people when they least expected them. There was a magic in those shots and they could often capture thoughts and expressions so beautifully. Many significant historical moments were caught just like that – the wailing boy at Tiananmen Square, the blue-eyed refugee on the cover of the *National Geographic*.

"You know if the same opportunity arose in the last few years, or decades even, I wouldn't have done it," said Dustin quietly, "And I regret that I did. I'm not proud of it."

He could see that Dustin was beginning to regret that he had opened his mouth at all, possibly thinking that Tom thought badly of him. It was awful, this constant worry about other people's thoughts.

"I had an affair too," he muttered. There it was, out in the open. And as soon as it had emerged, Tom desperately wanted to swallow it back down. He realised with horror that he had never uttered that sentence to anyone, ever.

"What?" asked Dustin, making a point to turn around in his chair and confront him head on. "And here you got me feeling all guilty and trying to defend myself for doing something awful. He slapped Tom playfully on the back. In his eyes, they were a team again. They were equals. He didn't understand the gravity of the situation. He didn't understand anything.

He struggled to keep his voice steady as he told Dustin seriously, "You were lucky. You were so lucky that your life carried on as you'd planned."

"What do you mean?"

But Tom was tired of the conversation. He felt more exhausted than he'd been since his arrival at *Sunshine*, and he could feel the tiny threads of panic beginning to weave their painful web in the corners of his mind.

"It doesn't matter," he said "It doesn't matter anymore."

To his huge relief, Clara suddenly appeared in the room. She looked different and it took Tom a moment to realise why – instead of her usual stiff blue and white uniform, she was wearing a bold, floral dress filled with exuberant greens and reds.

"I just came to see whether you might want to come with us to Church," she said, and it was only then that it dawned on Tom that this was a Sunday, and therefore her day off. "I don't know if you're a practising Christian, but I just wanted to say that you're welcome to come with us. Everyone is." Her eyes scanned the room at she said this, but he noticed that they quickly settled on him.

"Well erm, yes. Yes, I would like to," he admitted.

"That's great. Dustin?"

"No, thank you for the offer, but I'll pass."

Tom hurried back to his room, asking Clara whether she would give him a moment. She agreed, saying that she would wait outside.

He emerged, two minutes later in his crisp white shirt, tie and blazer, and immediately regretted it because the oppressive heat pressed down on him, causing beads of sweat to instantly appear on the back of his neck. But at least he looked presentable. He would play the part.

"There's somebody here that I would like you to meet," Clara said. "Lucy, Mr. Mason said that he would like to see you. There's no need to hide. Come out," she coaxed.

And then, to his amazement, a small dark head popped out from behind Clara's skirt.

"Hi," said the girl, smiling at him awkwardly and exposing a sizeable gap where her front teeth should have been.

"Hello. Nice to meet you," said Tom politely, "Is it OK if I walk with you?"

The girl nodded slowly, looked Tom up and down, and clearly deciding that he was alright to speak to, emerged fully from behind Clara.

She was small, even for a five-year old, with skinny arms and legs, her knees bruised and scabby. Her face was round and her cheeks large and dimpled. But it was her eyes that drew Tom in the most, because they were a beautiful deep hazel. They were strikingly similar to another pair of eyes that he knew so well, that it made the breath stop in his throat.

"It's not Father Wilfred," she told him, matter-of-factly. "Father Wilfred's on holiday, so there will be a different vicar."

And with those words she legged it down the street, her short legs splaying out awkwardly to the sides as she ran. Tom suddenly wished that he could bottle her childlike carefree joy and store it for her, so that she could use it later when life inevitably became tough and sad.

She had been right. The substitute vicar was young and painfully thin. His robes hung off his small frame, sack-like, arranging themselves into excessive folds which appeared as though they were drowning him.

From their front row seats (on which Clara had insisted), Tom could see his stern expression, and he fought the urge to turn around and walk out. But then the organ started, and the assembled crowd burst into song… and it was too late – he would have to stay. He settled down in his seat and found Lucy's hand absentmindedly placed into his. The clammy warmth helped to melt away his nerves.

Tom was very glad that he did stay. The vicar's voice was surprisingly gentle, and as he read the opening lines, Tom felt himself become completely and utterly engrossed. When was the last time that he'd been in church? It would have been what, twenty? Twenty-five years ago? When he first arrived in Chicago, he went every Sunday, even though he didn't understand everything that was being said back in those days.

He almost laughed when he heard the sermon about the Prodigal Son. Out of all the readings that could have been chosen, it had to be this one. Had the vicar seen him coming?

"Forgiveness is something that is often difficult to talk about in this society," he said gently from the pulpit. "We live in a culture of blame. We blame bankers for what has happened to our economy, we blame politicians for the level of unemployment, we blame our friends for not being in contact, or our partner for not being caring enough… The thing about placing blame, is that it's easy. It's so easy to do, and sometimes it very briefly makes us feel better.

But that emotion only tends to last for a very short time, because we realise that we can't feel good if we don't find it in our hearts to forgive. We're not good at forgiveness, and we're even worse at it when it comes to us. We find it extremely difficult to forgive ourselves for our own wrongdoing, and that in itself is a very, very bad thing. Because in failing to forgive ourselves, we grow bitter, we begin to hate the world around us, and we stop believing in our own ability to change.

I'm not saying it's easy, but we need to work hard at our own forgiveness in order to avoid falling victim to hate and despair. We need to share our feelings with others that you trust – I'm always saying to parishioners that they can come and speak to me, of course they can. But they also shouldn't be afraid to share their problems with loved ones…"

And then Tom couldn't see the vicar anymore, or anything beyond the small hand that was holding his, because suddenly his eyes blurred over, and the whole world became nothing but a mixture of yellow, summer light.

"Why are you crying?" whispered Lucy.

Chapter 16 – Joanna
Warsaw

It was a quiet Sunday. Joanna imagined that few people bothered to go out into the drizzle, if they didn't absolutely have to. The start of summer had brought with it an unseasonable amount of rain and the capital's inhabitants were desperate for a bit of sunshine. She'd decided to take the tram to Ochota – it was quicker than driving and it gave her the opportunity to scribble down some notes for the article. As she descended the steps at her stop, a glimmer of blue sky greeted her. The rain had stopped and she had a sudden urge to walk past her old flat.

She'd deliberately avoided this part of the city since her mother had moved out, as it had always generated intense emotions, a mixture of nerves, sadness and loss. Joanna associated this first home in the capital not only with Adam and his disappearance, but also with a different stage of her family life in which Monika was still hopeful, and still had a desire to build a life for her children. This was a happier time before her aunt had to step in to pick up the pieces and take Joanna to school by the scruff of her neck.

A woman sat hunched on the street corner, plastic bags round her feet, a ragged cardigan wrapped around her shoulders. She held a Styrofoam cup in her dirty hand.

Joanna dug into her purse and fished out a handful of coins. Her childhood nightmares prevented her from walking past beggars without offering them anything. The woman smiled up at her and mumbled something incomprehensible. Her eyes were heavy-lidded with long, curling eyelashes which gave her a slightly startled look. The short hair fanned out around her face like a greying halo causing her at first-glance to look middle-aged, when she was probably not much older than Joanna herself. Her pupils seemed slightly dilated, her vision unfocused.

Joanna noticed that she was mechanically stroking something furry in her lap and it was only when she leaned in closer to ask the woman whether she wanted something to eat, that she saw the ears and black nose, and realised that it was a dog.

"Is he alright? Is he ill? Do you want me to help…?"

But the woman continued to smile at her, not comprehending.

She later wasn't sure what made her do it, but her hand suddenly shot out and she touched the poor animal's head. It was cold and lifeless.

She wanted to pick the woman up and shake her hard. The dog was dead from hunger and starvation. It was nothing more than a bag of bones covered with loose skin and fur. Why hadn't she taken it to the vet? Why hadn't she alerted someone? Anyone? They could have helped. If she couldn't sort her own life out, that was bad enough, but why do this to an animal?

Her hand still hung suspended in the air and the woman stared at it dumbly. Joanna forced herself to stand up and walk away. This wasn't a situation for her to fix. Not this one. But she knew where the bitter thoughts had come from.

There was a period in her late teenage years, after her mother's condition had begun to deteriorate, when she would fall asleep every night with haunting visions of being reduced to the state of a ragged child living in the car park of central station. When she'd admitted this to Aunt Irena, she'd laughed, but Joanna had always suspected that without her aunt's sudden intervention, her nightmares may well have become a reality. In the woman's eyes she saw something of what might have been and it made the panic brew up inside her.

She walked slowly through the dirty streets towards her old home. The building must have been recently renewed as the concrete block which had previously resembled a grey airing cupboard, was now painted a lurid yellow. The double-glazed windows glimmered in their plastic white frames. The area was almost unrecognisable, apart from the large rectangular clothes hanger still standing in the front yard, which back in the day had been used to bash the dust out of carpets – a practice long since abandoned. It reminded Joanna of many weekday afternoons when she swung on it upside down, attached precariously to its middle pole by only the insides of her knees.

She could still visualise the giant concrete slabs which had been piled up in one corner of the shadowy courtyard. They must have been left over by some builders who had never bothered to discard them and they remained there, gathering cold wet moss in their cracks and forming a point of fascination for children from the local neighbourhood through the years. Joanna and her friends had a great time climbing to the top of the pile. They used to hold races to see who could climb the quickest.

Then of course there was the fateful day of the family picture. It was a hot summer. If she closed her eyes, she could still feel the angry beads of sweat on her forehead. It must have been about eighteen months after Adam's disappearance when she came back from school, and began working on her homework assignment which involved drawing a picture entitled 'my family'. To this day, she couldn't explain why she did it, but she carefully sketched a picture of just herself and Adam holding hands – no parents, no extended family, just the two of them.

Her mother saw it when she came into the kitchen to make dinner. Without a word, she took the drawing which her daughter had spent hours perfecting, and scrunched it up in her fist. Joanna had been so livid that she'd refused to eat and ran outside. She then proceeded to recreate the very same image with chalk on top of the concrete slab. She kept stepping backwards as she furiously chalked the legs and feet, and she was working at such speed that she lost her footing on the end of the slab and went toppling backwards to the ground. She could still remember the searing, agonising pain in her arm as she lay on the grass howling from a gut-wrenching combination of fury and physical pain.

Joanna wondered whether she would still find the remnants of the grass onto which she fell or whether the area had been tarmacked over. She walked carefully around the biggest puddles. The road that Mrs. Barska lived on was two blocks away, but it took her almost twenty minutes to tread her way to the front door.

She pressed the buzzer and waited. Nobody had picked up the phone when she'd rung earlier in the week, but she wasn't sure whether the number that she found in the phone book was the right one and decided that it was worth making the journey in person to find out for sure. But now she was physically shaking from the cold and beginning to regret her decision.

"Hello?" asked a male voice through the intercom. Relief rushed through her.

"Hello. My name is Joanna Malicka. I'm here to see Mrs. Barska," she said quickly.

There was a moment of hesitation, but then the door buzzed, and Joanna took this as a sign to step inside. She immediately realised that she didn't know which floor she should be aiming for and she stood helplessly outside the lift with its peeling layers of paint, unsure of which number to press. Luckily, a minute or so later, two teenage girls emerged from inside with a shivering sausage dog on a lead.

"Sorry, I'm looking for flat 58. Do you know what floor it is?"

"Hmm… it must either be the top floor or the one below."

Joanna eventually found herself outside the correct door, her finger on the doorbell.

"It's open!" a man's voice yelled.

She stepped forward cautiously and found herself in a darkened hallway with wood panelling on the walls and a giant hat stand half collapsing under the weight of umbrellas and bits of clothing. In the corner, a bookcase with glass fronted doors displayed yellowing tomes with torn spines, jutting out at haphazard angles.

This interior was such an exact replica of her own childhood home, that she experienced a physical shock, but it slowly dawned on her that this was what most homes would have looked like in the eighties. What was unusual was that the owner of this particular one had done nothing to it for thirty years.

She must have stood there for a good five minutes taking in her surroundings, before a man emerged from one of the side rooms. He was topless and barefoot, wearing only a pair of washed out workmen's jeans. He was clutching a young girl of about two, who had fallen asleep on his chest.

He seemed entirely unembarrassed by his state of undress and motioned with his hand for Joanna to follow him.

"I'm sorry," he whispered, "I've only just managed to put her to sleep. She's got a bit of a fever. I'll just put her to bed and I'll be right with you."

With these words he disappeared down the hallway humming a tune that she thought she vaguely recognised from the radio. The flat was exceedingly warm and was filled with the aroma of chicken soup that added to the general aura of nostalgia. Not wanting to risk overburdening the coat stand, she left her cardigan over the edge of one of the kitchen chairs.

The man came back and put on the kettle.

"Awful weather isn't it?" he asked, rubbing his palms together. "It's supposed to be summer. The weather people keep promising a heat wave, and what do we get?"

"Rain. And then they say at the end of each month that their forecast is 99% accurate."

"Yeah, it's always been the same for as long as I can remember. Don't know why we even bother watching it. Tea or coffee?"

"Erm… coffee please." She was entirely at a loss for why he'd not yet asked her why she'd come.

"So, unfortunately my wife is out. I'm surprised that she booked you in at this time. She doesn't finish her shift at the hospital until at least 5pm. But seeing as you're here, I'm sure I can look at your references and just let her know."

There was her answer. He had mistaken her for someone else.

"No, no," Joanna protested, "I'm here to see Mrs. Barska. Sorry I came unannounced, but I couldn't get through on the number that was in the phone book."

Out of the corner of her eye she spotted a small gilded picture of the Virgin Mary hanging just above the rickety bookcase and she was taken instantly back to her grandmother's house where the very same picture always looked down on her from above the door.

The man scratched his ear and gave her a peculiar look.

"Yes, but as I said, she's at work…"

"Ah… your wife is also called Mrs. Barska." She finally understood. "But I want to speak to an older Mrs. Barska who lived here. I'm guessing she could be your mother?"

"My mother? So you're not here for the baby-sitting job?" asked the man scratching his beard. Joanna couldn't help but notice the food remains embedded amongst the bristles. She was pretty certain that he'd had egg for breakfast.

"No, no," said Joanna laughing, "I'm afraid I'm not very good with kids. I wanted to see Mrs. Barska because she used to know my mother and I think she might be able to help me with something. Does she still live here?" She felt the increased pace of her heart as she waited for the answer.

"Yeah, she's in the other room," he said eventually, "But I'm afraid she's had the flu too. We've all been through it. Germs spread like wildfire in this heat. Anyway, I think she's sleeping at the moment. Does she know you were going to come?"

She couldn't help but detect a note of suspicion in his voice.

For a moment she considered lying, but it wouldn't be worth the potential fallout.

"Erm… no. She doesn't really know me. That is, she may remember me, but she certainly wouldn't recognise me. She would have last seen me when I was ten years old at most."

"Right…" said the man, placing the mug of coffee on the table in front of her. She could see the mistrust building in his expression. Perhaps he was beginning to regret letting her into the flat and was now seeking an excuse to make her leave.

She wanted… she *needed* desperately to stay.

"It's a really odd story. Please don't think me mad… When I was four, my brother went missing during one of the Solidarity protests. We were out in the street with our mother and he suddenly ran off. At least that's what we think happened. He was never found and the case was eventually closed. I don't believe he's…"

His frown suddenly relaxed, suspicion replaced with curiosity.

"Hold on… I think I remember the story. It was in the papers for a while. I must have been a teenager at the time… But it was quite a high profile case because it was during the strike."

"Do you really remember it?" she asked. She wasn't sure why, but she felt a sudden surge of comfort.

"I think so."

"It was such a long time ago though. You wouldn't believe it, but I work for a magazine myself and the editor has asked me to do a feature piece on missing people. He doesn't know about Adam of course. And, well, it's a good opportunity for my career, so I decided to take it. I've just started reading up on some of the other cases that I wanted to feature and it occurred to me that a couple of the ones that were solved – as in the people were found – as a result of TV footage."

"OK…"

"And this is such a long shot and I'm probably a mad woman, but I re-read some of my own interview minutes from just after it happened. And I mention that I was with my mother and your mother, and your mother's friend who had a 'zoomer'. I think in my childhood vocabulary a 'zoomer' could have been a camera. I just wondered whether your mother might be able to tell me who this friend of hers was…"

She realised from the look on the man's face that she was babbling incomprehensibly. Her Aunt Irena frequently had the expression on her face when speaking to Joanna's grandma who suffered from Alzheimer's.

"I realise it sounds highly unlikely, but it would make me feel better if she told me that her friend didn't have a camera at all, or that he'd wiped the film."

"I understand. Why don't I tell her you came and then she can ring you back when she's better?"

"Thank you," said Joanna, and scribbled her name and mobile number of the scrap of paper handed to her by the man. "I would be so grateful. It would really mean so much to me.

As she emerged back out into the crumbling block, it had begun to spit with rain once more. Would Mrs. Barska call her back? Joanna prayed that she would. But if not, she would just have to return in a week or so. This was a witness that she wouldn't give up on so easily.

Chapter 17 – Matty
London

The box had sat under his desk all day. There were several moments in which he'd subconsciously brushed his knees against it and felt equally reassured and anxious about its solid presence. He physically jerked in his seat when Arun rolled his chair over to cross-check something in a report he was working on and skimmed the edge of the box with his huge feet. He told himself that he wouldn't open it until he was in the safety of his bedroom. The office held too much risk. People might ask unnecessary questions.

By the time he embarked on his journey home, he was wound up like a coiled spring. It had been stupid of course to take the car into central London but it was the only way that he could get to and from Celia's quickly. Now, as he crawled through traffic on the Euston Road, he felt the anticipation build inside him, until it reached unbearable proportions. Eventually, he made it to the final stretch of Holloway Road and he parked up.

He ran up the stairs with it, two at a time, and after hours of agonising wait, he was finally alone with the curious package. He put his phone on silent wanting to have the certainty of being undisturbed. Ellie was out for dinner with a friend and wouldn't be back until late.

He slipped open the cardboard corners and breathed in deeply. The photograph of the man lay on top of the pile of reports. It was one of those disconcerting images, in which the eyes appeared to be staring right at you, no matter what angle you were looking from. Matty examined it again and flipped it over to look on the back.

There was a stamp of a photography studio: 'Vista Images, St. John Street, London WC1' and a faint scribble in pencil: 'LM, 24.04 1984'

A quick internet search confirmed that the studio still existed. However, with recent stringent data protection measures, Matty realised how unlikely it was that he would manage to get hold of any information about the photo.

He turned his attention to the school reports which he removed from the box and arranged in date order. He noticed that the one for reception was missing.

Year 1 Swallows. Miss Alicia Henderson.

Matty is quiet and shy, but he appears to be making progress in socialising and making friends. Like other EAL children in his class, he has gained confidence as his language skills have developed. His progress in reading and writing has been slow, but there has been a noticeable improvement over the course of the last term. He possesses good numeracy skills.

Year 2 Falcons. Mr. Michael Quinn.

Matty's reading skills are developing quickly and he is now at level six. I am confident he will be able to achieve level eight by the end of the year with reading support at home. His writing is developing at a steady pace, and he could benefit from further handwriting practice. He displays very good numerical aptitude – a level above the average for his peers.

He stopped reading, realising that he hadn't taken in the last two sentences. EAL? He racked his brain for what the abbreviation might stand for and not finding one, he typed it into the search engine.

EAL – In the British education system, an abbreviation of 'English as an additional language'.

There it was again. Nadia was right. He had sounded foreign.

He felt a strange numbness as he examined the report again, poring over each word, attempting to read between the lines.

'He has gained confidence and his language skills have developed.' Nadia had said it was a well-known fact that children absorb languages a lot quicker than adults.

The reports for Years 3 to 6 were much more regular accounts of his progress through the various stages with no mention of anything unusual. It was Year 1 that held the key, but the evidence began and ended in one paragraph.

There was an envelope which Matty hadn't noticed before lying at the bottom of the box. It had once been white but its edges had turned yellow with age.

He carefully opened the flap half hoping for a letter which would provide a simple explanation for what he had just discovered. But there was no paper inside, just three photographs featuring a young woman holding a baby. At first glance, he didn't recognise her. The Celia in the photograph had straight, bobbed dark hair – nothing like her current curled blond. But this wasn't why she seemed unrecognisable. It was the obvious difference in her expression.

The woman in the photograph was beaming, the corners of her pale green eyes creased up with happiness. The small boy in the picture looked as though he might be around two or three. In one photo he was pressing his face into Celia's neck. In another he was grinning, holding his hand out. There were some white petals in it, which he appeared to be showing the photographer.

For some reason it didn't seem immediately obvious to Matty that he was staring at a picture of his younger self. He was most focused on the fact that he didn't remember his mother looking so genuinely happy. She laughed frequently of course – when telling him funny stories from work, or when flirting with the waiters at restaurants that they used to frequent, but he had never seen in her this expression of pure, undiluted joy. What had happened between then and now which had rid her of this? His father?

Or maybe she'd been like this throughout his childhood and he just didn't remember it. There were two rows of fat photo albums lining the shelves above her antique fireplace in the living room – one for every year of Matty's life. She loved bringing them out to show her guests, but he was always bored, never bothering to look at the 'fixed in time' images of former sports days, of childhood picnics, holidays and graduation. The next time he was formally 'home', he would make sure that he took a closer look.

But what could he do in the meantime? What information could he extract from the box without asking Celia about it directly? His eye was drawn to the photo of the dark-eyed man, whose identity he was desperate to find out. But he realised that the only possible route of gaining information about it, was by contacting the photography studio. He could almost hear the voice on the other end of the phone telling him that he couldn't give out information due to customer data protection.

"Hi, what are you doing?"

Ellie came through the bedroom door, her hair wet, her old, fraying mac covered in a smattering of dark drops. He watched her cautiously as she hung in out above the radiator to dry, and moved into the kitchen to wring out her ponytail.

He wished that she hadn't come back so early. He needed more time to think, to formulate a plan. The box, although illuminating, provided him with so very little to go on.

"I'm alright," he lied, "You're back early?"

"I didn't go," she said quietly.

"What, why not? Did they cancel?"

"No… I didn't feel like it."

"Right, so what… so what were you doing until now?" he said. He knew somehow at that stage that the answer wouldn't be good. That he would be forced away from his search for the rest of the afternoon. Whatever it was that Ellie had to say could wait. It wasn't nearly as important as this.

But there she was, back in the room, sitting down on the edge of the bed in her wet jeans and giving him that look – the awful, accusing look of a wounded animal.

"I was just walking in the park. Walking around and debating what to do."

"About what?"

"Not 'what' but 'who'. Us."

He had known that the conversation was coming. It was inevitable. The situation would have to be addressed at some point, but he couldn't be dealing with it. Not today. Not now.

The pressure was building up again on the insides of his temples and he felt suddenly that there was a dark creature within him – a small, frightened, quivering creature which was standing at a fork in the road, unsure of which way to go. He could force himself to make a decision, but as soon as he went down one path, he could see that it too divided further along in another fork, and subsequent endless forks sprung out in all directions growing further and further outwards like an all-encompassing, destructive web.

"I think I'm not English. You know, not originally," he blurted out before he could stop himself.

"What?" Ellie stared at him as if he had lost his mind.

"Nadia said that I had an accent as a child and now these school reports… they confirm it."

"What are you talking about?"

She shifted herself closer towards him and finally looked down at the box, its contents splayed out around them. In the dull afternoon light coming through the window, he noticed that there were pale pink blotches staining her cheeks and her eyes were rimmed with red.

"Are you OK?" He touched her hand, placed it between his two palms. He couldn't bear it when she cried.

"Fine," she said, shaking herself free. "What is this about you not being English?"

He explained everything that he'd managed to find out, showed her his school report and the photos of him as a child. She read them silently and something in her expression changed. It was almost as if her anger had dissipated, or she'd found a partial explanation for his recent erratic behaviour, and she momentarily became consumed by curiosity.

"I think you should just ask Celia," she said eventually. "You deserve to know more about your background, the language that you used to speak… I don't think you should skirt around the subject. Maybe your relationship with her is so superficial exactly because you are so civil to each other all the time."

"You know what will happen – she'll refuse to speak about it. She'll get pissed off and probably leave the room."

"Then let her get pissed off! She can't avoid your questions forever. Plus, surely it's better than doing everything behind her back?"

"I don't know that it *is* better, you know."

"So how do you plan to find out?"

"I don't know… I suppose I could ring that photographer – I could go and see them with the photo. There's a small chance that they might be able to tell me something about it."

"Or you could see if you can track down this old teacher – Alicia Henderson. She might be able to tell you something more."

"But people don't remember stuff from that long ago, do they? To them it's all trivial. You probably won't remember your current class in five years' time, will you? Let alone in over twenty?"

"I think I'll remember more than you think. I spend every day for a year with those kids – their quirks are imprinted on my brain. Now I can second guess when some of them are about to misbehave before they even do it. And I think you're wrong – I think to some extent teachers remember every pupil that they ever taught. It's worth a try anyway."

She was right. It was definitely worth a try. But Matty couldn't envisage going on his own, speaking to people he didn't remember in the hope that they would remember him. Besides, he would look ridiculous, asking about things that he should have already known years before.

But the alternative of not knowing was far worse.

"If I find out where she works, will you go with me?" he asked weakly.

"Of course," she said simply. The wetness around her eyes had dried up. "Of course."

Chapter 18 – Tom
Chicago

"Thank you for taking me to church," he said to Clara again the following morning. "You know it's been a quarter of a century since I last went to mass, but I remembered everything."

She was shocked at this.

"You haven't been in 25 years?"

"No. Do you go every week with Lucy?"

He couldn't be certain, but he thought that he could see a glimmer of sadness pass across her face when he asked the question.

"Well, I have gone every week, yes. Always. As for Lucy – that's a more recent thing. For the last few months I've taken her every Sunday. It's to give my daughter a rest. She works all week you know, long hours."

"So do you."

It came out wrong. It seemed as if he were trying to gallantly defend her against the demands of her own family, but if she noticed it, she didn't seem to mind.

"I know," she said, "But I enjoy it, and her situation isn't easy."

She dropped the bag of laundry that she was holding and sat down in the armchair. Tom could see that she wanted to say a lot more, but was having trouble.

"I still don't understand how he could do it," she muttered eventually.

"Who?"

"Pete – my daughter's ex-husband."

"He left her?"

They were moving into dangerous territory.

"Yes. It was really only a couple of months after Lucy was born. I knew that things hadn't been right between them for a while, but I hoped that the child would change things, you know?"

Tom gave a non-committal murmur. The characteristic crawl in his stomach had started as soon as soon as they'd gotten onto the subject of the man's departure. He found himself wishing that she would stop speaking, that she'd finish gathering up the laundry and leave. They could resume later, when he would be more mentally ready.

In a moment of panic that gripped him with particular force, he considered pretending that he was very unwell and in desperate need of solitary rest, but he couldn't bear stopping her when she was mid-flow and clearly very upset.

"Did he meet someone else?" he asked, after a drawn-out pause.

"No. That was the strange thing. He hadn't. He just decided that he couldn't live the rest of his life unhappy. Those were the words that he used. And he moved out – far. He lives at the other end of the city now, somewhere in Schaumberg. It takes him more than an hour to travel to see them, which is why he doesn't come very often. I think that was his intention all along. He never bonded with Lucy. It's almost like he didn't know how."

"That's sad."

"Yes. And you know, on the surface you can't fault him. He pays his child support money on time and more than he has to. And he always seemed like a good guy to me. He was hard-working, he didn't drink – I was always particularly wary of the drinkers; you get so many young men these days…"

"I was 'a drinker' as you put it." The words had burst out of him before he could stop them and the colour flooded her face instantly.

"I'm sorry. I didn't mean…"

"It doesn't matter."

"It does. I keep promising myself that I will stop judging people, and then look what happens."

"But I deserve to be judged. In the end it was nobody's decision or fault but my own."

He felt light with the relief that the confession brought.

"When did you start?" she asked quietly.

"When I first came to America. I was only thirty-two. I came here and I was certain that this was the real start of my life; that from now everything would change. But things didn't turn out how I wanted for a lot of reasons. I couldn't find work for many months. Eventually, I was hired as a caretaker at a secondary school. I couldn't speak very good English, so it seemed that there weren't very many jobs that I could do. The kids at the school made fun of me, the pay was bad, and the woman who I was with – she left me. I was devastated. You see, she promised me things when we first arrived – she said that she would love me no matter what, no matter how poor we were. Instead, she found herself another man who earned much more than I did and that was the last I saw of her. She left me without even saying goodbye. I heard through a common acquaintance that she'd moved to Milwaukee to live with this property magnate who she'd met through a friend.

"That's awful. I'm sorry."

"Yes," he muttered. "That's when I started drinking. I had a friend – a fellow Polish man called Jurek. He was nothing like me, and looking back, I don't think he was a friend I would have naturally made in other circumstances. But at the time I was drawn to him, because I suppose he was a reminder of home. He would end up being both a blessing and a curse to me. You see, he was very successful. A businessman. He owned two car dealerships and he got me involved. That's the blessing part – I got a job that I enjoyed and that paid very well. It was an irony, because only a year after Lidia left me, I was earning good money – enough for her to be satisfied with. But the problem was we were both working extremely long hours and Jurek dealt with the stress by drinking.

Every day in the evening, when we shut the shop, he would bring out the bottle of vodka, and he didn't do shots. No, he would pour large, regular glasses, like you would drink water out of. He could handle those amounts – it almost didn't affect him and it was scary to watch. He could put away half a bottle and it would barely have any impact on him. But I wasn't used to it, at first anyway.

She was listening to him carefully, but there was no way of telling what she was thinking.

"And it got worse?" she guessed.

"Exactly. At first I hated it, and drank only because I felt I couldn't say no to somebody who had been so good to me. And then I realised that it numbed me, even more than work numbed me. I didn't have to remember any of the awfulness that had gone before."

"You mean the break up?"

"No, no. Well, the break up to an extent. But mainly things before Lidia – horrible things. Things that were my fault. Only my fault."

She raised her eyebrows then, but didn't ask anything else. He felt the flush of heat in his face.

"So yes, the drink helped. It was the only solid thing that was with me for all of those years. There were nights when I would come home and not bother having any dinner. I wasn't hungry. Instead I would sit in front of the TV and watch a film, drinking glass after glass of neat vodka, until I didn't *feel* anymore. The world would disappear in a cloudy haze and I would wake up the next morning, have another couple of drinks to halt the hangover and go to work. I functioned like that for years. I would top myself up during the day and for years nobody noticed. You wouldn't believe me, but they didn't. I functioned so well and I worked hard. The doctors told me that I would need a liver transplant, but I still carried on. I was scared of what would happen if I stopped."

"But you *did* stop?"

"Yes, eventually. It was a man named Mitch who made me stop. He and his wife were the people who brought me here. You might remember them from when they visited. I can't help but wish every day that they had appeared in my life sooner."

He was exhausted now. Exhausted from the vast flurry of words that had escaped his mouth – words that had lain dormant in the darkest recesses of his brain, slowly, ever so slowly eating away at him. He was dizzy with the release that they produced. There was a sense of lightness, but it was nothing like the blurred, cushioned elation produced by a third bottle of *Chopin* vodka. For the first time in years, he was clear-headed but free, wonderfully free, even if it was only a temporary freedom. The beautiful feeling enabled him to quickly, unnoticeably, slip into a restful, undisturbed sleep.

Chapter 19 – Joanna
Warsaw

The phone rang when Joanna was leaning against the wall of the shower attempting to wake herself up with an icy stream of water. Her insomnia was getting worse. She considered going to see her GP about it, but he would probably only give her sleeping tablets which would make her drowsy during the day and have no effect on her night's sleep.

She quickly stepped out to answer the call and cursed as she slipped on the bathroom floor, hitting her forehead on the edge of the sink. By the time she lifted the receiver, she felt mildly concussed.

"Hello?" she groaned.

"Anna Barska," said the voice.

With her pounding head, Joanna momentarily forgot where she knew the name from.

"You came round to my flat the other day..."

Of course.

"Yes... I just... I didn't expect you to call so quickly. I erm... sorry, are you feeling better?"

"I was never feeling bad. My oaf of a son is protecting me from the world again," the voice responded gruffly, but it was followed by a quiet chuckle.

"I don't know if you remember me…" Joanna began.

"Of course I remember you. I'm not senile yet. You want to see me?"

Joanna wondered whether the whole conversation was a figment of her concussed mind.

"Yes, very much," she breathed, "When is good?"

"Anytime is good for me. Retirement can be so painfully boring, I tell you. Breakfast? But no; I suppose you young ones have to be in the office at 8? I would die if I had to go into the office at 8 and sit there for ten hours…"

"No, actually. I'm working from home for the next few weeks. I could meet you for breakfast."

"Corner of Grojecka and Dickens Street. Ladybird Cafe. I'll be there at 8: 30."

"OK, but how will I…" her voice trailed off as she heard the dialling tone.

***

Thankfully, the cafe was largely empty. Joanna had imagined a tall, middle-aged and perfectly groomed lady, with sharp features and an air of tired elegance. Instead, she was presented with a small plump woman with dyed orange hair. Her grey roots were beginning to show and her saggy arms clutched at a dirty hessian shopping bag.

"Mrs. Barska?"

"Who else?" she asked, laughing. Joanna noticed that she was missing one of her bottom front teeth, which gave her a slightly cocky edge.

"Thanks for coming to meet me," she said settling down into the chair opposite her. She wasn't sure how to begin the conversation, but it turned out that she didn't have to worry. Mrs. Barska was the sort of person who could speak for both of them.

"You've grown into an intelligent woman – I can see that," she said, running her beady eyes over Joanna's face, "None of this young riffraff that you see nowadays in the streets. I always said to your mother that you looked like you've a brain on you. Not that she paid much attention to anything I said… and she probably should have done, really. It pays to listen to people who are worldlier than you are. "

"Thank you, but I…"

"…And that brother of yours. He was a right tearaway. Always wanted to be the centre of attention, always pulling your mother this way and that… No, you were quiet in your way, but so aware of everything."

Joanna was stunned. This was the first person, aside from Stefan, who spoke openly about her brother, without skirting around him or averting their eyes. This was a living, breathing person who had known him, but wasn't frightened.

"Mrs. Barska, can you tell me what you remember from the day he disappeared?"

"Goodness, nothing helpful, as you might have gathered. If I did, I would have let the police know years ago. I saw you in the streets with your mother. I left work early that day, like thousands of others. Waldek came with me. We shut up the shop, even though we'd just had a delivery of meat and you wouldn't believe how rare an occasion that was. It wasn't an easy choice you know. I mean a protest is a protest, but meat brings in the money. On any other day we would have had queues going down the road for kilometres.

Anyway, we went and all three of you were there. Your mother was waiting in the place where we'd agreed to meet and I spotted her right away in her neat little white coat and with that pained expression on her face. Adam was running around like a headless idiot of course, but he was in our field of vision… It was rubbish what people said later on about Monika being a bad mother, about not keeping an eye on him.

She was more vigilant than most. She just didn't have eyes in the back of her head and that's not something that she could be blamed for."

"Is Waldek your husband?"

The woman's eyes widened and she let out a hollow laugh.

"Waldek Bem. Thank Christ that I wasn't married to him! No, no. He was the owner of the shop I worked in. A hulk of a man, but strangely gentle. He'd signed up for the Solidarity movement, but his father scared him that he'd lose the business if he went out protesting in the streets. Of course, he didn't listen."

"And he was there that day?"

"Well yeah, he came out onto the streets. He wouldn't miss it. But what's Waldek to you?" she asked, gazing at Joanna sadly.

"Did Waldek… did he by any chance have a camera?"

At that point, a young waitress came over to their table to take their order. Joanna felt so frustrated, she could have kicked her for her awful timing. Mrs. Barska ordered her coffee and gazed up at the ceiling in a look of concentration.

"He *did* own a camera," she said, when the girl finally walked away, "My memory is awful, so I couldn't tell you for sure if he had it that day. It was a big, cumbersome thing… but you know, he would have wanted to document what was going on. He'd been doing interviews with people in the run-up to the event and he was very devoted to the cause, so he may well have brought it out. He always had this big idea that he wanted to produce something useful that future generations would read or view," she sniggered – "always had ideas above his station. Why do you ask?"

"It was something I said…"

"Huh?"

"Sorry, what I mean is, it was something that was in the transcript of the interview the police did with me, right after Adam's disappearance. I said that you were with a man who had a 'zoomer'. I think in my childhood vocabulary that could have been a camera?"

"Well, that was definitely the only man I was with on the day. As for the 'zoomer'…" Here she shrugged her shoulders, implying that she didn't know.

"Are you still in touch with Waldek?" Joanna asked. She felt her chest constricting.

"He died a couple of years ago. Brain tumour, poor bugger. Went to the doctor one day with a migraine, was on the hospital ward a fortnight later and then 'kaput'." She spread her arms out helplessly.

"It's hopeless. I don't know why I'm even bothering…" she suddenly felt like crying with the exhaustion of it all.

"Hey, hey." Mrs. Barska covered Joanna's shaking hands with her own wrinkled palm, "What a dreadful place the world would be if we didn't have hope. Waldek is gone, but you can get in touch with his daughter. She lives in Izabelin, just outside of town. I have her phone number somewhere. I had to call her when she was arranging the dreaded funeral. She's a lovely girl. Tell you what, I'll ring her for you and ask her to get in touch. She could at least tell you that she doesn't have his camera, or that she's destroyed it, and then you'll know for sure. You of all people know that uncertainty is what eats you up the most."

"Thank you," Joanna managed. She scribbled down her mobile number on a piece of paper and gave it to the woman.

"No problem. Sometimes you just have to be sure."

She was about to leave, but she hesitated and sat back down. The realisation suddenly hit her that she might never again have the opportunity to speak about her brother with someone outside of her family again.

"What else do you remember about Adam?" she asked, grabbing Mrs. Barska's hand.

She smiled at her warmly, her dark pink lipstick seeping out of the corners of her mouth.

"He was a trouble-maker. It's impossible not to remember him. He was always playing Indians and knocking over people's plant pots in the yard. There was a time… I'm sure your mother has told you about this… when he was messing around on the balcony and he dropped a plastic bag filled with water on the estate caretaker. It landed slap bang in the middle of his head from a height of about three floors. If that bag had been tied up, it could have killed the poor bugger!"

"And then what happened?

"Well, he was drenched of course and he came up to give your poor mother a good earful. I'm pretty sure Adam got a good belting that day, but it didn't stop him from acting up again.

Then of course there was the time when he raided the neighbours' basements with the 'street gang'. It wasn't his fault. There were older boys in the neighbourhood who took pleasure in forcing the little ones to nick stuff. They somehow managed to break into three or four of the cellars at the bottom of your block of flats and ended up eating all the conserves and jam that a few of the ladies who lived downstairs had saved for the winter. Adam denied any knowledge of it, only his clothes were streaked with red…"

Joanna wanted to laugh, but instead, she felt an aching emptiness. Why didn't she have her own memory of these events? Surely she was present at the time? Her vision of Adam was so brittle – it was a patchwork of other people's recollections and scraps of damaged photos. Beyond this there was nothing… nothing but identical genes that connected her to her brother.

"Was it an awful time? When we were young?" She'd heard so many different people speak about the 'Communist years' but everyone had a different story to tell. There were a rare few, like her own grandmother, who would say that they were the best years of their lives.

"Oh, they weren't awful, really. Difficult, sure, but not awful. Everything's relative, isn't it? We're spoilt now. But even now, nothing is certain."

"Sorry?"

"You know I've been naively happy these past few years," Mrs. Barska told her leaning in, as if revealing an intimate secret. "I thought that after all the years of censorship, the rationing, false full employment, drudgery, basic things missing from shops… that eventually we had reached the 'golden age.' We deserved it after all and Solidarity fought hard to get us here. We've started to catch up with the West. We finally had the same Hollywood films reaching our cinemas at the same time as the rest of the world. We could travel, we were welcomed into Europe. And then what?" She spread her arms. "One plane crash and the whole government's gone."

"Yes… Nobody saw that one coming."

"I sadly sense that it's the beginning of the end of these years… the good times. Mark my words. Maybe it'll be alright for a while. Maybe people will rally round in the face of disaster. But there is a lot of anger out there. It's like all the fury that people have been holding onto has begun to emerge. It'll boil over and then… well, I don't want to say what will happen, but it won't be anything good."

"Surely we have to be positive?"

She laughed, a short hollow laugh.

"Thank you anyway," said Joanna, smiling at her and gathering her things.

"Hey, I didn't do anything," protested Mrs. Barska.

"You spoke about Adam," she said simply. "It helped."

Chapter 20 – Matty
London

They surfaced from the subterranean depths onto a busy road in Hackney and Matty surveyed his surroundings with no recognition. He hadn't even an inkling of an idea about which way they should turn. Sweat broke out on the palms of his hands, and he wiped them quickly on the backs of his jeans.

Ellie had come with him, as he'd asked her to, and he felt suddenly awful for bestowing his burden on her. She hadn't deserved it, particularly considering the way he'd behaved over the past few days. He'd openly avoided her by spending every waking moment in the office, even after everybody had left and he genuinely had no more work left to do. Then he'd hurriedly muttered a few sentences to her before bed, mainly about how tired he was, and turned around to face the wall, thereby escaping any attempts to revisit the conversation. During this morning's tube journey, they'd spent more time with one another (bar sleeping) than they had done in the past week, and now they sat side by side, unsure what subjects were safe to talk about and flinching whenever one of them accidentally touched the other.

No matter how hard he tried, Matty couldn't explain to himself why his feelings for Ellie had changed. Had they changed? Was this what people meant when they spoke, dramatically about 'falling out of love'? (He'd always hated the phrase – he thought it lofty and pretentious). Or was it actually nothing to do with Ellie? Was it he who had changed at some basic, fundamental level? There had been moments not so long ago in which he would look at her and feel such a clear, deep contentment that he wanted the world around them to just fall away. It happened during simple tasks – her peeling the potatoes or testing out her next Year 3 science lesson on him, him coming back sweaty from football and engulfing her in a bear hug, them doing the weekly food shopping or playing an impromptu game of Sunday afternoon *Scrabble* over coffee – it was then that he felt that he didn't want the moment to end, that perfect snippet of time in which everything was in equilibrium and there was nothing else on earth that he needed. But of course, it could never last – a beat later and the world shifted, and the moment quietly vanished.

And then another moment had taken place – when he was standing next to that graffitied wall in the centre of a city he'd never been to before, and he felt suddenly, inexplicably broken. It was as if the wall had transported him to a different part of himself, a part that was bleak and cold and colourless, forever leaving behind that other part, which sparkled and shimmered with a wonderful, carefree light. And the most awful thing about it was that he felt hopeless – he didn't know how to bring back that essential piece of himself that had gone missing.

"Which way?" Ellie asked.

He fiddled with his phone in an attempt to bring up a map which would give them directions to the school. He felt suddenly angry with himself for having such a useless memory. If only it had been better, he wouldn't have to be desperately searching for people to help put himself back together.

"Here, let me do it," said Ellie, taking the phone from his hand. She indicated the direction and they began to walk.

As they turned into a quieter side street off the main road, something in his mind shifted and the buildings took on a sudden familiarity – but there was still something that wasn't quite right. He looked around frantically, attempting to conjure up a memory of walking here many years before.

"You're seeing it all from a different height," said Ellie, as if guessing his thoughts. "Remember you were probably half as tall as you are now. Wait until you get into the school and see the toilets. They'll seem tiny. You'll literally have to crouch down to wash your hands." For a moment, he thought that she almost smiled at the thought, but the expression was gone before he could be sure.

"It's this way, isn't it?" he suddenly asked, as his feet automatically turned into another road.

"Yeah, it should be just here and left."

"This used to be my route to school. When I was in year five, Celia let me go to by myself, which is weird for two reasons – first, I'm not sure that it's legally allowed, and secondly, because she was funny about letting me out anywhere on my own."

"Well, she must have grown to trust you enough."

She was right. On the whole Celia did trust him but she made sure that she knew exactly where he was at any given time – she would always make careful notes on who he was with, what he was doing and when he expected to be back. And she would have a strange look on her face whenever she was saying goodbye to him – her smile would falter ever so slightly and there was a glimmer of what he first thought was sadness, but which he later identified as fear. It was almost as if she was scared that this would be the last time that she would ever see him.

He felt a dull sickness in his stomach at the memory of her calling the police when he'd been an hour and a half late from football practice. He'd stopped off at his then girlfriend's house and his phone had run out of battery. He'd found a police car waiting for him and Celia sat on the front porch, crying quietly. She hadn't even been angry – she just pulled him in close and whispered in his ear, "Thank you. Oh, thank you."

"I think the front entrance is here."

The school was much nicer than he remembered. In his head, he had visualised a rundown, characterless block of a building. It seemed that a lot of renovation work had been done over the years. He vaguely remembered a small field leading up to the main building where he used to play football with Dan and the other boys. Now, the grass had been tarmacked over, and there was a red climbing frame by the front gate. The frames of the tall windows had been painted green, making the place appear like the home of an eccentric old lady from a children's book.

A sign greeted them outside the front entrance: *Leafview Primary School – a good school with outstanding features.*

"That's a weird slogan. It wasn't here when I was a kid."

"It's not a slogan. It's the mark they got in their last Ofsted inspection," said Ellie impatiently. "Loads of schools like to shout about stuff like that these days. It's to attract wealthier families."

He slowed down, suddenly frightened of going any further. He had an odd sense that the place might bring up some hidden memories which he wouldn't be able to make sense of. He didn't have to do this. He could turn back and go home instead, perhaps ring up the photography studio later if I felt like it. There was no reason for him to pile this sudden pressure onto himself.

"Ellie, I…"

"Come on." She glared at him impatiently and when she saw that he wasn't moving, she grasped him hard by the elbow. Somehow, just like Celia, she had the ability to make him obey.

Matty walked up the stairs resignedly, dodging past the few mothers running in late to pick up their waiting children.

"We have an appointment to see Mrs. Henderson," Ellie told the receptionist who was cradling the phone and frantically arranging a stash of reports at her desk.

A few minutes later they were ushered into a messy office, just off the main entrance hall. The woman behind the desk was much younger than Matty had expected but he recognised her instantly. She still had the large protruding mole on her upper lip which he remembered staring at when she checked the register. Ellie had told him during the painful tube journey that she'd managed to do some research on Mrs. Henderson. She had apparently worked at several other schools since teaching here, and had only come back a few years ago as the headmistress.

She was dressed in a fluffy white jumper which did little to hide her sizeable breasts. Her hair was blond and littered with a few specks of grey. Matty estimated that she could be in her mid-forties, which meant that she must have just started teaching when he was in her class.

"Sit down. Mr. Reardon, isn't it?"

"C…call me Matthew," he stuttered, suddenly feeling like he had been transformed back into his six-year-old self. "Thank you for agreeing to see me."

"No problem. You know, I was intrigued when you called. We don't often get visits from old pupils, particularly not ones who were here so long ago. I looked up your files – we never seem to throw anything away here, as you can probably tell by the state of my office."

"Really?" He could feel a sudden tension in his temples. "What sort of stuff do you keep?"

"Oh you know, reports, school awards, sometimes some photos of events like sports days and Christmas plays. Parents often come back to claim things after the pupil's left the school.

Anyway, I looked in yours and it triggered my memory. You were in the first class that I ever taught. That's why I probably remember you better than some of the others. The first class that you teach often leaves an impression on the teacher."

Her fingers flicked through some pieces of paper in the file, but they were upside down and too far away from Matty to make out.

"That's good." He had the sudden impression that his voice sounded distant and echoey. "As I mentioned to you on the phone, I'm trying to find out a bit more about my background… because, well… there are some things that just don't add up. I don't suppose many people remember much from their early school days, but I… found some of my school reports and I was surprised to see some of the stuff that was written in there."

"Really?" she asked, her brow furrowed, "But your reports were generally very good – I had a flick through them earlier. You were well-behaved, never any complaints. You won the Maths Challenge Award in Year 6," she said, taking out a yellowed certificate with a gold star at the top.

"It's not so much that… it's that I was considered – what do you call it?"

"EAL," Ellie prompted.

"That's it."

"Yes, because English wasn't your first language," she answered cheerfully. "'English as an Additional Language,' is what it stands for."

"I know, that's the thing that I was confused by…"

"How do you mean?"

He knew that he would have to explain it to her at some stage, but no matter how many times he'd rehearsed it in his head it sounded wrong. Any sensible person would ask why he hadn't spoken to his parents – surely they would have told him everything that he needed to know?

"I don't know what my mother tongue was," he blurted eventually after the silence had lasted unnaturally long.

As he'd predicted, a confused look appeared on Mrs. Henderson's face as she looked from him to Ellie. Her questioning gaze stopped on her face, as if she might offer a simple explanation, such as 'Don't worry – he suffers from early-onset Alzheimer's.'

"I was adopted when I was little," he began to explain, "and since then, I obviously didn't speak my mother tongue. I haven't been able to find out the identity of my birth parents."

She slowly intertwined her fingers and her eyebrows narrowed.

"I don't think you've come to the right place to find that out," she said gently. He could sense an undertone of anxiety in her voice, "Surely you should be going back to your adoption agency? Or the home that you were…"

"I've tried them already and they wouldn't give me the information," he lied, "Anything that you can remember or any documents that you can find on me… anything at all. It would be useful." He realised that he was speaking too fast. It was as if the words were rushing out of his mouth, spilling out in a torrent of helpless rage. The quicker he spoke, the more Mrs. Henderson drew away from him.

"Right… well this is really stretching my memory," she muttered. She unlocked a cabinet behind her and took a big bound book off the top shelf with the year '1990' written on the spine. When she opened it on the desk, he could see that it was a photo album. She flicked through the pages of class photos and stopped on one labelled as 'Year 1'. Then she ran her finger across the names below it and finding Matty, matched it with the other hand to the corresponding child.

"Ah." Her eyes widened. 'You were the boy with the terrors." She looked back at him as if noticing him for the first time.

"Sorry?"

She edged the album in their direction. It took Matty a while to locate himself. He was sitting in the second row, his straight brown hair falling into his eyes. His arms were folded across his chest as if in a gesture of defence.

"I was a terror?"

"No, no… you had 'terrors'. Sorry maybe that's not the right word for them, but I'm not sure how else to explain what they were. I remember them distinctly because I hadn't come across that many behavioural issues yet."

At first I thought it could have been attention-seeking, but then I saw that you seemed genuinely terrified. I think it first happened when we were in the reading corner and you'd fallen asleep, which is not unusual for kids that age. But then I got one of the other children to nudge you awake and you started to shake and scream. You were yelling something that I couldn't understand. I remember trying to lift you to standing position and you went rigid all over."

A wave of heat swept through his body and he felt a sudden sting in his cheeks. He wanted her to stop talking. He decided that he didn't want to know any more. The small, dark scared figure inside him winced at the words and coiled itself more tightly into a foetal position.

"How many times did this happen?" asked Ellie quietly.

"A few more. It always happened when you were sleeping or daydreaming and somebody roused you suddenly. I noticed that you were often quite tired and I wondered how aware you were of this state that you'd got yourself into. I actually remember worrying that… maybe you were trying to prevent yourself from sleeping at night because you were scared of what would happen when you awoke."

He closed his eyes and heard the blood pulse in his skull. He'd always been a great sleeper. It couldn't have been him.

"I was definitely worried about you," she continued, and I asked colleagues for support with what to do. The head advised that I speak to your mother about it at Parents' Evening – I remember her, a glamorous lady, white blond bobbed hair – but she brushed it off and she didn't like it when I suggested that perhaps it would be good for you to see someone to discuss what was causing these reactions… It's such a blurred line where a teacher's responsibility begins and ends."

Matty stared at her. She had remembered what Celia had looked like. Celia had spoken to her and she'd made enough of an impression for Mrs. Henderson to remember her. But if it had been him, surely he would have had some recollection of it? Anything, if only a tiny glimmer.

"Did… did Matthew go and see a doctor or a psychologist about it?" Ellie asked, taking over for him.

"I don't think so. At least if he did, it wasn't reported back to me. But it got better. About mid-way through the school year, as you began to get more comfortable in class, and you made new friends, you seemed to stop doing it."

"Just like that?" Ellie asked doubtfully.

A flicker of annoyance passed across Mrs. Henderson's face.

"I can't remember whether it was sudden or gradual… I'm sure it was a gradual, but noticeable…"

"And… and my language? Do you remember what language I spoke?"

She rested her head in her palms and closed her eyes. Matty felt like ten minutes might have passed, but in reality it was probably seconds.

"I can't be sure. I don't want to tell you something that isn't right. I'm afraid the years begin to blend into one when you've worked in school for so long. But…"

"Do you have a *sense* of what it could be?"

"I seem to remember that there was one girl in the class that understood what you were saying, but I couldn't for the life of me tell you which one," she said, staring at the photograph. "That's not helpful. I'm sorry."

They were interrupted by the arrival of the receptionist.

"Peter Lacey here to see you about his son," she announced.

Mrs. Henderson rolled her eyes, "I have to see this man – an unhappy parent."

"Can we take a copy of this?" Ellie asked, pointing at the class photo.

"Yes of course, Liz will do it for you," she said motioning towards the receptionist, "And you can take this," she said handing them the file.

"And here's my phone number? Please could you call if you happen to remember the name of the foreign girl?"

They emerged into the rush hour. Traffic moved at a slovenly pace down the street and tooting horns could be heard in the distance. The pain in Matty's temples had developed into a full on headache and he was filled with a dull, hot confusion usually associated with a hangover.

"I just don't know," he said aloud, "I just don't know anymore."

Chapter 21 – Tom
Chicago

Winter was coming. He could smell it in the air – it had a beautiful crispness that always arrived in Mysłowice in late October, just before All Saints Day. This year, it had come early and on the radio they were saying that there might well be snow by the weekend.

"Conkers!" Adam shouted, "We want to collect conkers! Will you take us? Oh please will you take us?"

How long had he been sitting down? No longer than ten minutes. He could feel the tiredness in his body – it seeped into every fragment of him.

But there he was – his little boy, with determination painted onto his three-year-old face. He was so confident that his wish would be granted, that he was already pulling on his hat.

"Have you asked your mother?"

It was a useless question. He knew that she would be in bed, as she increasingly was in the early afternoons these days, lying there quietly, listlessly looking up at the ceiling. He knew better than to move her.

"Yes," he sighed eventually, "Yes of course. Go and get your sister. We better go now before it gets properly dark.

Moments later the three of them emerged through the front door of the old greying block of flats, one warm hand in each of his. The cold air stung his face, and he contemplated returning upstairs to get another warm jumper, but it was too late. They were already off, flickers of navy blue among the red and orange leaves.

"Mr. Mason? Tom?"

The voice was muffled, unclear. It reverberated from the edges of his brain like whispers in an echo chamber.

And then he felt his head being elevated and his eyes slowly fell open.

A man's face loomed large before him. It looked familiar.

"Sorry to rouse you Mr. Mason. I was banking on you waking up before I had to leave… I hope you don't mind. I just wanted to check in on you. Nurse Clara was saying that you've been resting a lot recently."

Dr. Burgess. He straightened himself up, immediately embarrassed about having been asleep.

"Yes, sorry I…"

"No need to apologise. We got the results of your recent blood tests, and I just wanted to check what your pain levels were like."

"Fine."

"Really?" It could have been his own paranoia, but he thought that he detected a note of surprise in the doctor's question.

"What were the results?" he asked, the beetle crawl beginning in his stomach.

It was only when he asked the question that Tom realised how much hope he had built up over the past few weeks. His sickness symptoms had gone away almost entirely, and although his appetite hadn't quite returned, he was eating enough, and on the whole, he was feeling rather better. He only had one moment of shock a few days earlier when he had a good look at himself in the mirror and noticed for the first time how very yellow his skin was. It was the hue of ground cumin, giving way to a dark grey-blue just beneath his eyes. He'd turned away quickly and resolved to avoid his reflection at all cost. He chose to focus instead on the fact that, on the whole, he was feeling really quite good.

The doctor breathed in deeply.

"It's not good news I'm afraid, Tom," he said quietly. "But then again, it's only what we expected, isn't it?"

"How bad?" he asked.

"Well. I want to be frank with you, Tom. I pride myself on being frank with all my patients. But I mainly came to see you today because I thought that we might have to increase your pain medication. The reason for that is because your condition is in its very advanced stages. I really don't enjoy playing God and telling people how long they have left. I often get it wrong, I can tell you that. I have rarely got it *very* wrong, you understand me, but still nobody knows for certain."

"But if you were to say?" Tom persisted. He felt strangely calm, as if he were an observer, viewing the situation from the outside.

Dr. Burgess sighed. His glasses slipped down his nose, but he maintained eye contact at all times.

"If I had to say, I would tell you that you have a few weeks. I'm sorry it's not better news. I'm sorry it's not longer."

Tom pulled himself up higher in his bed. He swallowed hard. His eyes were drawn to the rectangles of light reflecting off the doctor's forehead, in the patches by his temples where he had begun to lose his hair.

"Thank you," he managed eventually.

"My job and the job of all the nursing staff here is to make those weeks as pain-free and as enjoyable as they can be. And you of course should ensure that you spend the time in the absolute best way that you can."

Tom stared at the doctor's face. He tried to make an estimate of how old he could be. Mid-thirties at most. How many times had he been forced to make this speech before?

"How do they do it?"

"Who?"

"Your other patients. How do they make sure that they spend the time in the absolute best way?"

He seemed taken aback by the question.

"Well… they tell their families and friends. I always say that it's so important that you tell the people who are close to you. I've seen many who have tried to hide it, you know. They think that it will spare heartache, but it's worse in the long run. It honestly is. Apart from that – see everyone you want to see, say everything you want to say and live the rest of your life. Remember that you have the chance to do all of those things. Some people don't. For some of the unlucky, death comes with no warning signs."

That night, long after the doctor had left, and after Clara had administered his pre-sleep medication, he lay in bed, replaying the conversation over and over in his head.

Only a few hours earlier, he'd been dreaming of the fall with its flurries of red and amber leaves, and now he was plunged into the very real possibility that he may not live to see it.

But strangely, the idea didn't bother him. He had seen the fall many times. He had experienced it in its fullness – the colours, the taciturn weather, the murky whiff of bonfires. There were no regrets there.

The real pain came not from things that he would miss, but from those which he hadn't ever experienced. All those unlived days, the unfelt emotions, the unforgiven sins. But it was too late for all that now. It was far, far too late.

He pushed the intrusive thoughts away, determined to fall into oblivion, but they came chasing back. It was as if suddenly, the carefully catalogued segments of his memory, which had been locked for as long as he could remember, came unstuck and flooded his consciousness all at once.

He battled them for a full two hours, but at 1.05am exactly, he capitulated. He forced himself out of bed and switched on the light. Then he rummaged around in his bedside table drawer for a torch that he'd brought with him from home in case of emergencies.

He pulled on his dressing gown and slowly, ever so slowly, made his way down the hallway to the lounge. The thick silence of the building scared him. He could hear nothing but his warm breath and the heavy pounding of his heart. It was mad of course, what he was doing, but Tom was beyond concerning himself with his mental state. In that moment, only one question circled over and over in his mind. Would he know what to do?

He had watched Dustin operate the computer many times and he thought that he could remember how to locate the site that he needed.

He dared himself to switch on one of the side lamps in the room, and he sat down heavily in the chair usually occupied by Dustin, listening out for any sounds. All was quiet.

He had always been the passenger. Now he would have to drive. The green light on the start button of the computer stared at him, unblinking.

Chapter 22 – Joanna
Warsaw

Joanna reread the last paragraph of the article, making a few editorial corrections. She'd lost track of the amount of time that she'd spent on it. Although the magazine wasn't due for print until the following Monday night, she had completed the first draft in the early hours of the morning when sleep had eluded her. She'd made herself a strong cup of black coffee and carefully selected the stories to feature, adding and then removing Adam's case several times.

After having met Mrs. Barska, she'd recognised her obsession developing again, the piercing thrill of a potential new lead in Adam's search. She'd tried her utmost to stifle it – she'd been in similar situations before, only to find that the information led to nothing and only left a dull, painful ache in its wake. She fully realised that including his case in the article would mean exposing herself to the awful risk of crippling disappointment, but she finally acknowledged that without it, the article didn't work. The rest of the content seemed to perfectly hang off it. In the end, her brother's disappearance became the leading case in the piece.

She'd titled it *All that Remains*, because it was curiously a phrase which was repeated in several of the interviews with relatives of missing people.

"These photos are all that remains of Lucjan, since he left all those years ago."

"All that remains are the few scraps of evidence that were gathered from witnesses on the day she'd disappeared."

"Hope is all that remains…"

Was that the right title? Surely in some cases even hope didn't remain amongst the desolation caused by a disappearance. Her own mother was certainly not a person who carried hope in her soul. She had given up on Adam many years before and this was something that Joanna could not forgive her for. Until recently, she thought that Monika had been very alone in her attitude, so she was startled to find that forgetting a missing person was something that was actively encouraged by support counsellors.

As part of her research, she had attended an evening session run by DELTA which was well publicised online and via police stations as 'free and effective counselling' for the families of missing people.

The session was in the traditional format of 'group therapy', a circle of chairs in a dimly lit upstairs room on the top floor of the old council buildings in the centre of Warsaw. The space was filled with a dense mustiness and the smell of wet clothes. Joanna was surprised to note the vast range of ages and backgrounds of the attendees. In the corner of the room a couple of old women poured out tea into fancy glasses with tiny handles which looked like relics from the Second World War. Her grandmother had had a very similar set, Joanna remembered. It was carefully arranged in a glass cabinet which stood in her hallway and she distinctly remembered her hands being slapped when she wanted to extract it for use in a playground picnic.

Joanna sat down next to a boy who looked no older than sixteen. He was fumbling desperately with the shoelaces of his Doc Martens which were tied into a multitude of knots.

"Hi. I'm new here."

"Hello," he responded without looking up at her.

"I don't really know what to expect. Have you been coming here long?"

"Uhmm… five months or so. The people are nice. They help you move on, you know, help you forget."

"Forget?" Joanna was struck with the force of the word, its brusque finality. "But… but what if you don't want to forget?"

But the boy was spared from having to answer through the sudden, sound of hands being clapped together to signify the start of the meeting. Cups of tea were offered around the room and one of the elderly ladies stood up and bowed her head in prayer.

"May the Lord bless those who are missing in our lives, protect them from harm and deliver them eternal peace. May he also bring us comfort in the knowledge that the life which he granted us continues and help us to move on so that we may live it to the full."

There was an echoed chorus of 'Amen' around the room.

"Welcome to Joanna who is joining us for her first session. Joanna, please feel free to share your story with us."

An uncomfortable silence filled the room as she explained Adam's disappearance. She realised with a start that she hadn't spoken aloud about what had happened for many years, and allowing the words to flow out of her mouth to a group of strangers, generated fresh anger.

When she finished speaking, she was conscious of an uncomfortable shuffling around the room.

"Thank you for that Joanna. It's obviously something that you still feel very strongly about," said the elderly woman who had led the prayer. As Joanna spoke, she sensed that the woman had grown increasingly uncomfortable, her hands clasped tightly in her lap, her fingers winding around the tassels of her jumper. "Would anyone like to offer any support?"

"You need to let go. You say this was during the Solidarity protests. That was what, more than twenty years ago? You have let this rule your life for long enough. You'll never have a life if you don't allow yourself to breathe on your own." This advice came from a pale, thin man sitting a few chairs to the left of Joanna. She guessed that the last line had become like a mantra to him – it had a tired tone to it. Part of his left eyebrow was missing and a neat pattern of piercings snaked their way along his large earlobes.

She was too taken aback to speak.

"As a child you have a certain expectation of the world. You believe that each new day will bring something unexpected and new, something to explore and perhaps retain for the future…" began a middle aged overweight woman sitting a few chairs away from Joanna, "Then a time comes when you realise that this belief is not necessarily the truth, the only truth. Life is full of loss. You realise that there is nothing that you can do but grow around these losses. That is the only way to survive. There is no other choice."

"But why do you think I have to let go of Adam? He doesn't rule my life – I have a flat, a job… I'm successful. Why should I give up on him?"

"I bet you don't have a relationship," muttered the youth next to her. The heat stung her cheeks. She deliberately pretended that she hadn't heard.

A couple of people in the room tutted and nodded their heads at her sadly, as if to say 'We were all like you once.'

"It's OK, Joanna. You're still at the denial stage, you're clinging onto a shard of useless hope. We're going to help you understand that your life is so much bigger than your brother…"

At that stage she couldn't listen any further. A black noise built up in her ears, a crescendo of despair which she hadn't felt since – when? Since Christmas all those years ago, when her mother had broken down. She ran out, forgetting her bag of groceries. She almost fell over on the way down the stairs, so eager was she to get out of the building.

So yes, hope remained for her, but for so many people it was no longer there. It had been stifled, thwarted by their own depression or by the nagging voices of others who told them that they should rip it up, stop self-flagellating, give themselves a fresh start. But she wouldn't change the title. It would be as bad as giving in to the counsellors and that would be the ultimate defeat.

Joanna was completing the corrections to the final case in the article, when the phone rang. Too engrossed to answer, she allowed the answering machine to pick it up.

She could hear a chirpy woman's voice through the thin wall separating her study from the kitchen, "It's Lena here. I got the message from Anna that I should call you. To be honest, I don't really understand what it's about, but then again I never can keep up with what Anna's saying.

Did you want to meet in town? You're welcome to come to mine if you prefer not to meet in public. I live at Number 4 Dluga Street, or you can type the postcode into the Sat Nav: 05 – 080. But then again you might not have a car, so you can travel by train and I could pick you up by the station? Sorry for going on like this – I'm not good with answering machines. Anyway, give me a call back to arrange a time." She recited a mobile number and hung up.

Joanna typed the postcode into her web search. It came up with a road outside Warsaw, in Izabelin. Yes! This was Lena, the daughter of Waldek, the man with the 'zoomer'.

Chapter 23 – Matty
London

"You know I'm the wrong person to be asking about this sort of thing. My memory's buggered mate," said Dan, shrugging his shoulders. He'd just come back from the barber's with a crew cut, nothing but a short ginger fuzz covering his head. Matty would usually have had a dig at him about it, but today he wasn't in the mood. He'd come to him in the desperate hope that Dan would remember something that would be useful to him, or that might trigger something in the dark, shut crevices of his mind.

When he thought about it now, Dan – even more so in some ways than Celia – had been a constant presence throughout his life. He had been there, solid and dependable, unchangeable, while the world around him was anything but. They had been in the same class at primary and then secondary school, and their paths had only diverged at uni, when he'd gone off to Cambridge, and Dan had stayed in London to study graphic design. And when Matty had returned after getting his masters' degree, Dan was there, waiting for him in the same house, being his same cocky self. There had only been one painful moment in their relationship when Dan's parents had separated and he and Nadia moved out to Tottenham. They were both scared that he would have to move schools, but amazingly he stayed, making the forty minute journey across London every morning.

Matty's memory was wonderful when it came to facts. Like a well-oiled mechanism it only needed to be fed a snippet of information to examine it, process it effectively, and use it to output something far grander or more useful than what first went in. It could memorise even the most complex equations, theorems and axioms, and later a whole array of stock market trends, but it struggled to remember people, actions and situations.

But the one situation of his childhood that he *did* remember was meeting Dan. He remembered being introduced at the start of term and sitting down at an empty desk at the front of the class, feeling scared, bewildered and alone. By first break he was ready to run home. Then, when he stood in the corner of the playground, doing his best not to look at anybody, and staring down at his feet, a hand suddenly reached out for his. He was forced to look up then and he saw a boy with a shock of red hair and more freckles than skin grinning at him. He beckoned for him to join in with a game of 'Bulldog' that he was playing with a group of boys at the other end of the football pitch, and that was it. From then on, he was never alone.

He clearly remembered suddenly feeling wonderful – whole and happy and calm. He was someone's friend and his pride at that fact was so overwhelming that he imagined it manifested itself physically, as if it had been written in something bold and shiny across the front of his uniform.

"Can you at least try? You remembered my 'weird' way of talking, didn't you?"

"Well, it was difficult not to."

"OK, so surely it would be difficult not to forget me having regular tantrums or panic attacks or something of that…?"

"What?" Dan's furry eyebrows narrowed in confusion.

"Our teacher from Year 1 seems to remember that I had 'terrors'" Matty told him, making inverted commas in the air with his fingers.

"You spazzed out?"

"I'm serious."

Dan noticed his mood and immediately stopped laughing. He followed Matty into the living room and accepted the pile of reports handed to him. He flicked through them quietly, self-consciously scratching his head.

"I need you to focus. Is there anything odd that you remember about me? Not 'odd' in the way you interpret that," he said before Dan started with his usual jibes, "I mean something unusual… foreign."

Dan threw him a questioning look.

"I don't know," he said after a long pause. "You're… you. I've known you for too long. If you see someone almost every day, nothing stands out…"

Matty exhaled and some of the awful anxious tension in his chest abated.

"These are weird," said Dan, flicking through the yellow cardboard folder that Mrs. Henderson had given him, "What even is this?"

He passed Matty a handful of sugar paper pictures, the paint cracked in parts where they had been folded. Matty had studied them as soon as he got home from the school and decided they didn't reveal anything useful. They were scribbles mostly – the indecipherable mess created by all children of that age, lovingly stored away by doting parents.

"How dare you? They're pieces of art," he told Dan, grinning, but he grabbed the paper back from him and looked at them again.

"What?"

"Nothing. It's just pretty dark. This looks as if you've drawn a tiny person stuck in the middle of a massive storm."

Matty looked at it again over his shoulder. Initially he'd only noticed the black and blue blotches, but now he could make out a shape that could indeed have been a tiny person, but equally could have been an ant or an accidental dark smudge.

"I know, but kids draw all sorts of random stuff."

"Yeah but usually not like that." He shuffled off into the kitchen and brought back a couple of beers and some curled pieces of paper. Matty recognised them as the laborious creations of Dan's six-year-old niece, Lizzie, stuck lovingly to the fridge with coloured magnets.

"Have a look at this," he said handing them to Matty, "There's a bit of a difference, right?"

He'd seen them so many times that he already knew what they showed – wonkily drawn houses and stick figures with arms coming out of their stomachs. Lizzie had even gone as far as labelling the different characters as 'Granny, Lizzie, Mum, Dad."

"What you doing with my pictures?" asked Nadia, filling the living room door with her awkward bulk.

"Just using them to prove to Matty that he's always been a psycho."

"What?"

She dropped her shopping bags, hurriedly washed her hands and inspected his drawings which he'd handed over to her. He noticed the shock that registered clearly on her face when she reached the one with the storm.

"I didn't speak to Celia," he told her before she asked, "But I did go back to school and I found Mrs. Henderson, our Year 1 teacher."

She raised her eyebrow, "And?"

"You were right… she said that I had a foreign accent. That's not even the oddest thing. She also told me that I had tantrums," At this, Matty noticed a sudden change in Nadia's face, a widening of the eyes, as if the spark of a memory was forcing its way through.

"You…" she started and then stopped, as if checking herself.

"You remember me having them?"

"Well…"

His head bolted with fear and hope.

"Anything you could tell me would be really helpful," he told her, jumping off the back of the sofa and looking her directly in the eye.

"You stayed round here loads when you were small…"

"I know."

"One of the first times you stayed, you woke up in the night screaming and you came to my room. I had to give you a blanket and I sat with you on the edge of my bed as you shook and shouted. I couldn't understand what you were saying, but I could tell that you were very distressed. What was strangest was that I couldn't be sure whether you were still asleep. You know that lots of people sleep-talk and sleep-walk and you seemed sort of knocked out… Eventually you quietened down and went back to sleep."

"What? I don't remember that," Dan chimed in.

"It happened a couple of times. I mentioned it to your mum and for a while she refused to let you come here." Nadia was now anxiously gnawing at the skin around her fingernails as she spoke.

"It's OK," he told her, desperate to coax out more information, "I know that she wasn't easy to get along with."

"She made me feel a bit guilty for making you upset, even though I told her that I was never in the room when it happened. She sort of implied that it was my fault. But you know… it's quite usual. Often when something bad happens to your kid, a natural reaction would be to try and find the cause of it. She was constantly worried about you with you being her only child."

She held his gaze for a moment longer and then she removed a fleck of dust from her top and collapsed onto the sofa, her sizeable stomach protruding over her thick leather belt. Even in appearance, she was the exact opposite of Celia.

"I know… She hates it when I ask anything about adoption. And I know it must feel odd to her, me wanting to know. It's been so many years, that it shouldn't matter either way, should it?"

"Well no. You have a right to know," said Dan in his defence.

"I just wished she'd told me some of these things," he said, pointing at the folder. This was only a half-truth. By now, he was convinced that Celia was hiding something from him and he was certain that asking her any direct question would cause her to block any chances that he had of finding out the truth.

"And your teacher didn't say anything more?" asked Nadia, taking a glug of beer out of Dan's bottle.

"Nope, nothing. All she said was that there was a girl in my class who apparently understood me more than anyone else. That doesn't mean anything though, does it?"

"Do we have a class photo?" asked Dan, "You could look for someone with a foreign sounding surname?"

Matty passed him the photocopy and he read all the girls' names aloud: "Kelly Bryan, Jessica Cole, Amanda Patterson, Kiera Goldman, Gurpreet Singh, Stefania Rutton, Eleanor Miston."

"Is that it?"

"That's all of them. I remember Kiera and Mandy well – used to fancy them. But yeah, small class. Only twenty in total, more boys than girls."

"Apart from Gurpreet, they all have very English sounding names."

"Stefania is a strange name," Nadia pointed out. "It's not your usual. Her surname is English, but she could have a parent from a different country."

"It's a long shot though isn't it?" Matty asked. He collapsed on the worn leather armchair feeling more than ever before that he was embarking on a hopeless task. His head sank into the slight dip in the arm, which he'd created with his own head over many years of staying over at Dan's. He remembered the year in sixth form when he'd spent more nights here than he had done in his own house.

"Yeah, it is," Dan agreed, "But you might as well find out. It's easy to get hold of people these days. I'll look her up for you on Facebook."

Chapter 24 – Tom
Chicago

"Come on. How long are you going to be thinking about it? We'll be dead before you take your turn."

"Yes – hilarious, Dustin," said Kyle, finally making a move with his king and rolling his eyes.

Tom had been asked to sit with them and be an independent judge of the game, as the two seemed to disagree on a vast range of rules and moves.

"I think that in future, we should put a time limit on how long you can think about a move. What do you reckon Tom?"

"Well, yes, it would be a good idea."

"In ten minutes we're going to have to pause the game anyway, interrupted Kyle. "My children are visiting. We can resume after dinner."

"Or maybe Tom can take your place?"

"No way. I mean, no offence Tom, but I've got my own way of playing and at this stage in the game, I don't want to give up my position."

"It's fine. It's honestly fine, Kyle."

He'd grown to like this meaty-faced, straight-talking man who provided such a great antidote to Dustin, who was forever hyperactive, jumping from one task to the next, never being able to settle. Kyle on the other hand was stoic and steady.

Tom found himself wondering what Kyle's wife and children would be like and whether they had already partially come to terms with the fact that their visiting days were numbered. But he didn't get the opportunity to see them because moments later, Kyle eagerly got up, pulled on his coat and was taken away for the afternoon by a waiting car.

"They're good to him," said Dustin, when he had gone.

Tom desperately tried to memorise the positions of the key figures on the chessboard to ensure that no sly manoeuvres took place during Kyle's absence.

"I can't complain about mine either, I suppose. They have a long way to travel, but Noah is coming to see me next week."

Tom said nothing. His only visitors in the two months that he had now been at *Sunshine*, had been Mitch and Sally. On their most recent visit, upon Tom's request, they brought with them some of his old books. Published in the seventies, their pages were yellowed, some of their spines crumbling. They were all written in Polish, and he yearned to see whether he could still read them and understand all of the words. He had started on one of them the previous night and when he realised that he could still enjoy it, the words blurred before his eyes, and he was surprised to find that his cheeks were wet. Yes, Mitch and Sally had been good to him and they were as close to family as he had.

"Do you ever wish you had any?"

"Any what?" Tom was so engrossed in his thoughts that he hadn't realised the train that the conversation had taken.

"Any children?" There it was – the bolt hit him square in the chest. He could lie, of course he could. But what was the point now?

"I do… or rather, I did."

"You did?" Dustin stared at him as if seeing him for the first time. "What happened? Where are they?" he asked carefully.

"I don't know."

"You don't know? Huh?"

Dustin looked at him with shock.

"Yes. I don't. I haven't seen them in years. I haven't seen them since they were very small."

"Right… Can I ask why?"

"It's very complicated. But it's my fault… it's not theirs."

"Did the wife poison them against you?" asked Dustin, angry now. "Holy smokes, is it because of the affair? Something like that can ruin things between you and her, but it shouldn't stop you from seeing the kids. That's awful. That's really low."

"No. No. It wasn't her. It's nothing like that."

He shut his eyes. He couldn't do this.

To his surprise, Dustin stopped talking. The silence spread between them, suspended on an invisible string.

"I have a question for you," said Dustin eventually.

"What?" he asked, with fear in his voice.

"Don't worry. I'm not going to ask you any more about what happened. I am just curious… do you *want* to see them again?"

"Yes," he answered, unthinking. "Yes, of course. But I can't… I've tried already."

"You've tried, how?"

"I've done what you showed me. I've searched for them both on Facebook. There's nothing."

He'd been exhilarated when he managed to log into the site on his own the previous night. His hands shook as he typed the names into the search bar. When Adam's name yielded no results, he didn't allow himself to loose heart. He tried Joanna. He imagined her to still be the more resourceful and organised one of the two. She was probably more likely to have a profile. But he wasn't sure whether social media was particularly popular in Poland. He doubted that it would be anywhere near as big as in the States. Nothing came up. He stared at the blank results page, and it was then that the true regret set in. It was regret at its mightiest. All of the previous times that he'd experienced it were poor, watered down versions of the real thing. He wanted to howl, but instead, he sat there silently at the computer screen and he sobbed.

He wasn't sure how long he'd been there, but he saw that the sky was lightening outside when he finally found the strength to shuffle off to bed.

"I'm sorry," said Dustin unexpectedly. "But there are other ways to reach them. You don't have any contact details for them? Even if they're old ones, they might still be worth trying, you know."

He shook his head. "No… when I… when I left, we didn't even have a phone."

Dustin's eyebrows shot up under his fringe, but he ploughed on.

"Right, well you know that this isn't the start and end of your search? There are plenty of other routes that you could try."

"It's the main one though, isn't it? You said. You told me that there were millions of people on there. If they're not there, then where would they be?" he asked grimly.

"Well, you can't just give up," said Dustin outraged. "Have you tried Googling their names?"

"No. What good would that do?"

He hated the prospect of further disappointment. He was already brimming with it.

"Well, it would give you a broad search of anywhere on the internet that they might appear. But look here – you don't have to do anything right now. How about you just leave me their names and I'll see what I can do."

He turned over one of their old scorecards and handed the pen to Tom.

"I don't know Dustin…"

"Well, look… If I don't find anything, I just won't mention it again. And if I do… well then we'll see what else we can do about it. It's win-win for you, my friend."

And despite all of his resolve and self-preservation, Tom found himself picking up the pen and scribbling down the two names. When he'd finished, he stared at the card, holding it down on the table before him. How long had it been since he'd actually written those very words? When would the last time have been? On a nursery school registration form?

He slid it in Dustin's direction and did his very best to forget what he had just done.

Chapter 25 – Joanna
Warsaw

Lena had been right. The house was easy to find. It stood out against the sea of dulled brown brick, its bold canary hue almost blinding in the sunlight. Joanna wasn't sure why she'd agreed to a meeting at her house. Surely, she could have just asked over the phone whether she had her father's camera or not? But she'd restrained herself – she'd deliberately put off the moment of finding out. She loved to stretch out those blissful moments of unawareness. As a child she would always shut a book she was enjoying and put it away for a day when she sensed that something important was about to happen. That way she could dream up the different possibilities, which was far more enjoyable than finding out the true outcome.

The woman who opened the door was small and thin, with a messy bun of red hair arranged haphazardly on top of her head and a pair of large thick framed glasses perched on the end of her nose. She looked as if she could be in her early thirties. A long cigarette hung out of the corner of her mouth and her resting facial expression implied mild anger or dissatisfaction. Joanna noticed with horror that she held something dark and furry in her right hand and was brandishing a short pen knife in her left.

"Hi," she said cheerfully and her face rearranged itself suddenly into a welcoming smile. "Sorry; I didn't realise that you'd get here so early. I was desperate to finish this before you came. The client wants it tomorrow."

The ferret-like object in her hand appeared to be moving and Joanna let out an involuntary shudder. She walked warily inside the building, following Lena who ushered her into the living room. A stench of decay hung in the air and the space was dark and stuffy. She had the distinct impression of entering a crypt.

"Sorry, I really need to air the house. I was just keeping the curtains drawn because it's better for the preservation fluids."

Joanna's stomach heaved. She fought the urge to reverse back outdoors.

When the curtains were finally open, she realised where the smell was coming from. All around her on the high-ceilinged walls of the room, on the huge oak table, propped up against the chair legs, were animal carcasses, or parts of them, laid open in a strangely artistic fashion.

"I'm a taxidermist," the girl explained, clearly amused at the expression on Joanna's face, "I'm getting these prepared for a show. I have my workshop here because I'm just starting out, so I can't afford to rent a studio.

She placed the furry creature down carefully on the table and Joanna noticed that it was a small black and white rat. The animal had been carefully arranged on a wooden platform, its hind legs spread apart and slightly bent in what looked like a jaunty pose. It was standing upright, its front paws raised together as if ready to receive a treat. It almost looked realistic, if it wasn't for the two pink caverns where the eyes should have been. These raw, fleshy indents made her feel instantly nauseous.

She forced her eyes away from it and instead took in the vast array of tools that Lena used in her trade. Propped up against the wall were huge rolls of wire. Boxes of toothpicks were scattered on the table, their contents spilling. There were scalpels of various sizes, superglue, cotton wool, spools of thread in various colours and tiny scissors.

"He still needs his eyes done. I just haven't managed to find the right beads. He was kept as a pet by two kids from a rich family. The parents wanted him immortalised. People are strange… but if they weren't, I wouldn't have a job," she announced cheerfully. "You know the process for doing this hasn't really changed since the late 1800s? All these technological advancements everywhere else, but here you don't need anything more than a steady hand."

"It's just…" Joanna shuddered, "not a job for someone with a weak stomach."

"Yeah, definitely not. Anyway, let's have a cup of tea in the kitchen. I promise I don't keep any furry friends in there."

"Thanks. Sorry, it's just quite scary. I wasn't expecting it."

"I know; it's my fault. I should have told you. People often have that reaction." She dropped the cigarette in the ash tray and switched on the kettle. The kitchen was small and homely, with a large old gas stove in the corner. Joanna's shoulders relaxed.

"So Anna said you wanted to hear about dad?" the girl asked.

"Yes. I mean, it's specifically about one event. Did she tell you about my brother going missing?" she asked.

"Mm, at those protests in 1988."

"Exactly. And I know that your dad was standing near us at the time and I just stupidly wondered… hoped that he might have had a camera."

"Well, yeah, of course," she said, surprised. "He documented all the big events in Warsaw that Solidarity played a part in. I think he wanted to be their official camera-man on the ground, if such a position ever existed. Sugar?"

"What? Oh, no thanks." The breath had caught in her throat.

"I sent a lot of his footage to the ECS in Gdańsk when it opened a couple of years ago," said Lena, placing the hot mug and a tray of biscuits in front of her visitor before lighting up another cigarette.

"The ECS?"

"The European Centre of Solidarity. It's a new version of the original museum that they had in the dockyards."

"Oh right. No. I hadn't heard… It seems like he was amazingly dedicated to their cause."

"Well… he was a firm believer in democracy, and he thought that this was the best way to actually achieve it. It was funny, because my mum didn't want him to go out there and get so involved. I don't think she really understood what all the fuss was about. Sure, there wasn't a huge deal of choice when it came to food, but we never went hungry. She had work and decent healthcare and a sense that as a family we weren't doing any better or any worse than our neighbours. Do you know that she even points it out to this day?"

"Points what out?"

"She still lives in our old flat and when I go to visit, we usually take a walk to the local market. There are two women who always beg in the same spot by the entrance to the underground, and without fail, mum always gives them at least 10 złoty each. She explained to me that if we still lived under Communism, this never would have happened. There wouldn't be people living 'in the streets' with nothing to eat. I think she almost sees it as a way of apologising for what Dad contributed to."

"I think that there are more people than we think who feel nostalgic about it, which I always find weird…"

"Not weird, but just what they're used to. That was the thing about my dad – he never wanted to get used to anything. He was always out wanting to change things. That's why he got so obsessive about the filming."

What did… what did his films look like?"

"What did they look like? Erm…" Lena cocked one of her eyebrows upwards, implying that she didn't understand the question.

"Sorry, what I mean is, how did he film events like this? Did he just scan the crowds? Did he interview the people taking part?"

"Oh I see, well yeah. It was a mixture of takes. It varied depending on where he was. He was there at the fall of the Berlin Wall and that was all action footage. People were so beside themselves that nobody wanted to stop and talk. 1988 was more peaceful so he got some speeches captured too."

"Do you still have it?" asked Joanna desperately.

"The filming of the protest? God yes, I have to keep it for my kids at least! It's all the build up to the fall of communism. Do you know how few people realise that Poland is where it all began?"

"I know… I can't believe that I was there to see it happen. But it was also the day that my own little world fell apart. Would I… Would it be OK if I saw it?"

"Of course," the girl seemed surprised, "but what…?"

"It's stupid…" she said slowly, "I just wonder whether my brother might be anywhere on there."

Lena took the cigarette out from between her lips and looked at Joanna with a strange expression. She held the gaze for longer than was comfortable.

"I'm scared for you," she said eventually.

"Sorry?"

"I'm scared for you because I see you so desperately believe that there is something on there. I had the same desperation when I believed that Dad would get better. It crushes you completely. It shatters your very core so you can't think properly anymore. I should warn you now that it's highly unlikely that your brother is in any of the footage."

"I know."

Lena sighed and left the room. She returned after a few minutes with a wooden box labelled 'Kwarc 1988'.

"What does 'Kwarc' mean?"

"It's the name of the camera. It's a Russian brand, apparently really expensive at the time. It also cost me a bomb to get all the film converted to CD format. But if I hadn't done it, in a few years' time there would probably be no way of recreating it."

She opened the box revealing hundreds of CD spines covered in shorthand which meant nothing to anyone but her. She muttered under her breath "May… 1st May."

"Is it in there?" asked Joanna under her breath.

"Yeah, but it's spread over eight CDs. There's surprisingly little storage on a single CD. Do you really want to watch them all? It'll take you ages."

"Of course. Would you mind me borrowing them to watch at home? I promise I'll take good care of them," Joanna pleaded.

Lena sighed heavily and lit another cigarette. "It's not them that I'm worried about; it's you. Take them," she said, pushing the stash in Joanna's direction. Just drop them off when you've finished. I'm always home at this time on weekdays."

"Thank you so much. This might be the start of something…"

"…or not," Lena whispered as her visitor ran out of the door, but Joanna was already out of earshot.

Chapter 26 – Matty
London

Matty was surprised at how easy it had been for Dan to locate Stefania online. He wasn't on Facebook himself, disliking the idea of everyone being able to gain an intimate insight into his life. But in situations like this, he acknowledged that it was useful to be able to message anyone you wanted.

Her strange name at least made them both certain that they had the right person. Dan had managed to find out that she worked for a small PR agency in Brixton and told her truthfully that Matty was 'exploring his past' and less truthfully that she was only one of several people from primary school that he was getting in touch with. After a short exchange, she agreed to meet Matty at the café below her office. He was half excited and half dreading the meeting.

He emerged out of the Brixton tube into glorious sunshine. It was just before midday and the roads were unusually peaceful. He watched a middle aged woman with thick dreadlocks smoking lazily in the doorway of a corner shop and nodded to her amicably. A shrill voice called her from an upstairs window and she answered something in a foreign language. All of a sudden she jutted out her hips and began to clap her hands together with glee, as a high syncopated rhythm started up within the building.

Matty's mind performed its usual curious cycle. It was something that had stuck with him since childhood, perhaps a method of combating the loneliness of being an only child. Every time he was out anywhere in public and his attention focused for a minute or two on one individual, he would make up a back story in his head of what their lives were like. That way, the old man with the muscular legs sunbathing on his balcony would become a retired circus performer dreaming of the elephants that he used to ride, and the blond woman with the briefcase on the tube in the morning would be a skilled bank robber carrying the tools that she needed to crack open safes.

Who was this dreadlocked lady? A dancer for sure – you could tell by her hips. Quite possibly an international performer, who had travelled the world, but decided to retire where she had grown up, in Brixton.

He and Ellie used to have fantastic play-arguments based around the ways that they imagined people's lives. Once, they had been walking through the outskirts of Tooting, passing curry houses and decrepit corner shops. Just before the turn into the road where their friend lived, they saw three young men sitting outside a Bangladeshi restaurant, still in their chef's overalls, smoking. One of them was wearing sunglasses, giving him an aura of a sixties gangster.

"Those three chilling over there. Clearly international art thieves…" he started, winking at Ellie, but her eyebrows narrowed immediately at his words. "No they're not. Look at the one with the long hair. He keeps readjusting his collar. He's clearly got a hidden microphone under there. I reckon that he works for the MI5. He's exactly the type that they would recruit. My only criticism is that he's *too* laid back. If you're a proper chef you're always stressed out, even on your breaks.

You're always thinking about those waiting customers and uncooked meals. I know because of Uncle Ben. He used to be Head Chef at some fancy restaurant in Devon…"

He was brought back to the present by a sign which told him that he was on Electric Avenue. He wondered whether this was the road that the song was named after. He'd never thought of it as a real place, complete with dirty asphalt and wig shops, and he felt strangely self-conscious, like a foreign passer-by in an unknown land.

He entered the café at two minutes after one in the afternoon, just as the lunchtime crowds had descended. Luckily the queue moved quickly.

"Hi, are you Matthew?" asked a soft voice close to his ear. The suddenness of it made him physically jump.

He turned around to see a willowy girl with long, knotted dark hair hanging down to her waist. She was dressed in skin-tight leather trousers and a loose sheer strappy top, through which you could see her red bra. There was nothing about her that even vaguely resembled the small, gap toothed little girl in his Year 1 class photo.

"Stefania?"

"Yep," she said, giving him a lop-sided grin. It was too strange. What was he doing here?

"Thanks for coming."

"It's OK. I was intrigued. You played me at my own game."

"What?"

"It's the tactics we always use on journalists. We offer them a smidgen of information, wave a little carrot under their nose, and hope that they'll come crawling."

Here she screwed up her face and made a sudden dangling motion with her hand that made him burst out with nervous laughter.

"Let me get this," he said, "What are you having?"

Eventually, they settled themselves into a booth and Stefania leant in, peering closely at his face. He felt suddenly naked, the raw rush of blood stinging his cheeks. It was the same sensation that he often felt when Ellie accused him of lying about something.

"Hmmm… maybe slightly, there's something about your eyes and the mole on your chin."

"What?"

"I'm figuring out whether I would have recognised you without you telling me what you were wearing. I normally have a pretty good memory."

"You think I still look a bit like this?" he pulled out the class photo. She studied it closely, a small smile playing across her lips as her eyes darted from one face to the other.

"I haven't seen this in years. God, I'm sure that there's a copy of this somewhere in my dad's house. I have to dig it up. Did you know that Mark ended up working with me for a couple of years? Small world, but most of these guys – I haven't seen since school."

"Really? Where did you work?"

"Oh it was a big news corporation. First job after uni; I hated it. It was the middle of nowhere. Had to walk for miles from the tube station and I barely got paid a thing. My boss was a complete arsehole. He was such a lech, stared down my top all the time, would sidle up to me when I was smoking outside. Once he even put his hand on my butt. That was when I had it. I put my fag out on the lapel of his posh suit."

Matty could barely keep up with the fast flow of words emerging from her small lipsticked mouth. He was growing tired of the conversation already.

"And you? What do you do? Let me guess… you look like you're some sort of I.T. geek, programmer, that sort of thing?"

He was horrified at this. On his days off from work he thought that he cultivated the air of someone casual and – if not quite stylish – then at least well put together. Certainly not a geek or a techie.

"I'm a trader," he said shortly, cutting her off.

"Oh," she was evidently put out about having guessed wrongly and he wasn't sure whether he'd imagined it or not, but he thought that her attitude towards him changed now that she got a sniff of his money.

"So why did you want to see me?" she asked curiously.

"Well…" As usual, he didn't know where to begin. "I'm trying to find out where I'm originally from," he said, cutting straight to the chase, "I was adopted and I've never really had a chance to get to know my origins. The place from which I was adopted doesn't exist anymore you see…"

"Right… Why only now?" she asked, rapping her electric green fingernails on the side of her coffee cup, "Sorry, it's not my business. It's just I was thinking, why start looking for your real parents in your late twenties, when you're already independent and… well, they're not such a big part of your life anymore?"

"Yeah, I know. I suppose I just wasn't very interested before. I was under the impression that whoever my real parents were, they didn't want me and that was that. But recently I came across a few things that made me think about my past. Not even my parents, but just everything… where I was born, what my heritage was, that sort of thing. And then I came across my school reports and Dan's mum told me that I used to have an accent…"

He stopped mid-way through the explanation when he noticed that she was giving him a strange look. Her thinly plucked eyebrows narrowed in the middle to form a confused 'v' shape.

"What?" he asked. He was beginning to develop a slight headache from the cacophony of voices in the background and the dense air in the café.

"Sorry, I just still don't understand – why now?"

"Well, for starters, I wanted to find out the language that I used to speak. Apparently there was a girl in our class who used to understand me and…"

"Are you serious? You don't remember us talking? You don't remember that I sang you 'Sto Lat' on your birthday?"

"What?" A painful spidery sensation of nerves developed in the pit of his stomach. It was like a merciless tickle from the inside – one that spread wider and wider in deepening concentric circles.

"No… I don't–"

"Polish. We spoke Polish. I had to translate for you at first because the other kids couldn't understand what you were saying. You only knew a few words of English to begin with. I don't know what you would have done without me…" she said, grinning, and finally taking a bite into her panini. Her lipstick left a small pale red half-moon on the thick bread.

He watched the cheese oozing from either side of the grilled bread, the highlighter yellow of processed cheddar. He had known all along. Of course he had. He realised that now.

"Polish?" His voice was quite steady, "You're sure?"

She rolled her eyes and smiled at him, chewing hard on the giant mouthful.

"I think I know what languages I can speak," she said eventually, sucking up the last bit of tomato left on her plate.

"But your name. It's…"

"Polish. After my grandmother. It's the Polish version of Stephanie. Naprawdę nic nie pamiętasz?"

The words were familiar, but he couldn't quite grasp their meaning. He gathered that it was a question from the inflection of her voice at the end, and the answer was just there, on the tip of his tongue, but it refused to emerge.

"I just don't understand how you can forget," she muttered, looking again at the picture. "You sat next to me throughout the whole of Year 1 – probably because I was the only one who could understand what you were saying. Dan wanted to sit with you, but Mrs. Henderson put us together so that I could help you. My mum loved you, I guess it's because you reminded her of her own childhood."

And there it was, somewhere in the depths of his mind, like the afterglow of a dream. A tall, thin woman at the school gates, ruffling his hair, asking when he would come over to watch videos. But he couldn't work out whether it was a real memory or a fiction that he'd conjured up to fit with the version of the past that Stefania had laid out before him.

"What was I like?" he asked her, suddenly fearful of the answer.

She narrowed her eyes, thinking.

"Sort of scared at first. I felt sorry for you. I think you reminded me a bit of my little brother."

Her face had softened. Gone was the mocking front that she'd presented when they first met or even the sudden appreciation when he revealed his profession. And he could see that without the overdone make-up and ridiculous clothes, she would be quite beautiful.

"I remember that you would often run off when we were asked to line up in the playground at the end of break-time. I had to help to chase you and coax you back into the classroom. Have you ever thought about why you can't remember…?" she asked quietly.

Of course he had. He thought about it every day since finding the reports and every time that he addressed the subject, the raw anger started up again. He had no answer to give her.

"Your surname is English," he said, changing the subject.

"Yes, my dad's from Brighton. English born and bred. My mum came over in the early eighties. Poland was still Communist and she wanted to get out… just for a bit initially.

She wanted to work, earn some money and then come back home. But she found a job at a hotel and then met my dad. And well… they ran off into the sunset. They've been broken up for years now."

She glanced suddenly at her watch, "I'm going to have to run, Matthew. I've got stacks of press releases to write before tomorrow. All my news is being pushed out by the bloody football."

"I bet. Thanks for meeting me anyway…"

"Listen, if you want to know anything else, take my number and give me a call whenever you want. I mean it," she said, looking at him seriously.

"Thank you." He took out his phone and punched in the numbers as she dictated.

She blew him a kiss on her hand, like a vampish Marilyn Monroe, and within seconds she was gone.

He left the café barely noticing in which direction he was walking. The blinding glare of the sun made him stop in his tracks. Polish. He was Polish.

Chapter 27 – Tom
Chicago

When he looked back on the event days later, Tom would find that it wasn't as sudden or as unexpected as he would have thought. In fact, he would realise that his subconscious mind had most likely planned it.

He was in the middle of reading Czesław Miłosz's *The Issa Valley*, lost in the beautiful descriptions of the remote countryside, when the photo fell out and hit him, quite literally, in the face. He picked it up carelessly and was about to discard it, thinking that it was merely an old postcard that had served as a bookmark, but his yellow, wrinkled hand stopped mid-flight.

His gaze met with two pairs of small blue eyes, printed on poor quality photo paper. Their faces still had the baby chubbiness about them, but they might have already turned three and there was a sense of movement about them that implied they had long ago started walking.

Adam was laughing, pulling at the sleeve of his sister's hand-knitted jumper, but Joanna was annoyed, or worried perhaps. He couldn't be sure. Her lower lip was jutting out slightly and there was the circle of a tear, making its way slowly out of the corner of her left eye.

Time stopped. And suddenly with a force so powerful that he could visualise himself there, holding the borrowed camera in his hand and arranging them both on the battered fold out sofa. Monika didn't want to do it. She didn't like anything that would disrupt her routine and most of all, as always, she just wanted to sleep. Their conversations lately revolved around nothing but how exhausted she was, how utterly and completely exhausted.

But he wouldn't pass up on the opportunity to borrow the camera from the Kowalskis next door – they themselves only had it for a week, as it was borrowed from a family member. He'd spent the last of his earnings on the film and had a crash course from Kowalski himself on how to operate it. Yes, using the camera wasn't the difficult part. You just had to wind on the film, make sure that it clicked into place, then clean the lens, spend some time focusing it on the subject, and you were ready. The difficult part was actually getting your subject, or rather the subject*s* prepared.

He'd asked Monika whether she might pose with the twins on her lap, but she flat out refused, so he was left with no other option but to position them on the sofa to the best of his ability. He spent at least half an hour trying to entertain them both, making funny faces and sticking out his tongue, but still, he somehow couldn't get them both smiling at the same time. In the end, he just took as many shots as he could in the hope that one of them would turn out fine.

When the film was developed a week later, he was devastated to find that the majority of the photos were ruined, either through over-exposure or the twins' sudden movements which caused blurring. There were two good ones though, and Tom got these framed, proudly displaying them on the main wall in their sitting room. And then there was this one – it wasn't quite as good because Joanna was crying, but it was clear, and focussed. He also liked the fact that it was truer to life than any of the others, because it showed their real interactions with one another. It was rare to get pictures like this, so completely and utterly unposed.

The photo had a crease down the middle from where it had been folded in the back of Tom's wallet for years. He couldn't remember when he'd first taken it out and tucked it safely among the pages of his favourite book. It became too painful to look at, and when he started working at the dealership, he didn't have time to read. As a result, the memories had been tucked so safely out of sight that he'd never had the occasion to revisit them.

But that day, they came back with a force that winded him. He held the photo in both of his shaking hands and his heart felt as if it were on fire.

"Mr. Mason?"

He didn't even notice when she'd entered the room.

"Are you ready for your tea? The doctor's changed your medication, so it's only two pills now. Let me prepare them for you."

And still he didn't respond; he was suddenly unable to.

"Is everything alright?"

She sat down on the edge of the bed and looked at him with concern. His tired arms had allowed the photo to drop onto the duvet and she picked it up gently.

"They're beautiful. Who are they?" she asked.

"My children. They're my children."

"I didn't realise that you had children," she said, looking at him seriously. He could see the unanswered questions in her eyes. *Where are they now? Why haven't they come to visit you? What happened? What happened?*

"I haven't seen them since they were four years old," he muttered.

"Why?" she asked. It was a simple question. In a different person's mouth it would have sounded intrusive, but not in

Clara's. And he surprised himself by finding that as terrified as he was, he might just be able to tell her the truth. It would be painful, as he would have to reveal it slowly, like peeling off a plaster that concealed a deep wound.

"I left them. I left them because I had been unfaithful…" he started.

"Right…"

And then the hot tears streamed down his face and he grasped hold of Clara's hand.

"It's OK. You don't have to tell me," she whispered, but he wanted to. He found that he badly wanted to.

"I did something awful. Something truly awful…" he said, almost inaudibly.

"I see…"

Her voice soothed the hammering of his heart.

"I was so young at the time, you know? Twenty-two when we married. Only twenty-six when the twins were born. I was very scared… I was so scared that my wife would die that day."

"Did she have a complicated birth?"

"Yes, very. I kept having a dream – the same dream over and over. A wall comes," he made a rapid pulling motion with his hands, "It moves closer and closer in my direction. I'm running, but I cannot move fast enough. It is a dark wall, a strange wall. I feel it's almost a person, with feelings… destructive feelings. I am so tired, my legs won't move any more. And then I fall and the bricks, they come down, they start to hit me. They fall, first on my arms, then my back and then my head. I dream that I want to get up but I can't… there are too many bricks."

"I think any psychologist would say that the bricks are your problems, weighing down on you."

"No, I think the wall is test… a test of strength and I fail. I often think that the wall was actually Lidia."

"Lidia?"

"The woman who I cheated on my wife with."

"Ah, I see. Did she make the first move or…?"

"I did. But that wasn't when the children were born. It was more than three years later. I bumped into her on the way to work. At that point I felt a horrible monotony in my life. I wanted to be an artist, a painter and I was angry that my life was so mundane. It was the same journey to the mine every day, the same twelve hours working in the dark, and then repeat. Week in, week out."

"Why couldn't you pursue your art?"

"Because it doesn't pay enough and I had a whole family to support."

"Of course. But you could have done it on the side? As a hobby?"

"No time. I worked from eight in the morning to eight in the evening. I was so tired when I got home that I sometimes couldn't stand up anymore. My wife was tired too. We argued. We had very little money from my work and she looked after the children at home. There was sadness in the monotony and anger in the sadness and fear in the anger… and in the middle of all this came Lidia."

"She made life exciting again?"

"Yes. We walked the same way to work because she started early at the hospital. And she was shy at first. But little by little I got through her many layers and I got to know her. Like me, she had another world that she wanted to live in, but she was stuck in that one. She wanted to be a singer. She took classes, but her father died and they no longer had enough money."

"So she became a nurse?"

"Yes. Every day we pretended. We'd meet up en route and she'd ask how my painting was going. And I'd congratulate her on her show last night… It sounds stupid, I know."

He realised he had tightened his grip on her hand, and released it slightly.

"And one day it happened. I hadn't slept all night because of the children crying and I was so tired I felt sick. We walked and I was dizzy, and she made me sit on a bench on the side of the street. She gave me water and she stroked my face, and suddenly I kissed her.

He studied her face for some sort of reaction, but there was none.

"I kissed her, and then I couldn't stop. It was a hot sunny day, no clouds. And I said to her, 'What if we don't go to work today? What if we go down and lie by the river?'"

"And you did?"

"And we did… I remember panicking that people would see us, but nobody went past our spot. And we did it again the next day. Of course I knew that soon work would want to know where I was."

He began to wheeze gently with the effort of speaking and the tiredness engulfed him in its warm, fuzzy blanket.

"Stop for tonight," she said then, "Have some sleep. When I come back tomorrow night, you can finish. I desperately want to hear the rest, but I also want you to have the energy to tell me."

He had barely started of course. He was still very far from the crux of the matter, but he'd made the first step. He had begun his confession. And now that he had started, continuing would not be so difficult and perhaps it would go some way towards stopping the awful, crumbling wall – the all-consuming burden of guilt.

Chapter 28 – Joanna
Warsaw

"It's a great piece of work," said Marek, "A truly impressive piece of writing, particularly for a first feature. We made minor corrections, but all in all, it's good to go to print. Get your hands on a copy, frame it, send it out to your whole family…"

He smiled at her. Marek never smiled and at first, she was so taken aback by his words, that she wasn't sure how to react. She half expected him to burst out laughing at any moment, and say that of course they weren't printing it – they had always planned a different feature to go there and were only teasing her to see how far she would go.

"Erm… thank you," she managed finally.

"These stories are very sensitively written," said Marek, "Readers like that. You give an emotional perspective which is really important with topics like this. You've really got into the minds of the families. Now… I have something that I would like you to work on. It's a project that I've had in the pipeline for a while now, but I think we'll finally be able to get moving on it."

"What is it?"

But then the phone rang, and she could tell immediately that it was something important by the way that Marek's brow suddenly furrowed.

"I'll ring you about it," he mouthed, as she got up to leave.

Now, sitting in her bedroom four hours later, all the elation that she felt following Marek's praise had gone. She felt a migraine coming on. She hadn't experienced such a throbbing pain in her temples since her final exams at university, during which she'd left the hall and been physically sick in the toilets. Yet her body refused to draw itself away from the screen. It was 10.36pm and she'd been staring at Waldek's footage for an unbearably long amount of time, leaving only once to go to the toilet.

She had worked methodically to analyse the chronology of the CDs, refusing to rely on Lena's numerical system. Eventually, she'd determined that the footage that was of interest to her was on CDs 3 and 4. She then spent two hours carefully watching the film, first at normal speed, and then considerably slowed down. Her eyes strained from closely studying every single child that came up on the screen, pausing the footage and enlarging the image so that she could study their faces.

She was amazed at how different the roads looked. The street corners that she recognised on her daily drive to work had peculiar shop signs, with announcements in the window, such as 'Meat on Tuesdays'. She remembered her aunt telling her that there was nothing available in the shops under Communism – that people would queue for hours if they'd heard from their neighbours that there was a chance delivery of some staple product. Seeing it all before her eyes brought the family's memories to life.

She saw men slapping each other on the back, neighbours greeting one other, toddlers leaning excitedly over the flags hanging out on their balconies. She couldn't imagine such a display of friendliness, of togetherness in the streets of today's Warsaw, despite the times being so much better. People had so much more to be thankful for today. There was democracy, Western shops filled to the brim with everything you'd ever want to eat, free higher education, constant rises in foreign investment. Even the global recession didn't seem to hit the country as hard as it did many of its European neighbours. Yet people didn't tend to rejoice in what they had. They were constantly after something bigger, something better. And they seemed to envy their neighbours rather than wanting to help one another out. Joanna was saddened by this thought.

She continued to watch as the camera jolted around. It seemed that Waldek had been walking for a while from Ochota towards the centre of town and then had stood on the corner of Emilii Plater Street and Jerusalem Avenue, overlooking the action.

The camera zoomed in and out on individual crowd members, particularly three young men who appeared to be leading the action. Joanna was convinced that she'd caught sight of a small dark head in the crowds. At one point she was certain that she'd seen Adam, only to find the little boy had a large red birthmark on the side of his face that had been initially obscured by another person's arm.

The slow, painful realisation dawned on her that she wasn't going to see him on the screen. She couldn't find herself, or her mother or Mrs. Barska, even though they'd apparently been only a few metres away. The more she'd accepted the fact, the more she relaxed into viewing the proceedings. She felt strangely engrossed in the atmosphere of the day. She longed to be once again part of the chattering clusters of people in the streets.

Just as her migraine was creeping its way to the front of her skull, Waldek's camera settled on the face of a young man with a thick moustache holding a flag. She stopped the film to read what was written across it: "Wałęsa for new Poland!" it proclaimed. From her futuristic, all-knowing perch, she couldn't help but smile. The man's demand had come true as Lech Wałęsa, the leader of Solidarity, had become the first president of a democratic Poland less than two years later.

His lips began to move at a rapid speed and only then did it occur to Joanna, that she'd been watching the footage without any sound. Studying the screen in minute detail, she hadn't even bothered to switch it on. The voice quality was surprisingly good. She listened mesmerised as the man raged against the Communist government, his short moustache twitching indignantly.

"They're dogs!" he shouted, "Dogs! Rising prices and arrests of innocent people is all that they're good at! We're demanding the release of Kornel Morawiecki!"

A quick web search of the surname revealed to Joanna that Morawiecki was one of the Solidarity leaders arrested by the government in November of the previous year.

At that point, unable to fight the mounting tension in her head, she walked unsteadily to the kitchen to swallow some aspirin. She lay down on the bed and covered her face with a jumper, blocking out the piercing shards of light that were bolting through her brain. The man continued to rant in the background.

"Today something will happen. There is a change in the air. We're not out here to be violent. We're just here today announcing that we don't accept…"

His protests were merging with the thumping in her head, growing gradually more distant. She couldn't bring herself to sit back up and turn off the sound and the angry voice was strangely soporific. She tried to force herself over the threshold into sleep.

But through the haze of his words, she made out another series of voices in the background.

"Nanna, why is that man weeing?"

"Shhh… don't look. That's vulgar."

"See over there. Why does that boy not want to go with him?"

"I don't know my darling."

"But he's hurting him!"

Joanna felt a cold and clammy sweat on her forehead. She sat bolt upright and stared at the screen. Nothing on it had changed. The man continued talking, answering some of Waldek's questions about previous protests.

She moved the cursor on the screen back by a minute. There it was, the young girl's voice.

"See over there. Why does that boy not want to go with him?"

"I don't know my darling."

"But he's hurting him!"

Joanna listened out desperately for anything further that she might say, but there was nothing until…

"I can't believe they managed to organise this! Do you know; I heard that there are similar strikes going on in Gdańsk, Dąbrowa Górnicza and Bielsko-Biała… Thousands of people involved."

"Really? Do you think that it will actually lead to anything this time?"

"Definitely! Mark my words. This is the beginning of the end; they're all saying it."

"But surely…"

Her mother's voice. Joanna was sure of it. The other woman was Mrs. Barska. They were close to the camera, just out of view. The end of their brief conversation was drowned out by the crowds breaking into sudden song.

Joanna stopped the film. She saw black spots before her eyes and felt that she was on the verge of passing out.

'He was taken,' was the thought that ran on a loop through her mind. She was certain that the girl's question referred to Adam. "Why does that boy not want to go with him?"

The outcome was painfully deflating, as her drowsy brain realised the virtual impossibility of searching for a 'him' of no age or description; a nameless man at an event twenty years ago.

And beneath it all remained the most awful desperate question: 'Why?'

Chapter 29 – Matty
London

Occasionally the dawns in even the grimmest parts of London can be dazzlingly beautiful, so much so, that for a few moments you might forget where you are. Out of the murky half-light hovering above the grotty streets, and the crushed cans falling out of black bin-liners, you see a tinge of pink, like the sky blushing. Then the blush spreads and eventually fades, and gives way to other colours, before finally spilling through into full daylight. In the back streets of Holloway, the sudden brightness springs residents into action.

Recently, he'd been half-way through his morning commute by the time the sun rose, so he'd missed the beauty of the dawn, and on weekends, he would, of course, sleep in. Today was a rare exception. Lately, sleep had eluded him completely, and at five in the morning he gave up trying and went out for an unplanned morning run.

Today, his feet pounded the pavement in sync with the heavy beating of his heart, and he watched as the murky charcoal grey sky began to fill with colour. By the time he'd reached Finsbury Park, he was doubled-over panting, but he'd formulated a plan. He needed urgently to locate the next piece of the puzzle. He was planning on calling the photography studio, but he decided that he would visit it in person instead. That way, it would be easier to suss out which member of staff might be the most willing to give out information.

Three hours later, he was already on Oxford Street, in one of the largest crowds he had ever encountered. Choosing a Saturday to visit the studio hadn't been his brightest idea. He dodged groups of tourists and frantic shoppers on Argyle Street and was pushed onto the road due to an overspill of pedestrians.

Eventually, he managed to force his way down Carnaby Street and into one of the side roads where the point on his Google Maps was directing him to. He checked the address again, just to be sure. Judging by the area, Matty guessed that it must be an upmarket establishment which had clearly done well to survive the recession.

He spotted the sign and walked through the unassuming dark oak doors, surprised to find himself in a small room, fitted at one end with a wooden counter.

The only other piece of furniture was a dark green velvet sofa with a carefully arranged display of gold silk cushions. The walls, from floor to ceiling, were filled with photos. Many of them were celebrities – singers, musicians, Olympic sports personalities and models, but in between them there were images of regular people. Some were headshots, others were taken in motion, others still were artistically posed.

"Can I help you?"

Matty wasn't sure how long he'd been standing in the centre of the room staring wide-eyed at the collage.

"Yes, sorry. I have a bit of an unusual request. I…"

He was about to launch into a carefully prepared explanation of how he had come by the photo in his pocket, when something caught his eye. The image was half obscured by the shoulder of the short, bespectacled man who had appeared behind the counter. His face was tanned and leathery, and he was entirely bald. The studio lighting made strange oblong shapes become reflected on his head. He reminded Matty of Picasso in his later years.

"That photo. Could I just see?" Matty pointed to the picture behind the man. His stomach lurched when he saw that he was right. It was the same man. Admittedly, it was a different shot of him – this one was in profile, but there was no mistaking that it was the same person. He had the same dimpled chin, the same dark, arched eyebrows and thin lips. Matty had spent a great deal of time studying the face in the privacy of his bedroom.

"I have this picture," he said, pulling the photo from his coat with shaking hands. He passed it to the man behind the counter who surveyed it with a look of surprise. He readjusted the glasses on his nose.

"You have a photo of Claudio. It's a lovely shot of him. Are you family?"

His stomach felt as though it was filled with lead. Of all the possible questions, he hadn't been prepared for this one.

"I might be," he muttered eventually.

"Sorry?"

"I found the photo in a box in our attic, when I was cleaning it out," he lied, "and I wasn't sure who it was. I saw your address on the back and I thought you might be able to help me find out."

"It's Claudio, my business partner," said the man, still smiling. "Ah yes, I can see that it was taken here. Perhaps even by me? It does look as if he's wearing the same clothes, doesn't it?" he asked, holding Matty's photo next to the one on the wall. "It must have been from the same photoshoot."

Matty stepped aside as two young women entered the shop. One of them was dressed in an elegant black fur coat and had a silk scarf tied around her head like a turban. The other was wearing a floaty yellow dress under a tight leather jacket.

"Jules, are they ready?" she asked excitedly.

Matty watched as 'Jules' took out a bound album and placed it on the table before them. He waited patiently as they looked over it, poring over every page.

"The smudge. Thank goodness you got rid of that. Second time lucky, eh? Right, could you remind us of the total including the touch up?"

The price was astronomical – a month of Matty's salary.

As he sat on the edge of the velvet sofa, he once again studied the photos around him. He could spot no other shots of Claudio, but he found one of Jules himself taken in the same style and against the same backdrop.

He never would have guessed that the identity of the man in his pocket would have been handed to him on a plate, and now that it had, he felt a sudden surge of anxiety.

When the girls finally left the store, Jules motioned for him to come forward.

"Did you want the photo reproduced?" he asked.

"No, I… I just wondered whether I could meet him?"

"Who?"

He looked hard at Jules. Was he senile or just eccentric?

"This man. I would like to meet him. You say that his name is Claudio?"

"Yes, Claudio." He gave Matty a sad smile, making tiny dimples appear in the corners of his tanned, wrinkled cheeks, "But Claudio departed from us… when was it? Eight years ago now."

Matty didn't immediately catch the meaning of the words. His first thought was that Claudio had left the business. It was only when the old man muttered the word 'cancer' that he understood.

"He died."

The tension that had gathered in his chest evaporated immediately, and with it came an unexpected pang of regret.

"Yes. I'm sorry to break it to you like this."

"Thank you. I didn't know him. I just found the picture and wondered whether he might help me find something out about myself.

He realised how ludicrous he sounded.

"Who are you?"

It was a gentle question, almost as if he was asking Matty to search inside his soul for his true identity.

"I'm Matthew Reardon," he said helplessly, "I'm a trader… er… I work for Chipston Capital."

He watched as the man narrowed his eyes and shook his head.

"I need more."

"Sorry?"

"More facts about you. You're not lighting any bulbs at the moment."

"I don't know what else to say."

"Where did you say that you found Claudio's photograph?"

"At my mother's house in Barnet."

"What's her name?"

"Celia… Celia Reardon."

Jules' eyes widened in a look of surprise and, Matty thought, recognition.

At that moment another customer came in and frustratingly their conversation was cut short.

"I finish in forty minutes," Jules told him. "Can you wait that long?"

Matty nodded.

"Meet me outside the shop."

***

Jules led him to a greasy spoon down a Soho backstreet. They passed groups of young lads – quite likely underage – assembling outside pubs, sipping on lazy pints. It was Saturday afternoon, after all. This was likely to be a precursor to their big night out.

"Ah Bibi, hello," he said raising his hand to a large-bosomed lady behind the counter, "The usual for me, please. And for you?" he asked Matty.

"Er... just a cup of tea."

They sat down on opposite sides of a lurid yellow plastic table, and Jules tapped out a nervous rhythm on its top with his fingers. Matty noticed that his nails were unusually long for a man and had a strange, talon-like shape, as if he had filed them into points. They sat in silence until the waitress brought over their steaming drinks.

The old man glanced up at him, but somehow had trouble catching his eye. He looked like he was on the verge of saying something but restrained himself at the last minute.

"So you're Celia's son. How is she?" asked Jules, staring into his mug.

"You know her?" asked Matty surprised, "You know my mother?"

"No, no," he said quickly, "I only met her once, but I feel like I know her very well... mainly from Claudio's stories. They were together for almost three years."

Matty felt his stomach turn. There was a dry tickle in the back of his throat which he recognised as the precursor of nausea. A cold suspicion formed in his brain.

"Was... was Claudio my father?"

"What?" Jules' pale, bushy eyebrows rose up on his forehead. "No. He definitely wasn't," he said shaking his head slowly from side to side, "I'm sorry to disappoint you."

A bubble of maniacal laughter formed in the back of Matty's mind.

"Then what?"

"What do you mean, what?"

"Tell me a bit more... How did they meet? What happened?"

He was already feeling the sting of disappointment. Claudio had clearly been just an old boyfriend of Celia's – hence the photo in the box. He was nothing to do with him.

The old man had a strange expression on his face.

"Claudio first met her… your mother, when they both worked in a small Islington theatre in the early eighties. He was still studying then – I think he was trying to earn extra money by working at the box office. Celia was – let's just say that she was keener on him than he was on her," said Jules. Matty got the impression that he was choosing his words carefully. A small vein pulsated just above his right eye.

"And they were in a relationship?"

"Of sorts. I always thought that it was a one-sided affection, but perhaps Claudio did really love her at one stage. I couldn't tell you that for sure. All I will say, is that he was definitely scared of her."

"Really?" Matty smiled wryly. Who wasn't scared of Celia? Maybe her celebrity friends, but everyone else, was intimidated.

"Yes, I'm sorry to say this, but she would threaten him with all sorts of things. There were many occasions in which he tried to leave her but somehow he always ended up going back. And of course the ultimate happened about a year into them knowing each other… and then he couldn't leave."

"The ultimate?"

"The baby."

Matty felt as if a sudden deafness had overcome him. He could make out the words spoken by the old man, but they were somehow nonsensical to him. It was as if he was outside the conversation, observing it from the point of view of a casual passer-by.

"You didn't know," said Jules to him. It was a statement rather than a question and he looked suddenly petrified, "I was sure that you knew, that Celia would have told you."

He said nothing, but motioned for the man to carry on talking.

"It was a little boy. For a while, everything was OK between her and Claudio, although they never married and he never even moved in with them. The boy was very ill from the beginning. He was born premature and there were complications…"

He knew immediately what was coming before Jules said the words.

"He died?"

"Yes… he caught measles when he was three and sadly he never recovered from it. Of course, Celia blamed herself for it – for not ensuring that he got his vaccination on time, for taking him to the hospital too late, for not keeping him warm enough when he had a fever… Claudio told me she was completely torn apart."

"And then?"

"And then Claudio went back to Italy for two years. He couldn't face coming into work… and truth be told I think he wanted to get away from her too. I ran the studio on my own for a while. My wife helped out when the kids were at school. Then eventually he returned and he was a changed man. The spark was back in his eye. We had an unspoken agreement that we would never mention Celia and Matthew again. It was just better for his mental health, you know?"

"Matthew?"

"Yes, that was the boy's name… Same as yours. Clearly, Celia liked it."

Matthew. Matty. The boy had been him, but not him. He couldn't handle any further information. He propped his forehead up on the table with his hands, took a deep breath and before he could gather his thoughts, he realised that he was crying. Hot, angry tears slid their way silently down his cheeks merging with the dregs of tea left in his mug.

He stood up quickly, causing a sudden, awful scraping noise, and ran out of the café into the darkening street. The ground had been shifted beneath his feet and he stumbled around, unsure of where he should be headed.

And then a sudden thought struck him. 'Matthew' written in cursive script on the back of the photos. The boy in those images… he was… he had been a different person entirely.

Chapter 30 – Tom
Chicago

"I have something," Dustin burst out when he entered the living room after breakfast. Tom was dozing in the corner, listening to Susie play the guitar. The soft medley of Beatles classics had a particularly soporific effect on him.

"What do you have?" he asked, momentarily panicked that he had just fallen asleep in the middle of a conversation.

"I have something on Adam Malicki," he said in a half whisper. "But don't get too excited, because it could honestly be nothing."

But Tom couldn't halt the sudden glimmer of hope that sparked up inside him as Dustin sat down next to him with a plastic folder on his lap.

"You were right – there wasn't anything on any of the social media pages, but I did find this article," he said, thrusting a printed out piece of paper in front of Tom.

Warsaw volleyball team wins league read the headline.

"What is this?"

"Just read the actual article and you'll find out," muttered Dustin impatiently, "It says that the captain of the team is Adam Malicki.

The Warsaw University Volleyball Team came second in the Bologna Eurovolley championships, just three points ahead of the winners from Sapienza University of Rome. Captain Adam Malicki said that he was very happy with the 'rather unexpected' result. He said…

Tom's eyes scanned the article frantically, but there were only details of point scores and the future of the championship.

Was it really possible that this was him? He was always so active, constantly moving, constantly wriggling and running around. Did he put all this energy into sport and succeed in volleyball? If this was him, then it would be a simple case of contacting the club that he played for. He wanted to embrace Dustin for finding this article, for giving him this undeserved route back to his family.

"There's a photo on the second page," said Dustin calmly, and Tom turned to it, scanning the faces of the team members. According to the strapline below, Adam Malicki was the young man standing in the middle holding the silver plate.

His euphoria evaporated as soon as he looked more closely at his face. He was old… at least ten years too old and his hair was very blond. It wasn't *his* Adam.

Dustin could clearly see the disappointment in his face, because he quickly took the sheet away and said, "It's not him. It doesn't matter. I'm still very early into my search. I have something on Joanna Malicka too. There are some records coming up from what looks like a university, but it's all in Polish and they didn't have a translation option on the page."

He handed Tom another piece of paper and waited patiently as he digested it. It was a blog piece from five years ago about Joanna Malicka's master's degree paper on 'How effective journalism can support police detective work.' There were bullet points outlining the details of the paper, and the contact details of Joanna's professor.

"This is it?"

"Yes, that's all I got."

Tom attempted to work out the dates. If she had done her masters' degree straight after her bachelor's, then she would have been what? 22 or 23? And this had been published five years ago. In theory the dates added up, just.

"What do you think?" asked Dustin eagerly.

"It's possible. Too difficult to know without a photo obviously, but there is a possibility."

"There is a number. Why don't you just call and find out?"

He was suddenly angry at how Dustin thought it was all so straightforward and wondered how he would behave if it were his own son and daughter.

"It's not that easy, is it? What would I say? They wouldn't give information on students to just anybody."

"Well, you don't know unless you try. There are different angles you could go with if you didn't want to reveal who you were. You could call to say that you wanted to get a job reference for her, because you want to employ her?"

The thought of lying in order to have a chance of speaking to his own daughter filled Tom with a sick dread.

"Let me think about it overnight. Let me think about it and let you know. And thank you for getting this for me. It means a lot."

Later that night he practised in his head the different scenarios of how the phone conversation would go. There was a high chance that the number would no longer be right, or that the professor who had worked there had left.

But what if she was there? Then what? Could he be honest? Could he say that he was Joanna's father and was trying to track her down? They wouldn't buy that. They would refuse to give out personal information, surely.

Could he assume that she went on to work in journalism? Could he really pretend to be an Editor-in-Chief looking to track her down with a job offer? It didn't seem plausible.

He was still debating his options when Clara came in.

"How are you feeling today?" she asked. He noticed that she looked more tired than normal, although she beamed at him in her usual way. He realised with a start that perhaps she could be much older than he'd thought, and a sudden selfish fear crept into his mind that Clara might retire before he was gone. It was a ludicrous idea of course, but he couldn't bear entertaining it for any amount of time.

"I'm fine, the same."

She handed him his pills and a glass of water. She placed the mug of tea down on the table, and then she sat herself in the deep armchair. He knew what was coming.

"I've come for the next instalment," she said quietly and smiled at him. "Tell me what happened after you went to the park."

And he found that in a strange way he'd been looking forward to this moment. It was as if, when he'd released his story to Clara, he would have achieved something vital that would bring him onto the next step, whatever that may be.

He closed his eyes to help trigger his memory..

"The weather got hotter and we continued to escape to the park at every opportunity. I'd missed three or four days of work by then. I rang in before Monika woke up, saying I was seriously ill with flu. I don't think they believed it, with it being 35 degrees outdoors. We hid ourselves in the shadows of the trees, and my heart raced at every flutter of leaves, every thump of footsteps on the path near us. I didn't know how long I could keep it up, but I didn't seem to think of practicalities like that.

Lidia brought sandwiches in her bag and some compote made from strawberries. I can still remember the sweet taste of fermentation. I felt so happy that I fell asleep with my head on her lap, and I think I rested properly for the first time in years. When we woke up, the sun had gone in and it was late afternoon."

He stopped then, hesitating on the brink of the precipice. This had been the easy part, ahead of his ultimate downfall, which he dreaded thinking about, let alone voicing. Her opinion of him would inexorably change, that was certain. But Clara looked up at him with her intent gaze.

"So you went home? Did… did your wife find out?"

He swallowed hard. "No… no," he said. "We ran out of the park and we walked back using small secluded streets. Lidia insisted. She knew that if anybody saw us it would all be over – in a small town, everybody talks. We were near the main square, almost home, when I overheard a conversation between two women. One of them was crying, shouting something about an accident. My instinct was to run over and help. I ignored Lidia, and all the risk of being discovered and I asked what had happened. I could barely piece together what she was saying, but in the end I understood that it was an accident. It was an accident in my place of work."

"What sort of accident?"

"A collapse."

"I don't understand. Did someone collapse?"

"Not someone – the land," he explained quietly, "I worked in a mine you see. It wasn't that surprising an event considering our line of work, but there was shock. There was widespread shock because it had *never* happened before, not in our mine. Nobody in the town had ever heard of anything like that happening on such a large scale."

"I found out from the woman that seven people had died. Her husband was one of my colleagues – he'd recently joined, and it was then that I knew that it was my group."

He noticed that his voice had become faster and angrier. He couldn't catch Clara's eye.

"I left Lidia and the woman then. I apologised, but I had to get myself out of there – I couldn't trust my reactions. I ran and ran until I had no energy left. Then I sat in a square in an unknown neighbourhood kilometres away from home, cradling my head in my hands. I was there for what could have been a minute and could have been hours. I thought this was it – this was the end. And do you know what the most awful part of it was?"

"What?"

"That my first feeling wasn't pain or grief, but fear. Fear in its coldest, purest form, of what would happen if I were discovered."

Chapter 31 – Joanna
Warsaw

"Listen to it again."

> *"See over there. Why does that boy not want to go with him?"*
> *"I don't know my darling."*
> *"But he's hurting him!"*

Joanna watched her aunt swallow. Her throat shook gently with the effort. Irena had learnt to be a woman of few emotions. She was skilled at hermetically sealing her feelings inside herself so that nobody could penetrate the firm, logical exterior. She couldn't afford to release them, she told Joanna once in a rare burst of honesty, as the spillage could be hazardous. She'd witnessed Monika's outpouring of grief and saw where that had led her. The last thing the family needed was another broken woman. Her only wish was that her niece wouldn't try her quite so many times.

"It could be anyone, Joanna," she answered casually.

"You know it's not anyone. You know it's him!"

"I don't *know* anything," she snapped, "Neither do you. The only fact you have here is that a young girl noticed a boy being hurt at the strike in 1988."

"No-o-o," Joanna answered. The word was long, drawn out and triumphant, "What I have here is a recording of a girl telling her relative about a boy who does not want to go with someone – that someone being male. The same male is hurting him. What's more, this exchange takes place seconds before mum approaches and has a conversation with Mrs. Barska. We know from police transcripts that she noticed Adam missing exactly after that conversation."

Irena's green eyes bore into her niece's face. Joanna had the distinct impression that she was trying to transfer a subliminal message to her, which was pointless, as they were alone in the flat. She was always frightened of staring into their emerald depths, because they so resembled her mother's. The only difference was that Irena's were alert and focused, Monika's glazed and wandering.

"I know you believe me. Why are you pretending that you don't?"

"I'm not pretending," Irena admitted eventually, rubbing her forehead, "I just don't understand what you can possibly do with this."

The enthusiasm that had consumed Joanna suddenly disappeared. She had anticipated the cold and doubting response, but she had also believed that Irena would provide her with the answer to that very question. She was the source of all reason, the only real adult of the Malicki family.

"What do you mean?" she asked weakly.

"Imagine you took this to the police and they reopened the case. What could they do? The evidence that you've provided them with leads to a witness with no name, a girl who was perhaps seven or eight at the time. Even if by some miracle she could be tracked down, she's not likely to remember anything from that day. Joanna, it was a passing comment."

"But there could be other witnesses. If I take it to the papers and highlight the police's incompetence, they will have to reopen the case to save face if nothing else! Other people might come forward with camera footage!"

"Calm down and stop yelling," pleaded Irena, "Listen to me. You would not believe how improbable it is that you've discovered this… this recording, precisely for the reason that so few people had cameras in Poland at the time – by that I mean ones that recorded footage, not just took individual photos. And if they did, they would have to be pea-brained to take it out into the streets during a protest. The fact that you have one recording is unbelievable, the idea that there would be another that captured that very same scene is impossible."

"So you think I should just give up? Because that's what you always seem to bloody think!" said Joanna, slamming her fist on the table.

"You're not going to take the disappointment again," she answered, her jaw rigid.

"Well, that's my choice."

"Your choice, but everyone's suffering."

"What?"

"Who picked it all up for you when your mother…? I for one don't have the strength to do it again for you!"

Suddenly, she could no longer stand the rigidness of the wooden chair that she was sitting on. She stood up, grabbed the CD that she had copied from Lena's original and placed it safely in its plastic case. She cast Irena a final glance.

Her aunt's face didn't move apart from the slight parting of the lips.

"For the record, I believe it's about him," she whispered, as Joanna walked out of the door.

She avoided the lift and instead decided to walk down the eleven flights of stairs to clear her mind. The way she saw the situation, she had two options. She could take the CD to Stefan, who could pass it onto his head of department, Sergeant Lasko. If Lasko didn't react, she could take it to the press. She had a couple of influential contacts at several national broadsheets, from a series of internships early in her career. But would they find it an interesting enough story to run? Doubtful. The other option was to do nothing.

Her mobile rang as she was stepping out of the front door of the building. She picked it up abruptly without looking at the screen, thinking that Irena had regretted what she said and wanted to apologise.

"What?" she barked.

"Joanna? It's Marek."

"Sorry. God, sorry. I thought it was somebody else."

"No worries. Listen – I meant to call you yesterday and then some urgent things came up, and… anyway. Do you have a moment? I wanted to tell you about the next project I had in mind for you."

She breathed out slowly and sat down on the front step to the building. She felt strangely deflated. A month ago she would have be excited about any opportunity that Marek had for her, but now there was nothing but numb indifference.

"Yes, yes of course." She attempted to convey a cheery excitement, but she could hear the hollowness in her own voice.

"Just to check – what are you working on at the moment?"

"Just a small piece of travel coverage for Dorota. I'll have it done by tomorrow."

"Great. So… I would like you to be involved in our new website. I'd like you to run its launch – you're the perfect person for it. You will have heard me ramble on about going international for a while now. Everyone's doing it. We can't be left in the wilderness. The first step is the website. We'll get all our business and feature pieces released in English and German, as well as Polish. We need to attract some foreign investment and generate a wider interest, you know?"

"Right…"

"You don't sound too excited?"

"No! I am *very* excited. When do you plan to launch this? Have you hired a web developer already?"

"It's typical, you worrying about the details. That's what's so impressive about you. Never fear, as I have signed a contract with a top web agency and I've got my eye on a couple of translators, although you're quite multilingual yourself, no?"

"Well, English I'm alright in. My German is terrible."

"That's not what it says on your CV," he said in a joking tone. "Anyway, the initial project plan states that we would aim to launch at the end of July. I realise it's little more than a month away. But I'm a fan of tight deadlines. I want you to have the wireframes for the homepage done in the next week."

But she was no longer listening. The idea suddenly occurred to her. Its brilliance lay in the fact that there was nothing to lose.

"Marek?"

"Yes?"

"Would there be a chance to feature my piece on the website?"

"We'll feature lots of your writing on the website. You'll be its prime contributor."

"But that piece specifically," Joanna pressed, "Because it's my first proper feature. It would mean a lot…"

She heard a laugh on the other end of the phone.

"And what a first one it was. Yes, by all means. It will look good if we have some content when we launch, to line our readers' stomachs so to speak."

"Thank you."

"Come to my office tomorrow at 10am and I'll give you a full briefing on the project."

"Great. See you then."

She shoved the phone in the pocket of her tatty wool coat and punched the air. The CD wasn't useless at all. In fact, she knew exactly how to use it.

Chapter 32 – Matty
London

He knew that something was wrong before he opened the door. There was a grey hollowness in the air, a sense of change. As he entered the narrow hallway he saw that his instincts were right – Ellie wasn't home. He called out her name anyway, just in case. Nothing. In the kitchen, he spotted the note telling him what he already knew, that her absence wasn't temporary. She hadn't just left to buy milk.

Gone to stay with mum. Need some time. E.

He rushed to the bedroom and found it almost clinically tidy. The bedside table on Ellie's side, usually overflowing with nail varnish bottles, scrunched up tissues and magazine cuttings, was empty. He could almost glimpse a shadow of her on the floor, sitting cross-legged, her curtain of hair shielding her face, as she swept her multitude of tiny treasures into an open suitcase. There was a faint muddy footprint by the door, still ever so slightly wet. She must have left shortly before he arrived.

How long had he expected this to happen? They had been avoiding each other for weeks now, expertly side-stepping the gulf that had appeared between them. And with the perspective of time he was able to pinpoint exactly when his feelings towards Ellie had changed. It was during the trip to Warsaw. It was there that he had begun to lose the version of himself that had loved her – the version that he'd believed was his true self, and which had turned out to be anything but. And yet, now that she'd left, the sense of loneliness was overwhelming. He slid under the covers still in his shirt and suit trousers and curled his knees beneath his chest. He fought the urge to cry.

As he lay there, the hum grew in his head, rising in volume and pitch until it was so loud that he couldn't bear the sound any longer, and then the avalanche of memories began. They flooded everything, drowning out the past that he knew about himself – the safe and uneventful childhood, the mundane days at school, the afternoons with Dan watching the football, the Christmases spent with Celia and her glamorous friends.

Instead, his mind seeped memories of people and sensations that were at once alien to him and as intimate and painful as razors tearing through flesh. He could feel somebody holding his hand, their small, tubby fingers linked together, woven into a tight zigzag – the sensation was so intense that he felt as if he were truly there, living it. Faces swam before him of people whom he couldn't name or identify, but who he knew were frighteningly, overwhelmingly important. An eager face of a young man looked down at him and then he was being lifted, with strong and yet gentle arms onto his shoulders, from where he could see the world from a new perspective.

Tastes appeared on his tongue out of nowhere of thick warming liquids with a spicy aroma. He smelled fragrances that he hadn't experienced in years. And underlining all these emotions was the confusion of, on the one hand, desperately wanting to block them, to push them back safely into the vault within his brain, and on the other of desiring more of them, like one might desire a forbidden fruit. The confusion led to sadness and a strange, bitter emptiness that he could only rid himself of through sleep.

He was awoken by a buzzing sound beneath his pillow and thought at first that it was his alarm. It was only when he managed to locate his phone that he realised he'd missed a call from Dan. He dialled his number.

"Sorry mate, was asleep."

"You alright? You don't sound good.

"I'm not."

"Right… Er, well I was just wondering if you wanted to go to the pub? I've been at the bloody museum all day and I need to bitch about the idiots that employed me."

"What?" His brain felt murky somehow. It was as if the words were flowing into his ear through a distorting prism.

"Well, alright – they're not idiots," Dan conceded, "But they're a royal pain in the arse. Come to *The Plough*? Just for one."

He'd ended the call without giving Matty a chance to respond – his usual tactic for getting his own way.

Matty climbed slowly out of bed. The sky outside the window had turned a pinkish grey. He'd been asleep for more than two hours. His shirt was badly creased, but he couldn't be bothered to get changed. He grabbed a worn hoodie out of the wardrobe and went out into the darkening evening.

The street was alive with high summer. He could hear the steady beat of Jamaican music emanating from the garden belonging to his downstairs neighbours. Somewhere further there was a faint whiff of bonfires and an undercurrent of something sweet. He felt drunk on the light air as he walked in the direction of the pub.

Dan was already at their usual table, waiting for him with a pint.

"Finally. I had almost given up waiting for you. The day I've had."

"What happened?" he managed.

"You know that museum?"

It took him a while to register that Dan meant his latest client – a small engineering museum that had recently opened in a previously disused tunnel in Shoreditch. He had so far spent an unfathomable amount of time working on a launch poster for them.

"Yeah. What's going on?"

"The bastard director hates the poster. I did the final edits that the manager sent through, was literally about to hit send so that the printers could start the run, and then I get the call to tell me that the director hates it. Apparently it's too out there, too 'jazzy', won't appeal to the target audience enough! He wants it to be more traditional so that the intellectual types lap it up." He drew furious inverted commas around the word 'intellectual' in the air with his fingers.

"So I need to take all of this feedback into account, and they've only given me a week to make the changes. They're such idiots, genuinely – they'll have nobody coming to their bloody museum. If they had any chance, it would have been through getting the young crowd interested – it's mainly students who live in those parts anyway, and now they've gone and screwed that up too. It makes me so mad! And you know what's worst is that I actually liked the manager, and she was hot too, you know?"

"Yeah?"

"What's wrong with you? You look like someone's died."

"Ellie's left."

Dan's eyes widened and he almost knocked over his pint.

"No way. What, just packed and left? Did you have a row?"

"No. She left when I was at work. She took all her stuff and wrote me a note saying that she's staying at her mum's. Why are you so shocked? I'm not."

"Look, I know that things weren't going well for a while, I just never thought…"

"What?"

"Nothing."

"No. Go on. Say what you were going to say."

"I just never thought I would see the day. I'm sorry"

"Don't be."

They stared at the table. A boozy, safe silence hung between them. He knew that Dan sensed his reluctance to discuss Ellie further.

"You found out any more about the… you know, the stuff from your reports?"

"Yeah, actually. It was the most surreal thing ever. Do you remember I told you about the photo of the man that I found with my reports?"

"Vaguely."

"Dark hair, moustache – looked around 35. Anyway, I looked up the photography studio online and by some miracle, it still exists and I went there. I thought it was a real-long shot that anyone would tell me who the photo was of but the owner recognised him straight away. Apparently it was his former colleague – who used to go out with Celia."

Dan's eyes widened as he continued the story and Matty found himself strangely emotional when telling him about the baby.

"Christ, what are you going to do?"

"I have no idea. I suppose the only thing to do is to confront Celia…"

"And you don't want to do that?"

"Not yet. Not the way that I'm feeling now."

Dan ran his hand awkwardly through his short ginger hair. He clicked his fingers, as a sudden idea appeared in his head.

"Hey, what about your grandmother? You know, Celia's mum?"

"What about her?"

"Couldn't you go and visit her, and see what she knows?"

"Celia hasn't spoken to her in years, you know that. So I haven't been allowed to speak to her either. Apparently she tried to cheat Celia out of some money. It's always bloody money, isn't it? Relationships made and lost on money."

"'Not allowed, not allowed,'" said Dan mockingly, "You're not ten anymore, are you? If you want to go and visit her, you can."

"Why would I want to? For all I know she might have dementia by now. She probably won't even know who I am."

"It's just a thought," said Dan shrugging his shoulders, "You know sometimes old people remember stuff that happened years ago, even if they can't remember what they were doing the day before."

He had to admit that the more he thought about it, the more he was willing to agree that the idea was worth trying. How old was he when he'd last seen Grandma Helen? Thirteen at most. He remembered the wrinkles filled in with powder, the layers of grey hair piled onto her small head, the faint aroma of Indian cigarettes. She was in many ways the exact opposite of her daughter – serious, quiet, thoughtful.

Then came the severing of all family ties. It came so suddenly that he wasn't even allowed the chance to say goodbye.

"We won't have anything to do with that woman anymore," he remembered Celia telling him. "Look at me Matty. Promise me that you won't speak to her when she calls."

The explanation for this change was unclear. He was told that it was something to do with money and he knew better than to ask for details. For weeks after the incident, Celia came back from work more agitated and snappy than he'd ever seen her. He remembered the phone ringing as she carefully checked the number on the display to make sure that it wasn't Grandma Helen.

And then it was as if she had never existed. Even the Christmas cards from her went into the bin unread. He had to fight the urge to pick them out and read their contents in secret.

Would she still live at the same address? Or was she now tucked into a small, shared room in some distant nursing home? He couldn't even discount the possibility that she was dead. Perhaps she had been dead for years and Celia just hadn't told him?

"I'll drop by her old house and see whether she's still there," he said aloud, surprising himself.

Chapter 33 – Tom
Chicago

"I've thought a lot about what you said the other day about the fear of being discovered. I think you felt that fear because of the initial shock of it all."

He suspected that Clara was just trying to lessen his guilt, but he appreciated it nonetheless. It gave him the courage to continue his story.

"It's true. The fear of being discovered came first, but then I couldn't get the image out of my head of all the men that I had worked with over the past four years. All those faces that I saw every day, sometimes clean and bright, but more often smudged with soot, drenched with sweat… I wondered whether they sensed the danger coming, whether they had any way of knowing that the world was going to collapse on them? I prayed that they didn't, but I knew that there was no use in praying at that stage."

"Were they good friends?"

He nodded.

"We sweated together hundreds of metres below ground every single day. We shared our food, our water, like brothers. And suddenly they were gone… and me? I was still there… and for what? For committing a deadly sin?"

"But you didn't intend…"

"I know," he interrupted, raising his hand. "But at that moment, I doubted everything. I had no idea how I could continue living with myself. As I sat there, I felt as if everything was shouting at me."

"How do you mean?"

He remembered the emotion distinctly. The enormity of what happened triggered an avalanche in his brain. He stepped out of his mind and in every speck of dust and every blade of grass, he saw the face of one of the men he worked with. They were screaming… screaming for him to save them from the rubble. And when finally the screaming stopped, there was a panicked silence and he realised how completely unworthy he was. Unworthy of his children, unworthy of his wife, unworthy of everyone who had ever known him. He lay down on the ground then in that hot, dirty square. He cried… and he grasped hold of the soil. He just wanted to feel something familiar.

"I knew that was the end of everything I'd ever known."

She didn't say anything then and he'd lost all sense of what she was thinking. But it no longer mattered, because he was nearing the end. He was very close now…

"I began to walk… one foot in front of the other. I remember looking up at a bird in the sky – a tiny swallow. It's been said and thought many times before, I know, but to me that bird meant freedom. It flew wherever it wanted and guilt meant nothing to it. I wanted to be that bird more than anything in the world, and that's when the idea first appeared in my mind. When I look back on it now, it seemed ridiculously easy – an instant. And it was just that. It was as if a switch was flicked that set the cogs in motion. I started walking and my feet… they suddenly took me not in the direction of home, but the opposite way – the way that led me back to Lidia's flat. I stayed the night there. I didn't contact my wife.

The… the next morning she went out early to pick up the newspaper from the shop, and there was my name and my picture. I was listed as one of the casualties."

"What?"

"Yes. They listed me as one of the seven men 'presumed dead.' My boss, to whom I'd reported my absence was one of the men who had perished and it seemed that nobody else more senior was aware of it. The landslide was so dangerous that they didn't attempt to recover the bodies. Families had nothing physical to mourn over."

"But you went back to your wife? You admitted to her where you had been that day?" Even as the questions were emerging from her mouth, Tom could see that she was already beginning to figure out the answers. The horrid, sickening answers were reflected in her face and, when he didn't assure her that he returned to Monika, she finally understood the colossal weight that he carried.

"I felt the wall descend on me that night. Not in a dream anymore, but in reality. I swung backwards and forwards between two places." He made a motion with his hands imitating the pendulum of a clock. "The shame came like a dense cloud across my eyes and it makes me stop here," he said gazing at a point to the left hand side of him.

"You never went back to them."

"No."

"So what do they –?"

"They believe I'm long dead."

"Do you – have a grave?" It was a question that he was often curious about.

"Maybe. I've never wanted to look. But I've thought about it a lot. I always hated going to cemeteries and seeing graves that were built, brand new, ready for someone to fill them. They had the person's date of birth and were just waiting for their death date to be carved onto them. It was almost as if these people were waiting to die. But, I suppose in my case it would be different. I would have both dates on there, although the grave would be empty."

She was sitting with her eyes half closed, her hands on her lap, breathing in deeply, and he was suddenly afraid. What if he'd made a dreadful mistake? What if Clara chose to turn him in to the police? What he'd done was essentially unlawful. He could almost visualise her standing up and telling him that the game was up. But she didn't move and her voice remained even as she asked, "And your children were only four then?"

"Yes…" he continued, relieved. "Yes. Adam was always moving, always energetic, you know? As soon as he started walking, he ran riot around the house. A couple of months before that day, I noticed that he followed me to work. I stopped at a crossing and heard this… this panting sound. I turned around. It was him. He just looked up at me and smiled. He had walked more than three kilometres on his short legs. Joanna was much calmer, but she did a lot of thinking, you know, just like your Lucy."

"And Lidia? You came to America with her? The relationship that didn't work out – that was with her?"

"Yes, we came to America and everything changed. She is an example of how a place can change a person. We barely lasted a year and then she left."

"And you ended up alone?"

He looked up at her then, desperate to see the effect that his words had had. Surely, she hated him now? The crawl in his stomach began as if on cue.

But she smiled at him, a sad smile. And then she passed him his glass of water, and gently arranged the duvet to make sure that he was comfortable.

"Thank you for listening," he said.

"Thank you for trusting me enough to tell me your story."

She smiled at him, and he could tell, despite his paranoia, despite how undeserving he was, that the smile was still warm; it was still the same.

Chapter 34 – Joanna
Warsaw

The sun shone brightly on central Warsaw as Joanna made her way across the city to *Magix*, the web development agency where Marek had booked her a meeting. She'd stepped out for the first time this summer with only jeans and a short-sleeved shirt on and she revelled in the warmth of the morning. But even the glorious weather couldn't fully lighten her mood, as she replayed the conversation with her aunt from the previous night.

Joanna had been excited to tell Irena about the website launch and to make up for their previous disagreement of the week before. They were both in a good mood and about to settle into a quiet dinner when she'd revealed that one of the first pieces would be her missing person's report featuring Adam's case profile. She'd debated whether to mention it, but she figured that Irena would inevitably find out when she read the piece online. She had long ago stopped buying every publication in which her niece's articles had been featured, but she still read the news online, and there was no doubt that she would see it.

"You can't be serious?" Her face was motionless, but the words were laced with fury.

"Of course I'm serious," she said calmly, "It will be read by people internationally. Do you realise that we've missed a vital opportunity all these years by never putting any information about his disappearance online? Plus, I'm going to put the CD footage on there showing that it was a kidnapping. I've already told Stefan about it. "

Irena sat down and put her face in her hands. Her shoulders began to shake and this frightened Joanna. A memory wormed its way out slowly from the dark confines of her mind. She visualised her six-year-old self, watching her aunt carry her mother into her bedroom. Monika had been so weak and so exhausted from her crying that she could barely walk herself. Joanna had asked her aunt when she returned to the living room, "Why do you never cry?"

"I do," she said quietly. "But it's only at times when I feel *very, very* sad or frightened." At the moment, things are not so bad that I need to cry," she said softly, and then she tucked Joanna up in her bed.

And now? Now, a time that warranted tears had clearly arrived and Joanna didn't know how to react.

"I know there was no internet when it first happened," she continued gently, "but why didn't somebody put something up more recently?"

"You know why," her aunt's voice came out in a croak, "You know exactly why."

"No, I don't. Anyone would think that I'm the only one who wants to find him." The ugly, angry animal inside her braced itself for battle.

"You just can't stop, can you?" Irena asked her. She was speaking through her fingers as if she was too disgusted to look at her niece. "You have this desperate need to keep churning and churning it up. You know that you're the one who's driven your mother to the state that she's in now. Not Adam, but you."

Her words were slow and level and they tore at Joanna all the more, because suddenly the anger from them was gone and all that was left was a weary helplessness. She could see the shock in her aunt's eyes and she instantly realised that Irena regretted what she'd said. She began to explain herself, uselessly attempting to soften the blow that she'd given, but by that point Joanna wasn't listening. She'd wrapped her cardigan closely around her and announced, like a small child that wouldn't give up until it had its own way, "It's my article and it's my job."

But as she'd left Irena's flat, all her confidence about posting the article had evaporated and after a night's sleep, she was now certain that she wouldn't go through with it. She would be making herself vulnerable to potentially hundreds of people contacting her about alleged sightings that would prove to be nothing. It would just be another element of the two-decade long search that would end in disappointment. By the time she opened the door to the glass-fronted office of *Magix*, she made a solemn promise to herself that she would stick with this decision.

She found herself in an open-plan room sparsely populated with red plastic desks and art deco chairs. To her left stood a clear Perspex coat stand in the shape of a flamingo with a single jumper hanging artistically from the end of its raised leg. Behind it, she saw a young man with shaggy blond hair sitting in a huge round wicker chair lined with a cloudlike cushion. He was typing furiously on a laptop so thin, that from a distance it could be mistaken for a plane of glass.

Nobody seemed particularly interested in her arrival. There were only two other people in the room, both with their backs to her, so she decided that her only choice was to address the mop-haired man.

"Could you help me? I'm looking for Mr. Wasowski."

He was so startled by her voice that his body visibly lurched forwards in the chair.

When he'd recovered from the shock he stood up and gave her a distracted grin. He was taller than she'd imagined him to be, with a broad back and the befuddled appearance of a man who was in the wrong job. Joanna could visualise him chopping wood or fishing – something outdoorsy, requiring a significant degree of strength. Yet here he was, huddled over a laptop.

"Younger or older?"

"Sorry?"

"What I mean is, are you looking for me or for my father?"

"Ah. Right. I don't know. I work for *Prawda*," she said helplessly. She was suddenly conscious of an unexpected heat rising in her face.

"Ah, that's not me. It must have been my father that you were supposed to meet with, but he's not here. There's been some emergency down in Krakow," he muttered, looking concerned, "What time were you supposed to see him?"

"Nine-thirty."

"Ah, well that's bloody useless, isn't it?" he asked happily. "I'll see if I can help instead. I'm Oskar by the way."

"Joanna." She watched his eyes widen as she explained that the project would essentially involve the launch of an international website.

"That's huge. I honestly don't know why he's not here for this, I'm sorry."

He rubbed his knees and gazed at her with such wonder that she wanted to burst out laughing. As a rule she didn't like direct eye contact with strangers and she tended to avoid it unless it was absolutely necessary, but there was something so childlike and disarming about his behaviour that she felt instantly at ease.

"Let me just quickly check something and then we can begin," he announced, clapping his hands. He peered into the screen of the wafer-thin laptop.

"Fine, fine. First meeting at two-thirty," he said distractedly. He grinned at her, and motioned towards a narrow door to their left. They walked into an entirely white room with two white circular chairs in the same style as the one that he'd been sitting on outside.

"Make yourself comfortable," he said indicating one of them, "Would you like anything to drink? Tea? Coffee? Beer?"

"Just a coffee."

When he left the room, she collapsed into one of the chairs, which was much more comfortable than it looked. She had a sudden desire to curl up into a foetal position and to fall asleep within it, its sides shielding her from the outside world like a cotton cocoon. She'd barely slept the previous night worrying about Irena and the argument.

She still had her eyes closed when he returned.

"Here you go. This should help to stimulate the electrons." The coffee smelt divine, earthy and rich. It reminded her of something. What was it? The memory was just there at the front of her mind, but it refused to surface.

"Electrons?"

"Yes." He laughed. "I know it's not biologically accurate, but when I was younger I always visualised the human brain as a being formed of tiny particles – hundreds of thousands of them. When you were asleep they all lay neatly in rows, completely still. When you woke up, they would jiggle around a bit, but it was only when you were coming up with an incredible idea that they would be positively buzzing and jumping off the internal walls of your brain. I ended up calling them electrons because I liked the word when I heard it in a physics lesson."

She laughed – a belly laugh that seemed to come from the very depths of her insides.

"That's brilliant."

"Well, it'll be brilliant if we actually come up with something," he admitted. She noticed then that his eyelashes were remarkably blond, almost white. They were strangely in fitting with the interior of the room. The whole scene seemed ethereal somehow, as if the two of them had decided to take a voluntary break from reality.

"So tell me some of the most basic ideas that you've had about this website and I'll make a note of them," he instructed. Joanna noticed that he didn't have a pen or paper and wondered whether he planned to memorise everything that she said.

"Right, so we want it to be internationally relevant – so that it puts Polish news on the global map. There will be headline news of course, but also more interviews, feature pieces and in-depth reports on specific subjects."

"For example medical research? Like the discovery into the workings of the spinal cord? It's an incredible achievement, isn't it?" He looked at her, pleased with his recently acquired knowledge.

"Yes, yes of course, but also research in other areas – social research, for example, or historical."

Joanna continued to outline her vision for what the site would look like. From the moment that Marek had told her about it, she'd seen it as her own project, something that she would develop, run and grow over the years. She was of course realistic about the fact that Marek would need to sign off on everything, but she was confident that he would like her ideas. She was already strangely protective of the project.

She glanced up after talking for a considerable time and was shocked to see Oskar frantically scribbling her ideas on the walls using a thick red marker pen. To her far right he was beginning to draw out what looked like the potential homepage of the *Prawda* website.

"What are you doing?"

"I'm bringing your ideas to life. Well, not quite to life yet, but this is the first step. We've got the broad outline here and it's enough for me to be able to come back to you with some proposals. I'll run a stage site and you can then come back to me with changes that you want to make. No doubt you'll have quite a few."

"What's wrong with a pen and paper?" She felt immediately bad about her mocking question.

"Nothing," he grinned. "My father commissioned a weird interior designer to renovate this place and he came up with the idea of walls that you can write on. So we might as well make use of them… and it's a strangely pleasant sensation to write with these pens. Have you ever written with biro on a banana?"

"No."

"Well, it feels a bit like that. But try it – the banana I mean. It's good. The good thing about the walls is that if you change your mind about something you can rub it out and always have a working version."

"Right. I suppose…"

"So were you thinking you would have this behind a paywall or do you want it to be accessible to everyone?"

"Definitely to everyone. We want it to come up as high as possible in search rankings."

Her initial scepticism died away as they worked through the layout of different formats of news pages, spaces for digital advertising, biography boxes for the writers, decisions on colour schemes and various language options. He seemed to know exactly what questions to ask and many of them Joanna had to note down to think about, as she didn't have an immediate answer. She was wondering when she would have time to get different prospective advertisers on board when Oskar surprised her with a different query.

"Time for lunch?"

She glanced down at her watch. She had just spent three hours in a white box with a stranger. Although for some reason which she couldn't explain to herself, he didn't feel like a stranger. He appeared honest and simple – not in that he lacked intelligence (of which she could see he had plenty), but in the sense of being open to the world, presenting himself exactly as he was. She came across few people like him in her daily life.

"I didn't realise it was already that time," she muttered getting up.

"Will you let me get you something to eat to celebrate a good morning's work?"

The spidery sensation of panic appeared in her stomach but only for a moment. How many times had she refused at moments like this? She had felt a strong physical attraction to many of the men who had asked her, but she still declined because she was fearful that they would strip her of her independence. No, independence was the wrong word here. She was scared that they would force her to give up her search.

But this time seemed different. She had a sense that agreeing wouldn't signal the end of anything.

"Yes," she heard herself saying, "Yes. That sounds like a good plan."

Chapter 35 – Matty
London

He left the tube at Upton Park Station and made his way slowly down the road between the market stalls and the old council estate.

As he neared the West Ham football stadium, a sudden memory came to him of buying football shirts with Dan from a garden vendor. They were still there – the funny, rickety stalls set up in people's front gardens. He wondered whether these businesses were legal or whether the seemingly relaxed men manning the stands had a plan of action in place in case the police came snooping. He recalled watching a TV documentary in which an illegal street seller of ripped DVDs suddenly covered his stand with a thick plastic sheet onto which he'd pinned old clothes pretending that he was setting up an impromptu jumble sale.

For nostalgia's sake Matty stopped at one of the stands and bought a bag of cola bottle sweets. The sour sugar grated on his teeth and reminded him of the football matches of his childhood which he'd watched in the pouring rain, hood up, sticky sweets in his pocket, voice chords strained through screaming.

But then the memory morphed suddenly and unexpectedly into one of him running through a field kicking a ball, but not with Dan or any other of his school friends. He was with a girl of roughly his own age and as they ran together, she fell over – he could see her passing through the air before his eyes, her short legs wheeling frantically, before hitting the ground with a sickening thud. There had been blood, a lot of it. It had seeped from the pale skin of her knee in vast quantities, and she screamed with the unexpected pain of it, and then, for some reason unknown to him – for he was entirely injury free – he began to scream too. And they screamed together, as if they were one person, until someone came, a tall, comforting presence, and scooped them up, pulling them into safety.

His head reeled from the memory as he made his way slowly down one of the smaller side streets. Who was the girl? She was vital somehow, essential – and he stopped walking suddenly, as it to collect all of his energies into producing more of the memory. But there was nothing. He wanted to hurl his body against the brick wall in front of him with the frustration of it.

The closer he got to Helen's house, the more he was certain that she would no longer be there. When he turned into her road, a small man appeared in front of him pulling a canvas shopping trolley. Matty watched as he carefully stepped around the puddles on the pavement, his battered shoes performing a nifty dance.

As much as he dug in the depths of his memory, he couldn't conjure up the house number. It was a green door – that he knew for sure, but in the intervening years it could have been painted or replaced several times.

The man stopped so suddenly that Matty almost collided with him.

"Sorry," he muttered and shuffled past.

To his right was a series of almost identical houses, stretching down the entire length of the street. He almost burst out laughing. It would be impossible to select one from amongst them.

"Excuse me!" he shouted after the man, "Do you know Helen Reardon?"

The old man turned around mid-stride. He was wearing vari-focal lenses that had turned a murky brown in the sunlight. Matty couldn't see his eyes, but he felt the suspicious gaze.

"Why?" he asked after a pause.

"I'm… I'm her grandson."

The man doubled up coughing. He tried to lean on his trolley, but instead knocked it over, spilling the contents into the road.

Matty jumped to rescue a bag of oranges that had fallen onto the pavement. He carefully put the groceries back into the bag – a strange assortment of canned soups, spices and root vegetables.

"Are you alright?"

"She's number 37," the man said between coughs. Matty noticed the fear in his eyes.

"Thank you. Do you need a hand…?"

But the man had already waved him away and was trudging slowly up his garden path into the crumbling building.

He couldn't believe that Helen still lived there and he realised that he hadn't prepared himself for what he would do if he managed to locate her. The door into which the man had disappeared was number 31 which meant that she was only a few houses away. Now that he knew she was there for sure, he could always turn back and return later. He was surprised to note the crawl of anxiety at the base of his stomach. No, it was now or not at all.

He noticed with surprise that the front garden was well maintained. A pale cream rose bush blossomed on the left of the path and ivy in different shades of green surrounded the living room window. Apart from the front door, which had been painted a more demure shade of brown, the house looked very much as he remembered it. He realised that he was holding his breath as he rang the doorbell.

Time passed and there was no sound from inside. She wasn't home. But then suddenly – a low murmur followed by a sneeze. The door swung open. An echo rang in his ears.

"Yes?"

She was tiny, so much smaller than he had remembered, so raisin-like. Her wrinkles etched miniature rivers into her face and her hands shook. She had on a woollen dress up to the knee and lacquered shoes with a slight heel. He almost laughed when he saw them. They were the sorts of shoes that children wore. The pink lipstick was applied haphazardly as before, and smudged at the corners.

"Hello."

"Matty?"

She'd remembered.

"Yes. I… I came to see you about something important," he said, readjusting his glasses.

"So I see. Come in." Her lips exposed a set of brilliant white teeth, a little too perfect.

He followed her through the narrow hallway into the kitchen and he could see straight away that nothing there had changed at all. The red hooks were still there in the ceiling, supporting the vast assortment of various pots and pans. The eccentric table with the multi-coloured legs stood, as it had for years before in the centre of the room. He remembered drawing it as a child, carefully selecting the right colour of crayon for each of the legs Only the white paint on the kitchen window was slightly chipped and peeling.

"Tea? Coffee? Or cocoa?" she asked, winking at him, "Do you still drink it at your age? You used to love it."

He hadn't. Not since he'd last been here.

"I'll have a cocoa, thanks."

She bustled around the kitchen, taking things out of cupboards, filling the kettle. He watched as she scratched her head and was shocked to see that it moved ever so slightly. A wig. He should have guessed. The grey strands were arranged too perfectly for it to be real hair.

"How have you been?" he asked. The awkwardness had vanished in an instant and he felt blissfully comfortable. It was like coming home.

"In truth, a bit lonely," she said, "but I can't complain. At my age I'm still in good health and I can walk on my own two feet. I know quite a few people who can't. And you Matty? Good job? Married?" It was as if no time had passed between them at all.

"Well… job is OK, not great but pays well. I'm not married. In fact I'm single – it's only a recent development."

"Ah, well never mind. You're ever so young," she said, lightly touching his shoulder, as if to verify that he was truly there.

He could almost see the shadow of his younger self, sitting at the table as she bustled around the kitchen boiling the milk on the old gas stove and then carefully mixing the brown, sweet smelling powder into it, until it all dissolved into a blend of liquid goodness.

"You have your whole life still ahead of you," she said, smiling at him reassuringly. There was nothing but kindness about her. No anger, no admonitions about why he hadn't come to visit for so long. "Everything will change. At your age things are in constant flux, I know it better than anyone. They're still in flux for me now if you can believe that. And… your mother?"

He wondered how soon the question would come.

"She's the same, you know. She still works at the agency, still lives in the same place."

"Ah." She placed the steaming mug in front of him. It had a pattern of multi-coloured Easter eggs on it. She sat opposite him and sipped from a dainty teacup with a chipped saucer.

"I've missed coming here. I'm sorry…" he muttered.

A sunbeam came through the window illuminating the motes of dust spinning in the air between them.

"I've missed you too, Matty," she said after a pause. "What made you come here today?"

He considered lying and saying that it was because he felt bad about not seeing her all these years that he wanted to rebuild their relationship after years of neglect, but he knew that she would see through it in an instant. She was sharp and witty, and he felt ridiculous even considering telling her anything but the truth.

"I was hoping that you would help me discover some things about myself."

Later, looking back on the moment, he would be sure that he saw a flicker of fear in her eyes, but she remained calm, her expression much the same as before.

"What sort of things?"

Matty began by telling her about the school reports followed by his visit to see Mrs. Henderson. He omitted the part about secretly going through the documents in Celia's room as he feared his grandmother's reaction to his stealthy behaviour, but he explained his reason for seeing Stefania and eventually he got onto his visit to the photography studio. Here, he had to stop several times, as his voice shook so badly that he could barely get his words out.

Throughout the explanation, Helen's grey eyes increasingly widened and her manicured fingernails tapped out a steady rhythm on the wooden table top.

"I just thought that you might know more. You were there when I was adopted, right? Can you tell me anything that would help me to track down my real parents?"

She laughed then, a hollow, humourless, disbelieving laugh.

"You don't realise what you're asking, do you?" She took a calm sip of her coffee, her wrinkled little finger sticking up in the air.

"What do you mean?"

"Your mother doesn't know that you've come to see me?"

"No."

"Ah. I thought she wouldn't. Matty, I… I shouldn't say anything more on that subject. I've been told all too clearly that it's not my place to do so. What has happened, has happened. I've learnt to accept that. And you have come away more or less unscathed."

She seemed to be observing him closely, watching his every minute movement. A dull, sickening anxiety began to build in the pit of his stomach.

"What do you mean you've been told? Who told you?"

"Matty, why do you think your mother and I don't speak?" She peered at him curiously."

"Because… I don't know. Something to do with money. I've never asked and she never went into detail."

"Money? Pssh… I have more money than I know what to do with. I still get royalties from Jack's books you know. Besides, I would never take your mother's money. I'm not materialistic enough. What more do I need in life?" she asked, spreading her arms wide. "You didn't really believe that it was the real reason?"

It was ridiculous of course, now that he thought about it.

"I never knew what to believe."

"Matty," she said, looking straight at him with defiance. She was angry now – he could tell by the vein that stood out on her wrinkled neck. "We stopped talking because I found out something that she didn't want me or anyone to know. It was a complete accident but it changed everything. I questioned her and she pushed me away, accused me of trying to turn you against her."

"So this was something to do with me?"

She pursed her lips. All of a sudden he remembered that same expression from when he stayed here when he was small, in the half term holidays when Celia was working. The expression implied that Helen was quietly debating something.

"I won't tell her," he muttered quickly, "We don't have that good a relationship." He was about to add 'any more' but he realised that their relationship could never have been called a good one. Clearly Helen was aware of that.

"When I still worked at the theatre, there was a young actress called Esme," Helen began, "a beautiful girl – dark hair, amber eyes, face like an absolute doll. She was in her mid-thirties and she'd fallen in love with a woman. It took her by surprise she said, as she'd always been attracted to men and there had been reams of them over the years, queueing up outside the green room door after her shows. But she had met this set designer called Rachel and it was as though nobody had ever measured up. She invited me to their civil ceremony and it was a beautiful affair. You could tell they were very much in love. Anyway, one day as I was fitting her costume for the summer performance of *Measure for Measure*, she told me that she and her partner were thinking of adopting a child. 'Ah' I said. 'Now that's something I know a bit about. My daughter adopted my grandson.' She asked me how Celia had gone about it and I promised to look into it for her."

He could sense what was coming. Somewhere in the murky depths of his consciousness, he had known it all along.

"And you asked Celia?"

"Yes. She wouldn't tell me; she fobbed me off."

"So what did you do? Did you contact the adoption centre?"

"Yes. Not just the adoption centre, but the children's home, the social services… The more I found out, the more desperate I became in my search."

"You didn't find anything." It was a statement rather than a question. He already knew the answer.

"I didn't find anything. There was no record of you ever having been adopted, no record of the adoption agency that Celia named ever existing."

"So what did you do?"

"I confronted her about it, of course. I told her to come here because I didn't want you to be a witness to our conversation. She told me that she'd given me the name of a false agency because she 'knew that I would meddle'. She wouldn't reveal the name of the real one. The more insistent I got, the more furious she grew. Her cheeks developed this patchy redness. She always had the same reaction when she was a little girl and I would discover that she'd stolen some sweets or lied about something insignificant."

Helen's fingers shook but her voice was steady. Matty had a sudden urge to hug her, to grip her tightly in his arms and thank her.

"When I demanded the truth, she banned me from speaking to you. She said that she would contact the police if I did. We haven't spoken to each other since."

"What else did you find out?"

"Nothing. Absolutely nothing, Matty. The rest is supposition."

"What about the first child that Jules from the photography studio told me about?"

Helen's shoulders sagged and for a brief moment, he thought she was about to cry. But she merely cleared her throat and continued.

"Yes, she took the death very badly. Very, very badly. Celia had always been vulnerable as a child, but this was different.

She was withdrawn, lethargic. She took a good few months off work – prolonged sick leave. She started mixing with some strange people who she met at the pub and Claudio had enough of it and left. Then she met Cal."

"Cal?"

"Yes, a very strange man. He'd served a prison sentence for petty theft. I thought he was a very suspicious character from the first time I met him. Anyway, he was paranoid that the police were onto him for some other crimes and he persuaded Celia to pack in her job and go travelling for a few months. He told her he knew people in Sweden and Denmark."

"And Poland?"

"I don't know Matty… perhaps Poland too. My knowledge ends there I'm afraid."

They sat together in silence for a few minutes. The information seeped through Matty's pores. It was fragmented, unclear, but it was more than he had ever known.

"What happened to Cal?"

"Oh they came back when Celia's money ran out and then he left her of course, soon after she adopted you. But by then, her spirits lifted."

"I was a replacement?"

"Yes." She said it without a hint of apology.

"What do you think really happened?"

"I honestly don't know, Matty. For all I know, Celia might be telling the truth. She could well have adopted you through another legitimate route that she doesn't want to tell me about. But why?"

"Or equally it could have been illegitimate."

"Yes. But there's no evidence. You understand, I couldn't have turned my daughter into the police without any evidence. Besides, she wasn't mistreating you. You were fed, clothed, doing well in school. I bit my tongue and accepted the status quo. I'm sorry – perhaps it was the wrong thing to do."

There was a faint trace of wetness in her grey eyes.

"I would have done the same," Matty admitted and held her bony hand, like a withered bird's claw nervously clutching onto the side of the table.

Chapter 36 – Tom
Chicago

When he'd first arrived in America, that long-awaited land of promise, Tom was amazed at the novelty of accumulating wealth. As a young man living under a very different regime, he had toiled long hours, but always for the same pitiful money – just enough to live on but nothing more. On occasion, if he put in days of overtime as a favour to his boss, he might have been given a couple more clothing tokens than his usual allowance – but even that had to be arranged in secret so that nobody would be accused of any underhand, capitalist leanings.

But in his new home, the rules were overwhelmingly different. It turned out that the harder Tom worked and the more hours he put in, the more money he was given. Sometimes it wasn't even a linear equation, because apparently overtime warranted a higher hourly rate. So for somebody like Tom, who'd had hard work bred into them, there was a genuine chance of bettering yourself, and he grabbed this chance tightly in both fists.

Of course, he'd gotten off to a slow start, but once he'd become established in the dealership, his bank balance continued to steadily rise. Over the decades, he'd accumulated more money than he could ever imagine having as a young man. Even his final bill at *Sunshine* would barely make a dent in the stash that he had squirrelled away. He felt suddenly embarrassed by the enormity of his fortune. Because this was really the mass total of his accomplishments, the mass total of *him*. Other people had family, they had relationships, they had circles of friends and concerned acquaintances, where he had nothing but cold, hard cash. It wasn't much to show for a life. He needed to do something.

On Saturday morning, Mitch and Sally took him to his home in Cardinal Drive for the day, to sort through the belongings that he hadn't had a chance to deal with before his move to *Sunshine*.

"We can do it for you," Sally had protested a week earlier when she'd seen him. "I can sort through everything and then give you a report of what I'd done."

"I want to be there," he'd protested gently, and then, when it looked as if she wouldn't change her mind, he pleaded, "Come on, let me – for the last time."

And they'd taken him in the end, although he needed to use a wheelchair because he was too weak that day to walk even the short distance to the car.

It was a strange feeling being back in his old living room, which, to all intents and purposes, looked exactly the same as it had done when he left it. The place had all been aired and Sally had clearly done some cleaning, because there was not a speck of dust in sight. She'd even tidied away his books and cleared the condiments from the kitchen table so that the house had a showroom feel about it and, if he were honest with himself, this is what it would soon become. After his belongings had been tidied, boxed up and given away, the house would become a home for somebody new – another retired couple or a young family with children. Mitch and Sally would have new neighbours, and he would most likely be gone.

But Tom had a plan. He had been thinking about it constantly for the past week. And it helped that Sally was in the right profession to help him. He approached her when Mitch was in the midst of carrying boxes of books into the removal van to take to The Salvation Army Centre.

"Sally – I have a question for you. I would like to rewrite my will. Could you help me?"

"Oh?" Strangely, she wasn't surprised. Perhaps she thought that he was planning to leave some of his money to *Sunshine*. At present, his will left a few of his more valuable pieces of furniture, first edition books and paintings to Mitch and Sally, and his house and savings to a selection of charities which had helped him when he'd first moved to the States and at times didn't have enough money to eat.

Sally, who had worked for many years in a top law firm in the city, agreed to arrange a quick appointment for him with one of her former colleagues.

"He's very good," she assured him, "I should know, because I trained him." Neither she nor Mitch asked him any questions and he could have easily returned to *Sunshine* having divulged nothing else, but his revelation to Clara had moved something in him, and he resolved that he wouldn't leave his best friends without having shared the truth with them.

And that is exactly what he did. They reacted with shock and some concern, but ultimately their treatment of him didn't change. They both hugged him closely when he'd finished and they offered their help outside of arranging the changes to the will.

"Thank you," he'd muttered with disbelief at their generosity, "but other than that I'm alright. I have a friend who is helping me with my search."

***

The trouble was that when he returned to *Sunshine*, Dustin wasn't there. He wasn't around at dinner and he failed to show up in the lounge after breakfast the following day. Tom's concern for him grew and he eventually resolved to go and check in on him.

The sight that met him was worrying to say the least. He found the remains of Dustin's breakfast still on the bedside table, and his friend lying on his side under the thick duvet. The curtains were still drawn even though it was almost 10 o'clock, and there was a strange, musty smell that hung between the four walls – the acrid stench of sweat mixed with something medicinal.

Tom dared to pull back the curtain slightly to allow in a small beam of light inside, and he sat down heavily in the armchair.

He breathed in deeply. Five heavy breaths in and five heavy breaths out. It was the strategy that his mother had taught him when he had become panicky as a child. Usually, it was before an exam at school or a situation in which he would be faced with a large crowd of people with whom he would be expected to speak. The breathing helped to clear his head and enabled him to push his intrusive thoughts away. Because recently, Tom had become frightened of death. It was a sudden and all-consuming fear that eked into every crevice of his body, causing a dull, persistent ache.

It arrived, unannounced, quite suddenly. But, if he were honest with himself, he knew the reason behind its arrival. Before he'd come to *Sunshine*, before he'd met Dustin, his greatest annoyance stemmed from the fact that cancer had stolen his retirement. Everything else that mattered was carefully stored away in that compartment of his memory which became more hermetically sealed with every year that passed. That was of course, until he'd arrived here and everything changed, until Clara and Dustin made him realise that maybe, just maybe, he wasn't too late.

"I can see you, you know. Sitting there quietly fretting."

Tom couldn't help but burst out laughing.

"How long have you been awake?"

"All the time that you've sat there. I like observing people when they don't realise that they're being observed."

"And what did you notice about me?"

"Well, I've been lying here trying to figure it out. On the one hand you seem quite excited about something – I can tell by your eyes – but on the other hand you're fretting."

He was shocked by the accuracy of Dustin's analysis.

"I'm fretting because of you… because of your state," he explained, honestly.

"*I'm* not," he said honestly, struggling to lift himself up by his elbows. Tom rushed over to help him arrange his cushions. A horrible, hacking cough broke through his body causing him to momentarily double over with the strain. "We both knew that it was going to happen, didn't we? We just didn't realise that it would be so soon."

His voice was measured, calm.

"I'm sorry…"

"You shouldn't be," he said, winking at him, "It's just annoying that I might not be able to see you finish what you started. And I had another clue that I haven't been able to investigate."

"You don't have to worry about that anymore," said Tom gently, "It's my problem and you should be focussing on yourself and your family."

"It's kept me going these past couple of weeks. It gave me purpose like nothing has in such a long time. Here, take this," he muttered, handing Tom a Post-it note attached to the glass that lined his bedside table."

Tom picked up the note. There was only one word written on it in barely legible handwriting: '*Prawda*'.

"It means truth in Polish," he said to Dustin, "Why is it a clue?" He was beginning to think that his friend was either beginning to lose his mind, or was trying to convey some sort of deeper message to him. But it seemed not to be the case.

"Does it? I didn't know that," Dustin admitted, "I didn't think to look it up. It's the name of a newspaper, or a magazine, or maybe even some sort of online news portal. Anyway, her name is all over it."

"Are you serious?" The stir of excitement that had begun in the pit of his stomach over the last couple of days and which he had attempted to suppress as a means of self-preservation, now burst its banks. He told Dustin about his call to Joanna's university professor, which he'd eventually persuaded himself to make the previous day. He had been entirely honest. The professor was still a young man and he sounded kind. On Tom's request, he had described Joanna's appearance and character:

"Tall, dark wavy hair, large blue eyes. She was always quiet – never spoke in any of my lectures – but she was near top if not top in the year. Her writing was outstanding and she had a confidence about her when she spoke about subjects that mattered to her. I'm sure she's going to go on to have an outstanding career."

It wasn't much of a description, but it had been enough to convince Tom that this was his daughter and he bathed in pride at the compliments that the professor paid her. Unfortunately, the man knew only of the local paper that she'd worked on immediately after leaving university, and he was certain that she'd moved on from there after her six month placement had ended.

"I was about to start searching all publications headquartered in Warsaw," Tom explained to Dustin, "but it seems that I might not need to now." He folded the Post-it note happily.

"Promise me that you'll finish it," said Dustin suddenly. "Promise me that you will. That you won't allow yourself to be stopped by fear at the last hurdle."

He was looking at him with an intensity and seriousness that was so out of character, that Tom felt immediately anxious.

"You'll be around to see me do it," he insisted, but as the words escaped his mouth, he realised that even he didn't believe it.

"Can you ask one of the nurses if you can borrow a laptop?" Dustin asked, ignoring him. "Then we can have a look at this together? You can sit here," he said, patting the edge of the bed, and you can search yourself. If you get stuck I'll tell you what to do.

Tom shuffled out of the room immediately in search of Clara.

"She's sorting out the deliveries," said Maria, when he poked his head round the door of the office. He explained to her what he was after, and managed to get one surprisingly swiftly.

Maria pulled a stack of them from a small locker behind her desk.

"We have quite a few of them. Nobody seems to want to use them anymore. They prefer the desktops. It might be because of the WiFi. I must warn you that it's pretty bad. It cuts out quite a lot in the lounge, but you might be better off if you're in one of the bedrooms."

He carried the device carefully into Dustin's room. They had used laptops all the time at the dealership. All of the information about the models of the cars, the sales figures and accounts, were held in these frighteningly small and flat boxes of plastic, metal and wire. For some reason, Tom was convinced that they weren't reliable and he would keep his own handwritten paper copies of all the most important records carefully stowed away in files within his desk drawer.

"How many hours do you spend doing this?" asked one of his store managers. As Tom was his boss and superior, he addressed him with respect, but there was an unmistakable note of incredulity in his voice.

"Not that long," Tom had lied, "And it's vital that we keep this information safe. It can't be trusted on those," he would say, motioning towards the laptops.

The air whistled in the store manager's nose as he breathed in deeply.

"But it's all backed up," he would tell Tom. "Even if the whole building burned down, complete with all the laptops, and all your paper, we would still have the information."

"How?" asked Tom, not comprehending. The thought of a fire was enough to make him break out in a sweat.

"It's all online. It exists in the ether."

To this day, Tom couldn't get his head around this. He couldn't understand how billions of articles and pages of information could exist in the invisible "ether", and that humans had been powerful enough to develop it. If they had, surely they could also find a cure for Dustin, or for him? When would the day come that civilisation would have come far enough that disease would have been eliminated? It wasn't for him to experience. But he marvelled at the fact that he could still benefit from the wonders of the internet.

Dustin had shuffled himself over to the right-hand side of the bed, making a space for him. He sat down next to his friend, still feeling the warmth of his body on the mattress.

"OK, go to Google and type in *Prawda Joanna Malicka*. We'll go from there."

Chapter 37 – Joanna
Warsaw

www.prawda-mag.pl

All that remains

Joanna Malicka speaks to the families of some of the highest profile cases of missing people in Poland.

"All that remained of him were the photos and the spreading emptiness in our little flat," says Marta Gierska, the mother of Roman, who went missing at the Legia stadium aged 11. She considers herself one of the lucky minority of parents whose children were found, despite being registered as missing for more than 18 months.

Every year, there are over 15,000 cases of missing people across Poland. Common reasons for disappearance are physical or mental illness, reactions to domestic or work-related pressures and abduction. Around a third of cases are linked to some form of criminal activity.

Adam

Only 1% of those annually registered missing are children under the age of five. Adam Malicki, whose case was opened on 1st May 1988, falls into this category. He disappeared during a protest march in Warsaw which he attended with his mother and sister, and he was last seen in the area immediately around Central Station wearing a short-sleeved shirt, blue dungarees and brown lace-up boots. He was aged four and was just under a metre tall.

Adam's mother initially believed that her son had just got lost in the crowds. She insisted that he knew his address by heart and would be able to make his way home from the station. But 24 hours later, there was still no sign of the boy. Within the week immediately following his disappearance, the police search was broadened to cover all parts of the capital, and witness statements were taken from Adam's family, friends and members of the public who had participated in the protest.

Initially, a number of false leads offered hope to the family, but it was soon established that none of the people questioned had actually witnessed Adam's disappearance. His sister was the last to see him, as he ran into the crowd holding a red and white flag. His case remained open for another five years.

Sergeant Lasko who oversaw the investigation believed that the boy may have been mistaken for the child of one of the protest leaders, Mr. Minski, and for this reason could have been kidnapped by a member of the opposition. No evidence supported this however, and the four year difference in age between the two boys rendered the theory unlikely.

Artists' portraits of Adam as he was likely to have looked with each passing year appeared in the local Warsaw press on the anniversary of his disappearance, until the search was officially declared closed in March 1993. To this day, Adam has not been found.

His mother, Monika Malicka suffered a nervous breakdown following his disappearance, and has never fully recovered. Adam's sister recently uncovered footage taken by an amateur journalist during the process, in which there is a clear recording of another child speaking to a relative about the boy being led away, supporting the case for kidnapping.

Izabela

"We'd had an argument that morning," explains Izabela Owsiak's father, "It was stupid. She wanted to go on holiday and we just didn't have the money. I thought she was just going into the yard to play, but she never came back. Izabela had just turned nine when she was reported missing.

To read the article in full, please <click to expand.>

If you have any information to share about the cases included in the above article, please <contact us>.

He'd put it up and there it was – the lead article. Unable to decide about whether or not to post it, she asked Oskar to do it for her. She had left the decision in the hands of somebody who she'd known for barely a couple of months.

"It's an excellent piece of writing and it makes absolute sense for it to go up. And aside from your mother, you're Adam's closest living relative. If you say that your mother isn't in a position to make any decisions then the choice is ultimately yours.

"But that's the thing… I don't know what I want. I can't make these sorts of decisions myself. I just wish that somebody would choose for me."

So Oskar made the decision for her. And that was that. Within a week, the article had received more than three thousand comments.

Chapter 38 – Matty
London

"Hi."

"Hi. Come in." She grinned at him and he instantly felt the muscles in his shoulders ease up. He noticed with surprise and relief that she looked, on the whole, quite normal. He'd been half-expecting her to have the washed-out look of somebody who had lain in bed crying for the past week.

"I've missed you," she said eventually, "but not in the way that you'd think. In a good way."

"In a good way?"

She gave him an awkward hug. Her arms felt cold to the touch.

"I'm sorry," he mumbled and stood awkwardly beside her, neither of them wanting to make the first move from the corridor to the living room.

"What for? You didn't do anything wrong. I mean, it's not like you cheated or anything." She let out a forced laugh.

"No, but I wasn't…"

"We weren't right, it just took us a while to realise it. And that's fine, you know." She shrugged her shoulders in an exaggerated way and finally walked into the bedroom. She sat down on the bed that had so recently belonged to both of them and surveyed the surroundings. Nothing had changed, apart from her clothes which now lay in a heap ready for her to bag up and take away.

"You're not upset?"

"Of course I am, aren't you?"

"Yes," he answered truthfully.

"But we're not devastated and that's probably more of a sign than anything. Do you want to hear something that will make you laugh? The kids in my Year 2 class told me today that they thought I was seventeen. When I told them I was nearly twenty-seven, they said it was impossible because I didn't look so very old. So there you go. They've told me I'm still young enough to get on with it."

He could feel himself smiling.

"I'll grab my stuff. I have the car parked on double yellows outside. I'll make sure I transfer this month's rent to you as soon as I get paid."

"Ellie?"

It was so easy. He couldn't believe the suddenness of it all.

"Wait… what will you do?"

She shrugged and smiled at him again, a genuine, warm smile.

"I'll move in with mum for a bit. It'll give me a chance to save up some money and maybe eventually get my own place. And it's good that the school holidays are coming round the corner. I'm thinking of going to Italy – maybe to a language school for a month. And after that, you'll find out because I'll be in touch. I'm not ready to cut you out completely."

He was helping her to lift the suitcase that he'd carefully filled with all of her clothes the previous night, when the doorbell rang.

"It's open."

His stomach lurched. Celia stood in the open doorway looking so unlike her usual self that it took him a few seconds to realise who she was. She was wearing a pair of jogging bottoms and what looked like a pyjama top beneath a long mac which she had neglected to fasten up. It flapped around her like a winged animal. Matty realised with a start that it was possibly the first time that he had seen her without make up.

Ellie dropped the suitcase she'd just finished packing and it fell to the floor with an echoing thud.

"Mrs. Reardon, are you OK? What's happened?"

Celia ignored her, her eyes boring into Matty. He realised instantly that she knew.

"The documents. Where are they?" Her voice was so throaty and quiet that he could barely make out the meaning of her words.

"Which documents?" He'd been expecting a question about him visiting Helen.

Celia shuffled into the kitchen and perched on the edge of one of the seats, cowering like a wounded animal.

"Your papers and photos and Matty's…"

Ellie looked at her confused. "What do you mean?" But he understood her meaning exactly.

"You mean the other Matty… the first Matty?" His voice was hollow. It was as if it belonged to somebody else.

Celia looked at him with befuddled shock. She clearly hadn't expected him to figure out the identity of the boy in the photo.

Her arms dropped to her sides and for a long time neither of them spoke. Matty found that he couldn't hold her gaze.

"I wasn't feeling very well," she whispered eventually. "I wasn't well at all. It was a terrible tragedy – you must understand that."

"What was?" asked Ellie.

Celia looked at her bewildered, as if she'd already forgotten her presence.

And then her tinny voice reached him through the veil of fury that was mounting inside him, slowly, but steadily: "I'm sorry. I'm so sorry… He was so frail and small… only three. Children are not meant to suffer like this."

She leant against the doorway and stared fixedly at the opposing wall. "He had a cough and such a dreadful rash. It spread all over him very quickly. I thought at first that it was just my vision – that the spots were appearing before my eyes. I got him to the hospital and he was getting better; I really thought he was," she drew in a deep breath, "but he was so run down that he caught a hospital virus. He was still there one minute in this deep fever, and then… and then…"

"What are you talking about? I'm afraid I don't… I don't understand," said Ellie, her expression panicked.

"He persuaded me to do it. He took me away on holiday, 'to help me forget', he said. I could tell how fed up he was with me being so tired constantly and so low. So this would be a new start for us. But I didn't feel better when I was away, and everywhere I went I seemed to see my little boy. It was in Warsaw that he did it. I was in the hotel, asleep and he brought you back," she said. "And you were in tears and I was going to take you back. I *was*. I really was. And then he persuaded me. He said that the world was continuing to take and take from me and I got nothing back, so why shouldn't I take something too? Why shouldn't I take? After all everyone else seems to. Everyone…"

There were thick, bulbous tears falling down her cheeks as her body slid to the floor.

"You should have given me back!" He wasn't sure when he'd moved across the room to speak to her, but he was so close now that he could hear her heavy breathing. She stared up at him and flinched, as if cowering from the gaze of an abuser. She opened her mouth several times, wanting to say something, but then shut it again helplessly. The minutes stretched out in a painful silence as the anger fired up in his loins. It was an emotion unlike anything that he had ever felt.

It filled him completely, pressing out from the inside, coiling round his organs like a snake, refusing to let go.

Before he knew what he was doing, he grabbed Celia's wrists and held them by her face. Her body tensed and froze, only her hands shuddered in his grip. He could feel the fast rhythmic pulse. The mask that she had so firmly held in place over the years was torn off, exposing the frail and soiled being beneath.

"You're not to leave this place, until you tell me the absolute truth, DO YOU UNDERSTAND?" The words were spitting out of his mouth, rushing off his tongue in angry waves, "There will be no more fakery, no more question-dodging, no more manipulative, bloody guilt-tripping."

"Matty, stop it! Calm down. Sit down and talk…" Ellie begged, but he pushed her aside.

He noticed that a red welt had appeared on Celia's wrist where he had grabbed her, and he loosened his hold slightly, shocked at his own force.

"I'm so sorry," she whispered. "I'm so sorry. He convinced me that it was fair."

"Fair? Don't ever say that again." He could hear the cracking in his voice. Something awful, unthinkable would happen if he didn't get what he wanted. "I'm going to ask you some simple questions and I want simple answers. It's the very least that you can give me, after everything."

She didn't react, but he carried on.

"Who did he take me from? Who were… who *are* my family?"

But she was shaking her head. "I don't know, Matty. I honestly don't know. I don't think even he knew. He just took you and brought you to me. At first you resisted me. It took weeks to gain your trust, but one day, when we had come home you… you eventually took my hand and looked up and something important passed between us, an understanding."

"You just took me? You took me just like that – away from my real mother, my family?"

She winced then.

"I am your real mother, Matty. I've brought you up. I've been there for you. Haven't I been good to you over the years? Haven't I been good? I've always treated you well, even though at times it wasn't easy. It wasn't easy at all at first…"

The nausea was rising through his stomach, but he needed to know. He needed to hear it all.

"Did they ever look for me?"

"Who?"

"My family. Did they ever look for me?"

"No," she Celia, staring straight at him. Their eyes locked and he could see that she wasn't lying. And there was something else in her stare. A defiance. *They didn't care enough about you to look*, her eyes seemed to say.

It was too much then, far too much.

"Who am I?" he screamed at her.

But she only smiled, a vague, fleeting smile which made him want to punch her in the face with his full force.

And then there was no emotion anymore, because he could contain it no longer. He leaned over the kitchen sink and was violently sick.

Chapter 39 – Tom
Chicago

Dustin died peacefully on a particularly hot July Wednesday, when the sunflowers in the front yard were not only in full bloom, but so open that they were beginning to lose their petals. No amount of expectation could have prepared Tom for the overwhelming sense of loss. He felt this loss selfishly, as if this new found part of himself that Dustin had uncovered was being slowly, and painfully ripped away from him, like the sticky plaster on a wound which had just begun to scab over. But the pain only strengthened his resolve that he would fulfil his promise to his newest, but at the same time, closest friend.

He chose not to go to the funeral, but instead he sat on the bench by the table at which he'd first seen Dustin, and he soaked up the sun's rays, opting for this private way of remembering him. He looked over the fields surrounding his home shimmering yellow with rapeseed in full bloom and in the distance, the landscape of high rises, beyond which he knew were the waters of Lake Michigan, and his past life, the life of self-imposed forgetting. There lay the years of aggressive car sales, the drinking, the forced camaraderie with people who were good to him, but with whom he actually had very little in common. His real life, his true self, lay far beyond that barely visible slice of the city, past Indiana, Ohio and West Virginia, past the unrelenting North Atlantic Ocean on a very different stretch of land that he felt, at the same time, remote from, and so close that he could almost sense it beneath his feet as he closed his eyes.

That morning, Dustin's three children had come to *Sunshine*, either to pay the last bills and collect their father's belongings, or to invite the nursing staff to attend the funeral. Tom observed them closely as they waited for a taxi to pull up outside of the front entrance to the clinic, two women and a man. They looked as if they were all in their early to mid-thirties. Too young to lose a parent. The son looked very much like Dustin – he had exactly the same colouring and similarly bad posture. In fact, they were so alike that Tom almost expected him to come over, slap him on the back and invite him and Kyle for an impromptu game of poker.

The three of them, huddled together on the porch made him think of his own children. Was there anything of him in them? Dark hair and eyes? Fine, long, painter's fingers? Workaholic tendencies? A penchant for alcohol? A deep-rooted self-criticism? Tom had expertly pushed questions like these aside throughout the years, but the image that he'd begun to form of Joanna and Adam over the past few weeks refused to give him any peace. And the question of his son's whereabouts loomed particularly large in his mind ever since his discovery the previous week.

All that remains. He'd first come across on Monday when he was alone in bed with the laptop. His heart bolted when he realised it was one of his daughter's articles. The title made him expect a report on missing and reunited relatives – a news feature that interested him due to the tiniest, most unlikely possibility that Joanna could have known about *him*. But he soon realised the impossibility of it, and carried on reading through pure enjoyment of his daughter's writing which flowed beautifully and exuded both confidence and compassion. The pride that he felt was unlike anything he'd ever experienced.

The first case study was of a missing boy, who'd disappeared during the Solidarity protests in the 1989. It took Tom a few moments to register the child's name and then the knot of panic tightened its grasp on his stomach. He closed his eyes and began to count backwards. His fingers shook on top of the duvet. It could have been somebody with exactly the same name as his boy, but he knew almost immediately that it wasn't. It was *his* Adam who had gone missing just over a year after Tom had disappeared himself, suddenly, inexplicably, surrounded by people. Like his father, he had vanished in plain sight, and the tragic irony of this struck Tom with a sudden and unexpected force. It was as if fate had conspired to make his family continue to suffer after his own wrongdoing.

His thoughts flew to Monika. How would she have dealt with losing first him and then Adam? She would have fallen apart. She was already half-broken when her family was whole. The guilt flooded him, but it strengthened his resolve.

And here he was, ready to be jolted into action when the time came. He looked at his watch. Less than two hours remained until the offices of *Prawda* would open. He had checked the time difference twice just to be certain. He hadn't prepared at all what he would say because every time he forced his brain into thinking about it, into formulating a prospective script, he found that something within him shut down. He could almost visualise the protective iron wall coming up, shielding the most vulnerable parts of him from the piercing pain that would inevitably come with exposure.

He breathed in deeply to steady the hammering of his heart and clasped his hands tightly together on his lap to prevent them from shaking.

And then unexpectedly a warm arm curled itself around his shoulder.

"I'm sorry," Clara whispered, "I'm so sorry."

He turned to her, confused as to what she was apologising for, and then he saw her black tailored dress ready for the funeral. She looked calm and beautiful, as always.

"We knew it was coming – and I for one see death approaching so many times," she told him, "But when it does happen to someone you'd grown to love so much, it never makes it any easier."

"No. It doesn't."

"You know, next week will be six years since I've started working here. I clearly remember the death of the first patient that I was caring for."

"Who was it?"

"It was an old Asian lady. Her name was Mrs. Sohta. Dilpreet Sohta. She was in her late seventies and she had a brain tumour. By the end, her doctor told me that the headaches must have been excruciating, but she only ever asked for the most minimal pain relief. And what was most inspiring about her was the fact that she was always smiling, always in a cheerful mood. She had trained as one of the first female pilots in India and had seen so much of the world. I was embarrassed to admit that I hadn't even heard of some of the countries that she'd been to. Yemen, Turkmenistan, Bhutan…

"'It's unlike anything else,' she would say, 'the moment that you're sitting there in the cockpit ready for take-off. It's freedom – that's the best way to describe it – an enormous, wide, all-consuming freedom. I would give anything to sit in that space again.'

She didn't. Later, after I got the news, I drove out into the small military airfield just north of here, and I stood, leaning against the car and watching the planes take off. And I somehow imagined that was where she was now, soaring through space, the air carrying her weightlessly somewhere, to wherever she wanted to be."

He imagined Dustin. What would Dustin be doing in his version of the afterlife? Challenging the archangels to a game of poker, no doubt. Maybe staring down at him, haunting him until he fulfilled his promise. The vision made him smile.

"I'm going to contact my daughter today," he told her, suddenly. He felt the need to voice his plan, so that he wouldn't be able to back out, he wouldn't be halted by fear.

"Really? What are you going to tell her?"

"The truth. You know… I read an article that she wrote about missing people, and Adam was among them."

"Your son?" she said, and her eyes widened.

"Yes. He went missing during a protest in 1988. He hasn't been found. I need to speak to her… about her, and of course, about him too. I can't imagine what she and her mother would have been through."

"It must have been terrible." Clara looked at him, concern on her face. "Do you think that you should just call her yourself and announce everything from the outset?"

"I don't know. Probably not," he admitted. "But I have no other way. And not much time."

She took her hand away from his shoulder then and stared into the distance, thinking.

"I could do it for you, if you like," she offered after a pause. "I could contact her and gently explain the situation. It might be better coming from me, you know. It would be less of a shock to her, I think."

He was taken aback by this. And then Clara took his hand and squeezed it, and he knew that she was doing it mainly because she could see the monster of fear hidden behind his eyes, and she could also tell how hugely he wanted this to work – he yearned for it more than anything that he had yearned for in his life. And he loved her for noticing this and for offering to do it on his behalf without him even having to ask. He trusted her entirely and completely.

"You would do that for me?" he made sure.

"Of course. I can't promise anything, Tom. You understand that? But I will tread carefully, and I will do my very best."

He handed her the slip of paper with *Prawda*'s details. He noticed with embarrassment that it was sodden, and that the sweat from his hands had made some of the ink run, but Clara just folded it wordlessly, and slid it into one of the deep pockets of her nun-like uniform.

They sat together in silence for a few more moments, looking together at the wide, boundless beauty before them. Then Clara stood up.

"I have to go to the service now," she said, "but I will do this as soon as I am back," she told him. "I'll let you know when I have some information."

Chapter 40 – Joanna
Warsaw

He stroked the small of her back in a way that reassured Joanna and brought with it the possibility of sleep, which an hour before would have seemed unfathomable.

"Will you stay here tonight?" she murmured hopefully, but she was already certain of the answer. Unlike any of the previous men that she'd let into her life before him, Oskar always stayed until the morning, wrapping himself around her unself-consciously, his limbs interlaced with hers. At first she found it uncomfortable, but she soon realised that she couldn't fall asleep any other way – she melted into the warmth, familiarity and safety of the embrace.

"Of course," he said, surprised at the question. "Tonight more than ever because I'm worried about you."

"Why?"

He breathed in deeply and she smelt the warm fug of menthol cigarettes.

"You're counting on this woman to tell you something revelatory. And in all likelihood, she may just be another false lead."

"I know. I know."

"I'll be here no matter who she turns out to be," he whispered. He kissed her gently on the back of the head and she suddenly wanted to cry for reasons that she couldn't explain.

They'd been together only a month, unofficially together without anything being agreed by either of them. Oskar understood. What was more, he appeared willing to share her attention with Adam. Not once did he tell her that she should stop searching for him, that it was a hopeless and ridiculous way to spend your life. He was entirely self-sufficient. He didn't demand anything of her. There were moments in which she craved for him to be angry at her for cancelling dinner or for losing her train of thought in the middle of a conversation, but he remained happily moored. And always she thought that he would be on the verge of leaving, that he would eventually get annoyed with how panicked, how unsettled she could be. She would call him, expecting him not to answer, or turn up at the restaurant they'd agreed to meet at, expecting him to have stood her up, but his voice was always there, his warm, cheery 'hello' after no more than two rings, his eyes busily studying the menu before she'd even arrived.

Tonight she slept only because he was there, but she woke up early staring at the green light cast by her mobile phone. She suddenly had the urge to switch it off and to pretend that she had never received a cryptic email from an unknown woman on the other side of the world.

She took the mobile with her into the kitchen and made a cup of coffee. Out of the corner of her eye, she could see the contour of Oskar's body gently rising and falling. She was envious of his restfulness, his freedom from fear and anxiety.

How had this woman read the article? The English version was only due to be released in the next week. She imagined her looking up Adam's name and then translating the article online, all of the pieces of the puzzle suddenly falling into place for her. But what puzzle? What did she know? Joanna didn't even dare entertain the possibility that the woman had met her brother.

As always, her imagination conjured up a grown man, a male replica of herself, long-limbed in a sharp suit. She added an American accent and a tan to her revised version of Adam. Wasn't Chicago hot for the majority of the year? His skin would react well to the sunlight, just like hers.

When the phone rang, she felt physically nauseous. It took all of her resolve to press the green button.

"Hello?"

"Joanna?" She pronounced her name with a harsh, exotic 'J'.

"Yes, it's me. Do you… do you know about my brother? Is he alive?"

There was a drawn out silence on the line and her stomach lurched with the sudden premonition of bad news.

"Your brother? I'm sorry… I, I don't know anything about your brother. Is he unwell?"

There was surprise in the voice. Not surprise, shock.

"What?"

"I was calling about… Joanna, I work in a hospice. I'm calling about a man that we're looking after here. I believe that he's related to you. He's got cancer, and he's hasn't got long left I'm afraid. He's expressed a desire to reunite with his family."

"Is this Adam?"

"Adam? No, no his name is Tom. He is… I believe he may be your father."

She laughed. It was a laugh of relief, a laugh masking disappointment. The woman had clearly got the wrong person. She didn't know anything about Adam. Adam was safe – untouched in her mind. He sat there undisturbed.

"You have the wrong person," she told the woman calmly. "I don't have a father. I mean, he died when I was just a child, years and years ago."

There was a sharp intake of breath on the end of the line.

"I know," the voice said, "And it's my job to persuade you that this is not the case. Please bear with me. I'm going to tell you only what I have been told by him and of course it's up to you whether or not you believe me."

Chapter 41 – Matty
London

He lay face down on the bed, somewhere on the uncomfortable border between sleep and wakefulness, unaware of whether he'd been in the same spot for hours, days or longer. Even the very concept of a day became a mockery. Time didn't run forwards anymore. It had turned itself into something solid which he could press himself against and feel it push back, a thick fluid that sent ripples of memory and recollection to and fro. He was viewing the world as if through a tinted window, the stupor only occasionally broken by a trip to the toilet or a long gulp of from the dirty water bottle on his windowsill. 'Tell me!' he wanted to shout 'Tell me who I am!' But he didn't know who he was shouting to or what response he expected.

All he knew was that something awful was happening to him. Familiar things took on a new shape and like a child left alone in the dark, he was suddenly anxious about the surroundings that he had known for years.

The phone and doorbell had rung interchangeably and he'd answered neither. Eventually, the battery on his mobile ran out and he was grateful for the quiet.

From the darkness of sleep a memory formed. He was a small boy standing before a mirror. There was another child with him, a girl. He stared out, stared into this dusty mirror and saw himself staring back. Then, suddenly, the feeling that he was outside of his body, looking at himself from the inside out, the strange yet comforting realisation that he was more than the sum of his body parts. He was a being with an independent sense of self.

Over the long hours that followed, the memories kept coming and he was learning how to sort through them and how to anticipate their arrival. He had categorised them into two groups – those involving the girl and those without her. There were fewer in the latter category and they consisted mainly of incidents in which he was alone. He could see himself hiding, under tables, in cobwebbed corners of rooms, beneath the splintered slats of a bed, and screaming – screaming so hard that his lungs hurt, that he feared his insides would be torn out of his small body, but still he carried on, because the alternative was worse.

Those involving the girl were much more pleasant and he attended to them eagerly when they arrived. She was a soothing presence in his mind, and she provided a sense of solidness, of dependability. He would hold her hand and he felt that she knew him better than anyone else in the world.

He could contain these small snippets, and deal with them individually but he struggled with the collective. He realised with horror that they were arranging themselves into a snake of memory, slippery and uncatchable, which wove its way through him like something desperate to maim him, to feast until the bitter end of the last remaining shreds of his identity, until he no longer knew himself. He may as well not exist at all.

His stomach ached with an emptiness that was beyond hunger. He wondered how long it would take for him to lose consciousness through lack of nutrition. Of course he could speed up the process if he also stopped drinking. He toyed with the possibility of no longer being, of joining the realm of the invisible. Would anyone miss him? Dan? Ellie? Perhaps only briefly, but they would quickly move on. A low, hollow laugh escaped him.

He needed a wee. He could no longer fight the urge. He lifted himself slowly from the bed, his knees bending unnaturally, as if suddenly unable to support the weight that they were asked to carry. He felt dizzy as he forced himself down the corridor. The floorboards blurred before his eyes. He would fall down, he wouldn't make it through the bathroom door. But he did. He did. On his way back, something on the front doormat caught his eye. A square piece of blue paper folded carefully with his name scrawled across it. Ellie's handwriting.

He reluctantly picked it up.

www.prawda.pl/ludzie_zaginieni/AdamM

p.s. If you don't answer when I come at 7pm today, I'm getting a locksmith. I know you're home and I suspect you're not eating.

Something coiled up inside Matty, as if his body was bracing itself, preparing for battle. He went back into the bedroom and switched on the computer. It took him three attempts to input the web address, as his sluggish brain had trouble with translating the carefully written letters into typed text.

Finally, the page flickered into life. He scanned the tightly packed foreign script and wondered whether he had made a mistake, but no – the web address was correct. Individual words on the page stood out to him but he could make no sense of their meaning. It was an article, he could tell that much, and the picture that accompanied it was of a group of people hugging. It was a stock shot – the teeth a little too white, the contours of the faces too uncomfortably straight.

A slow burning anger rose up in his stomach. What was this? Why had she sent him a page that he couldn't understand? He was about to shut down the window when he spotted them in the corner – a series of little flags, versions of the site in different languages. He clicked on the union jack.

'All that remains' – A study of missing people.

He began to read.

Chapter 42 – Tom
Chicago

"Your move," he said, looking in Kyle's direction, but really not looking at him at all. A week had passed and they had decided to resume playing, partly in Dustin's honour, and partly to distract themselves from the problems that lay heavy on their tired minds. Kyle's wife, a seemingly healthy middle aged woman, had experienced a seizure the previous Monday and had spent two nights in hospital. Her condition had stabilised, but doctors were still unsure of what had caused it in the first place. Kyle was fretting about his wife and grieving for Dustin, and Tom was grieving on two accounts – for his friend, of course, but also for his own family.

The past week had seemed longer to him than entire years of his life, and he had experienced a vast spectrum of emotions. When Clara had first offered to contact Joanna on his behalf, he was filled with a warm, hopeful joy. He clung onto the minute possibility that she might want to speak to him the very same day, but when she didn't respond, he understood. He even berated himself for his own selfish impatience.

But then the days had continued, and the nights. The helpless anticipation stopped him sleeping and he existed in a painful, purgatory-like state that prevented him from thinking, from doing anything, even from just being.

By the fourth day after Clara had made the phone call, the awful realisation began to dawn on him that she may never contact him at all, and he sat on the edge of the bed at three in the morning, utterly consumed by panic. And why was he surprised? Why did he feel the raw loss of her all over again? If anyone had the right to rage, to fury, to unquestionable accusation, it was her. Her silence was fully justified, fully understandable. But he worried that he had done a terrible thing, that he should never have asked Clara to contact her at all. It was a selfish request that may have entirely unbalanced her after she had clearly already suffered so much with her brother. He could read that suffering in between the lines of her article and he could visualise her writing it, her brow furrowed in concentration, her determined fingers fluttering across the keyboard. He thought about contacting her again. Perhaps it had been a bad idea to try to reach out to her via Clara after all.

You have no right. You left them. You're nothing but dust to them. You're a useless, feckless excuse for a father.

And he allowed the voices to come. To consume him entirely, to eat away at the last shreds of his dignity and self-worth.

When he could no longer take them, he had tried to read. He began with the local paper, but every news story, even those entirely unrelated, would remind him of Joanna. He picked up *The Issa Valley* instead, and was about to lose himself in one of his most favourite extracts, when the photo fluttered out like a dirty butterfly from among the pages, and the faces of his children stared at him through the half dark.

And suddenly, among the raging waters of his mind, a thought appeared, a buoy of hope. What if she didn't hate him? What if she hadn't even crossed into the possibility of hate, because, she quite simply, did not believe him? Or rather, she hadn't believed whatever it was that Clara had said to her.

He took the photo carefully then, between his finger and thumb, and he made his way weakly down the corridor to wait for her outside her office. He sat there on the floor, his knees huddled close to his chest, and he waited for the dark sky outside the window to soften with the first blush of pink. When the shy light eventually came through, it illuminated his feet first, in the battered slippers, his thin legs and angled knees, and finally his hands, clutching the photo from both sides. He gasped when he saw them.

Over the past weeks, he had been avoiding reflections at all costs, and his renewed vigour to find his family made him listen to his body very little, if at all. Only once did he catch a glimpse of himself, entirely by accident. The tap in his sink wasn't working and he had to use the bathroom down the hallway instead. He looked up while brushing, not expecting to see his reflection, and he recoiled at what he saw. He was so thin that his skin seemed to barely cover the skull beneath it, his eyes so deeply sunken, that they were drowned in shadow. On his shrivelled neck, a large, single vein stood out and he saw the pulse beating in the scooped-out hollow of his throat, as if there were something inside that was trying to push its way out.

And things must have gotten progressively worse. He could see it through Clara's increasing concern about his warmth, and also through the bagginess of his clothes. A week or so ago, he had noted with a start that he was now wearing size 'small' pyjamas, when only three or so years ago, he would be spilling out of a large. And now these bony, bird-like claws, these pitiful withered bags of vein and bone, were the final reminder of how very little time he had left until there would be nothing left of him at all.

"Oh my goodness! What are you doing here? Tom, what happened?" She was already lifting him up, checking him up and down for any visible signs of injury. He heard her exhale loudly when she didn't see any obvious damage, and she swung her arm around him, indicating that they should begin the journey back to his bed. But he resisted her.

"Let me sit in your office," he begged her, "Let me come in just for a moment. It's important."

He felt the tendons loosen in her arm as she released her grip and allowed him to follow her in.

His hands shook as he sat down opposite her at the desk.

"What is it?"

"Can you send this for me?" he asked quietly. She took the photo from him and, recognising what it was, placed it carefully between them on the table.

"She hasn't responded," she said to him, in the same tone of voice as she had used the day before, and the day before that.

"I know. But she was like me," he told her calmly, "She was like me and I believe that she still is. She just needs something – some semblance of proof to enable her to open up her mind to the possibility."

"And you think this will…?

"Adam was more like his mother and Joanna was more like me. She was quiet. She thought about things carefully before she did them, and she felt things very deeply right from the beginning. But she had strength inside her, a quiet strength. She would stand up to people when she had to but she needed proof that they were in the wrong…"

The memories multiplied as he spoke. "There was a boy in her class with some sort of deformity which made him limp. He had to wear a special shoe on one leg with a thicker sole and he was always sad. She used to come home and tell me about it and she said that she thought other children were picking on him. 'Why don't you tell them to stop?' I asked her, but she said that she hadn't seen them do it. It was only when she witnessed one of the incidents that she stood up to the bullies. Her classmates were shocked because normally she barely said a thing. Then suddenly, one day she opened her mouth and started to shout at the girl who was picking on her friend."

"I'm not sure whether this will work," Clara said honestly and he knew she said it because she didn't want to get his hopes up.

"I know," he said, "but I cannot leave without having done *everything*."

And she had sent the photo. He'd imagined that she would send the original by post and a part of him was distraught as it was his only copy. By she merely took it from him and placed it in the scanner on her desk.

"I will send it," she said, "I promise I will. But please don't ask me again if there has been any response. I will tell you if there has," she said, sadly.

"Thank you," he said, shuffling out. She tried to help him back to his room but he stopped her.

He didn't ask any questions. And here he was four days later, his mind numbed by grief. He'd agreed to play the game with Kyle to avoid continuing to stare at the small but spreading damp patch on the ceiling of his room, which seemed to be his only occupation. But he was regretting it already, because he didn't want to be here. He wanted to slowly disappear, to fade into the background of the room, silently, with no pomp, no fuss. He waited for Kyle to make his move, and he allowed his head to loll gently onto the back of his chair.

He was exhausted, every crevice of his body filled with a dull ache. The warmth of the room caused his eyes to droop and sent him into a light, fitful sleep.

The next thing he knew, a figure was hunched over him, jerking him awake. He vaguely recognised the face. It belonged to one of the younger nurses.

"Call for you," she said, handing him the cordless phone.

He took the receiver from her, expecting Sally's voice. They had recently altered his will. It just required a couple of final checks.

"Hello?"

"It's Joanna," said the small voice on the other end, in Polish. The world blurred and shifted.

"Yes?" he asked weakly, the word foreign in his mouth.

"I'm sorry I took so long. I… I wanted to speak to you. Are you, are you still willing to speak to me? Am I not too late?"

His breath stopped in his chest, but he forced himself up on his feet and he walked as quickly as his legs would carry him back to his room.

And it was only when he was there, in the privacy of his own four walls, that he allowed himself to slide down the back of the door onto the floor, and he cradled the phone tightly to his ear.

"Never," he said. "Never." And for the first time in years, for the first time since he had left his family home for the last time, his heart sang.

Chapter 43 – Joanna
Warsaw

The air was still at this hour, thick with rising heat. Joanna's watch said that it was barely ten in the morning, but because she'd been awake for hours, she felt a sort of confusion that was often associated with jet lag.

The airport seemed bigger and busier than she'd remembered. Before them a group of teenagers had just returned from a school trip. Their parents swarmed the arrivals hall shouting out names. Joanna bumped into one of the mothers who was so eager to reach her newly-arrived offspring that she seemed not to notice the bustling swarm around her.

"His plane has barely landed," Oskar reminded her, steering her by the elbow towards a row of metal seats.

"It'll take them a while to get everyone off and then he'll have to get his luggage. He won't be out for at least half an hour. Steady. Here, have some water."

But she pushed his hand away. She could barely breathe, let alone drink anything. How many years had she waited for this day to arrive? How many times had she played out the scene in her head only to dismiss it as a hopeless fantasy?

"What if he's not there? What if he hasn't arrived?" she asked breathlessly.

"Look at me," said Oskar, grabbing her by both hands and lowering her into the chair, "he's definitely arrived. He texted you just before he got on the plane and we now know that the plane has landed. That means that he's here, probably already in this building."

He was right. Of course he was right. Her sweaty palms gripped the side of the seat and she counted in her head to slow her breathing. The lights of the flight display seemed to multiply before her eyes.

She heard somebody shout 'Adam!' and she jumped immediately into standing position. But then she spotted the origin of the voice and realised that the call was meant for one of the youths from the school trip. It was a common name. She paced backwards and forwards, fighting the urge to sneeze.

Then, in a sudden burst of remembrance so powerful that he could have been there holding her hand right now, was four-year-old Adam, sneezing into a striped handkerchief. Dishevelled dark hair, a tattered shirt, trousers that were already a little short for him. He sat on the couch sneezing and blowing his nose, and immediately she knew that she would soon share in this cold, in the same way that she'd shared his chicken pox and mumps.

Did he remember things like this? He certainly said that he remembered her. They had spoken for four hours on the phone when he had first called. Initially, it seemed unnatural to her that the conversation had to be conducted in English. Adam said that he understood a lot of Polish words, but he felt he couldn't speak the language.

"What do you remember?" she asked him breathlessly a few minutes into their conversation.

"I remember you… I remember us playing in the snow. I have this image of us building a snowman and somebody coming to destroy it. I think it was some older kids from the neighbourhood. And I think you cried? Did it happen or did I just make that up? I can't tell what's a real memory and what I just made up."

She cried then, and laughed through her tears because she was of course imitating her four-year-old self.

"You told me it was OK because you would just build me another one, but better and stronger. You said that you would do it on our balcony so that nobody could get to it."

"Yes! I… I remember that."

"What do you like doing, Adam? And where do you work? What are you good at?"

The questions were never-ending. She wanted to know everything about him, to spot the similarities, to have something to verify their connection.

He laughed softly.

"I'm a trader, but really… I don't know what I want to be. The job is not what I thought it would be. I like loads of things. I'm good at playing the guitar and I like writing I suppose… It's amazing that you're a journalist. You know, I love to write too. I've always thought that one day I might sit down and write a book. People say it's never too late, don't they?"

There were many similarities that she could sense over the crackly mobile connection. It was immediately clear that they would get along, they would understand each other.

"Are you with someone at the moment?" she asked him.

"Do you mean whether I'm in a relationship? No… not anymore. I was, until quite recently. And you?"

They talked about life in Warsaw and London, about their school days and their friends.

"I have to see you," he said at the end of the conversation. "When can I come?"

"Any time! Come at any time."

Maybe she should have told him to wait a few weeks? Just so she could be a little more prepared? She could have given herself time to sit down and write what she wanted to say. She could have calmed herself down, rather than being this juddering mess. She'd been an idiot to drop everything and just come to the airport two days later.

The school trip swarm was dispersing and the arrivals hall emptied out. The sun beamed relentlessly onto the floor, reflecting in the black tiles beneath her feet. Joanna shaded her eyes with her hand. A person was walking towards her, a head of dark hair, a pair of angular shoulders.

"Is it him?"

A warm certainty filled her.

"Yes, yes it is."

And then he was there, in her arms. And all the time and distance that had separated them was gone.

Chapter 44 – Adam
Warsaw

She took him gently by the elbow and led him in the direction of the dimly lit room. It wasn't clear whether this was altogether a wise idea, but Joanna had told him that there was no real alternative. The woman sitting among the four walls at the end of the corridor had spent half of her life awaiting his return. Half a life. He somehow couldn't equate those three words with his own person. Had he ever meant that much to anybody?

Perhaps to Celia, but to Celia he had always been an idea, the embodiment of a very different boy who had grown into a disappointing adult. Through him, she mourned her own child. Here was somebody who yearned for the real him.

Over coffee that morning Joanna pressed her own hand into his, so hard that her nails dug into the back of his fingers and he half-expected small red droplets to appear on the surface of the skin. Her face was filled with something vast and important that she couldn't express. But he understood. He was embarrassed at first at the awkwardness of her communication – the fact that she had to speak to him in English because he'd forgotten their mother tongue. But he soon realised that language was irrelevant. They barely needed it.

"Her mind isn't there anymore," Joanna told him. "You must understand that. At least not in the way that it was. She barely utters a word and even if she did, she wouldn't… she wouldn't understand you because she doesn't speak English. So you need to…"

"Don't worry. I'll be gentle," he told her.

"I just don't know. I just don't know anymore…"

"Don't know what?"

"I don't know whether she will recognise you."

"It doesn't matter," he lied, "I just want to see her. It won't matter if she doesn't…"

His stomach felt as if it had filled with marbles, small glass globes weighing down his bowels, bringing with them the churn of a cold sickness. The old version of him was not nervous – distracted sometimes, frustrated often, but never scared. He had always prided himself on his calm levelheadedness, but today he felt as if his own mind had left him. What if he couldn't go through with it? What if he wasn't able to go into the room?

Joanna's eyes were boring into his.

"If you're thinking you can't go through with it, we don't have to do this today. But if you want to do it, I'll help. I'll make sure that you go in there."

He was struck by the way in which she could instantly guess his thoughts.

And here they were. They had made it as far as their mother's home. He already felt an enormous sense of achievement.

Joanna had taken him via a roundabout route, through the neighbourhood outside their old house. They had walked down a very unremarkable street which opened out onto a series of squares, each surrounded on three sides by dirty four-storey blocks of flats. The area was being renovated and scaffolding had been erected around many of the buildings. Matty noticed that two walls had already received a fresh coat of lurid green. He realised with a start that they were frighteningly close to the area which he'd visited with Ellie.

"I wonder who chooses the colours?" Joanna asked, laughing. Once again, she had picked the question straight out of his head. She launched into a description of the latest mad renovation ventures in Warsaw, and he was listening carefully until suddenly, something compelled him to turn into the square to their left. It bore no real difference to those they had already passed. Some wilting geraniums were struggling against the wind in one of the far corners and besides them there was nothing but yellowing grass.

But against this sparse backdrop images began to emerge in the craters of his memory. Small feet pounding soil, a blue rubber ball, a dirty watering can – no, two watering cans a couple of metres apart. They formed a goal. He was running, racing against somebody and then his foot connected with the blue and the ball flew perfectly, beautifully landing just within the boundary of the can. Euphoria. Heavy breath, the feeling of harsh, scratchy bark against his back as he rested in the shade.

Where was the tree? There were only the geraniums here, no tree.

"Are you OK?" Joanna's voice reached him as if through a haze. But he couldn't answer her, because just then something caught his eye – a smudge of brown against the yellow. A tree stump. His fingers touched the wood, and for a moment, just a moment, he felt that he belonged.

***

The nurse on the reception desk nodded towards Joanna and they exchanged a few sentences. He desperately wanted to grasp their meaning, but they spoke so quickly that he couldn't catch individual words.

"She's in a good mood today apparently," Joanna told him as they'd walked down the corridor. "She's eaten her breakfast herself and she's just had a sleep. So hopefully you will catch her at her best."

But through her optimistic tone, he could sense the fear.

"You're worried she won't remember me."

"Yes."

"It doesn't matter."

"But to me it does."

"We can come back and try again tomorrow."

She propelled him gently towards the door and closed her eyes. And then his hand was on the doorknob and he was walking in. The door shut behind him. The outside world was carefully closed away.

The woman sat in an armchair with her back to him. Her body rested limply against the backrest and he wasn't altogether sure whether she was awake. From where he stood he could see only her shoulders and the back of her short, grey hair.

He walked around to the front of the armchair and realised that his eyes were half-closed as if he was trying to shield himself from seeing everything all at once. Deep down, he hoped that she was asleep so that he would have the chance to see her first. But as he sat down on the footstool opposite, he noticed that the woman was already stirring, and within moments, her pale, watery eyes were wide open. They roamed over his face and there was something in them that quietened the cowardly, frightened creature in his chest.

Her face was surprisingly young and provided a stark contrast to the grey hair. The painfully thin arms clutched the sides of the armchair, the alabaster skin clinging tightly to the bone. He had a sudden, awful image of how easily they could break. Her body was feeble and weak, almost hollow, but there was something in those eyes that told him her mind was still there, buried but present. He wanted to say something but the words refused to trip over his tongue.

"I... I came..." he began, and he was furious to hear his voice cracking. But then she placed a withered hand on his and wrapped two fingers tightly around his thumb. The blood in his head pulsed and he looked up... There were tears in his mother's eyes.

Chapter 45 – Tom
Chicago

Tom always felt that the best part of travelling anywhere, was coming home. As a young boy, when his grandparents had taken over his guardianship, he was allowed to go on summer camp, on occasional field trips with school, later even on impromptu seaside holidays with his friends. But no matter how much he had enjoyed these periods out of his usual existence, he always looked forward to his homecoming.

His favourite part was the first few days back, in which he would find everything as he had left it, but at the same time worthy of double his attention. He would reorganise his belongings in his tiny bedroom, and rejoice at having this little piece of the world all to himself. Even things that were normally irritating, such as the cupboard door that would never stay shut, or the quarrelling neighbours downstairs, couldn't affect him on these days – he was filled with a contented calm.

And when he re-met Joanna (as that was how she viewed their phone conversation – as a second meeting), he couldn't put into words the enormity of what he felt, but if somebody had asked him, he would say that it felt like coming home – the best homecoming that he had ever experienced.

The next day he woke up, and in those first moments of wakefulness, he would be reverted back into the world of before Joanna's phone call – of fear and dread, and dreariness, because surely it wasn't possible that after twenty-two years he could have reconciled with his daughter? And then he turned over and looked at the photo on his bedside table which Joanna's boyfriend had taken of her and Adam at the airport, smiling, and the letter that he had received from his son, and a reassuring warmth spread through his insides. The letter was written in English – a better, more eloquent English than Tom could speak himself. How strange and how very lucky that they were able to understand each other despite not being able to communicate in their mother tongue.

He looked again at the photo. Here were two people who were really just extensions of himself, flesh and blood humans with familiar faces and wonderful, open expressions. They were also proof of something that he had produced which was not tainted or grubby, but pure and kind, and bursting with life.

And two days later, he got a message from them both to say that they wanted to see him in the flesh, that they were desperate to meet him – they would try and make the journey in early September, in just three weeks – and his heart felt as it if were about to burst.

Clara had insisted on holding a party for him, in celebration and he normally wouldn't have done – it wasn't something he enjoyed, but this time he agreed.

"We spend so much time focussing on everything that is wrong with us," she reminded him, "and too little time celebrating the good things, the amazing things. And you have *so much* to celebrate."

So they gathered in the sitting room with Kyle, and Susie and the others, and he invited Mitch and Sally to join them, and they drove up especially even though Mitch was recovering from a recent hip operation. Susie played *Octopus' Garden* on her guitar, and they sang and ate the lemon drizzle cake that Clara had baked especially for the occasion. He was filled with amazement and gratitude at all these people who cared for him, who had been rooting for him. He passed around the photo that Joanna had sent for everyone to admire. 'My children,' he said to them all. 'They're my children.' And they all marvelled at the photo, even though of course, to most of them family photos were an everyday thing, like eating breakfast or taking the rubbish out. Sally squeezed his hand, and in that moment, he was so inexplicably happy that he wished for it to last forever.

After the party, he was too tired to walk so Clara wheeled him out onto the porch for some fresh air. It was one of those summer days when the air was resplendent with a pleasant heat. It was warm, but not hot enough to be oppressive, and when he closed his eyes he could hear and taste and smell the world around him. The spicy scent of the camellias that lined the garden fence reached his nostrils, the citrus of the cake was still present in his mouth and the memory returned, quite unexpectedly.

They were sitting on the red picnic blanket, the four of them. Monika wore the green dress that he had given her. He'd worked for five Saturdays in a row to earn the tokens for the beautiful fabric and then he'd taken it to the seamstress to make two dresses – one for her and the other, tiny in comparison, for Joanna. And for Adam, he got a football made of soft pale leather, hand-stitched, which he insisted on bringing everywhere with him.

They were still poor of course. There would still be days in which there was nothing but onions in the shops and they would struggle to feed themselves, but on that particular day in that wonderful July, they sat on the picnic blanket and ate biscuits and drank weak lemonade, and he was happier than he had ever been. The image of the four of them – Monika lying back and laughing, her face turned towards the sun, the children chasing each other on the grass – began to fuzz over slightly, but the emotion that it generated remained. The pure unadulterated joy. And then he saw himself standing up. He needed to leave, he had to go back to work. But he was reluctant to do so – he stood suspended, still holding Monika's hand, and then he began walking away, waving to them.

And somewhere within the deep caverns of his mind he knew that he, in his current guise, was also leaving, that he would be gone imminently before he could… before he had a chance to… But there was no before anymore. There was only the present and it was filled with a brilliant light.

Chapter 46 – Joanna and Adam
Chicago

What is a home? Your own four walls? Somewhere to lay your head with the knowledge that you have a roof above you to protect from the elements? Or was it more than a physical structure? Was a home really just the combined power of its inhabitants – inhabitants who might form a family, who might be bound by the force of love? And if he was lacking these, could it be said that Tom truly had a home? Joanna's mind raced with these questions, extravagantly.

Yet there they were, within the home that their father had left to them. They'd been given the keys by a beaming elderly lady called Sally the day before and she'd asked, to their surprise, whether she could still come and tend to the garden.

"Tom would always leave the garden to me, you see. He would do the weeding and then he would sit there with his paper," she said, indicating the partially rotting wooden chair, "and I would plant all the seasonal bulbs according to colour. Sometimes I would just step over the fence and carry on my work when he wasn't home. He didn't mind."

When she spoke of him, the corners of her eyes were bunched up with joy, and Adam was forced to revise his initial imagination of his father as somebody who was serious, stern and lonely.

Sally had invited them to dinner and they both asked the greedy question, "What was he like? What was he *really* like?"

"Oh he could be an annoying one at times," said Mitch, the man mountain who was Sally's husband, "Holy smokes, did he wind me up with some of his views on politics and the economy. But he was a fine man, a real fine man. He was kind to everyone he knew, and patient, even with those people who he couldn't tolerate – the ones who were feckless and unproductive. He was harder working than anybody I knew."

"What will you do with the house?" Sally had asked, "Do you want to sell it?" There was a note of trepidation in her voice, and they quickly reminded her that if they did decide to sell it wouldn't be now, it wouldn't be yet. They were only at the start of their journey of getting to know Tom.

This evening they had finally felt ready to take the walk that they'd been planning ever since their arrival last week. They could have taken public transport for at least some of the way, but they chose instead to enjoy the late warmth of the September night, and to digest everything that they'd found out.

"Do you think he was happy here?" asked Adam. They were practising a new way of communicating now – he speaking to her in English and she answering in Polish. It was surprising how much he understood. Only infrequently did he need to ask her to translate.

"I think he probably was, in his way."

The sky was darkening as they passed through the elaborate entranceway. The air was suffused with a rare calm and the faint buzz of cicadas could be heard in the distance. They could taste the sea on their tongues if they breathed in deeply.

"Why did he come here, to the States, in the first place do you think?"

"He was scared," said Joanna, without hesitation. "You know he was only a couple of years older than we are now. And he'd done something which meant very little to him really until the accident which suddenly made it into something enormous."

"In other circumstances, I might find it difficult to forgive him," he said, "but somehow I don't blame him. I can't."

"No. I thought I would when I spoke to him on the phone, but I couldn't. He sounded so… so warm and so kind. We could blame him for being scared, for being impulsive, but I think he suffered enough for what he'd done. It sounded as though he'd blamed himself every day since it happened. My only question is why he didn't *do* anything. Why didn't he contact us – before? Much earlier?"

They had slowed down now. The ground was still wet underfoot from the morning rain and the uphill path was paved with pebbles. Small fir trees lined it on either side and they reminded Adam suddenly of Celia and her meticulous gardening. It was an oddly distant memory, as if it was associated with an entirely different person, a different life.

"Because it's difficult, isn't it?" he told his sister, "Because doing nothing is easier. I couldn't get out of a relationship even when I knew for certain that it wouldn't work. You get stuck in your small life, between your four walls and before you know it, there's no way out. You've locked yourself in."

"It takes something huge for you to break them down?"

"Exactly. Unless you're you," he said grinning. "You were always acting on the stuff that made you most scared."

"No," she shook her head. "What made me most scared was that I'd gone mad and was wasting my time searching. And it was safer to carry on just because there was a tiny possibility that I could be right."

He didn't say anything then, because she knew how he felt about her finding him. He was glad – so infinitely glad that she'd continued throughout all those years. Although late at night, before falling asleep, he also realised that *he* had played a pivotal part. She had posted the article, her final outstretched hand – but he had taken that hand, because it had reached out to him like a rope in a dark well, when he had lost himself.

And now, unbelievably, here they were, side by side, like they had been in their father's blurred photograph. The sky around them was heavy with dusk, but it was still light enough to make out the letters on the pale marble tombstone.

Tomasz Malicki
Born 27 February 1957 Mysłowice
Died 12 August 2010 Chicago
Here is all that remains

Virginia Prize for Fiction

AURORA METRO BOOKS

www.aurorametro.com
Twitter @aurorametro
Facebook aurorametrobooks

More fiction from Aurora Metro

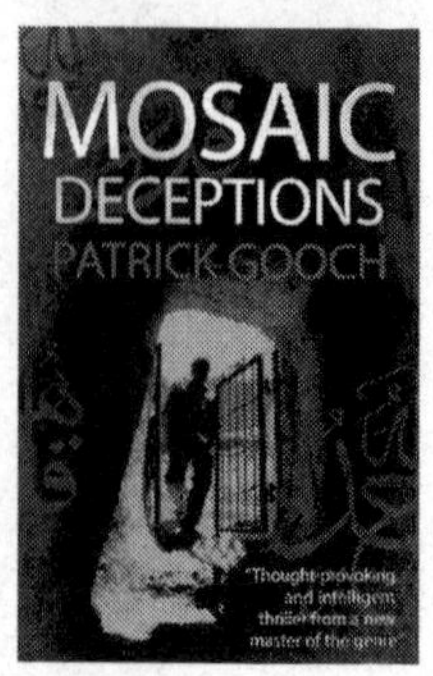

To find out about other titles from Aurora Metro Books please visit our website

www.aurorametro.com